K-PAX V

OTHER BOOKS BY GENE BREWER

K-PAX

K-PAX II: On a Beam of Light

K-PAX III: The Worlds of Prot

K-PAX: the Trilogy, featuring Prot's Report

Creating K-PAX

K-PAX IV

K-PAX Redux

Ben and I

Murder on Spruce Island

Watson's God

3 Stories and a Novella

The American Way

Wrongful Death

"Alejandro" in Twice Told

Three Early Novels

Becoming Human

K-PAX V

The Coming of the Bullocks

Gene Brewer

Rev. date: 04/25/2014

To order additional copies of this book, contact:
Xlibris LLC
1-888-795-4274
www.Xlibris.com
Orders@Xlibris.com
551293

"Thou shalt not kill."

– God

PROLOGUE

When a mental patient calling himself "prot" showed up at the Manhattan Psychiatric Institute in New York in 1990 claiming to be from the planet K-PAX (in the constellation Lyra), I took him on as my patient, thinking him to be an interesting case of psychotic delusion. I spent weeks trying to analyze and treat his psychosis before ultimately discovering, through hypnosis, that he was actually a secondary personality of a man whose wife and daughter had been raped and murdered five years earlier. It hardly entered my mind that prot could also be what he professed to be, namely an alien visitor from a faraway world. Even when he "disappeared" in 1997, I was still doubtful, despite the fact that his "departure" was witnessed not only by me but by several of my colleagues, as well as many of the other patients, and even a couple of CIA agents who recorded the whole thing on a video device of some kind.

My uncertainty evaporated in 2005, however, when a second being from the same planet appeared on the doorstep of our retirement home in the Catskills. "Fled" stayed only a month, but this was time enough for her to gather nearly 100,000 of the great apes (she closely resembled a large chimpanzee herself), and a number of assorted humans, for the return trip to her native planet. And more than enough time to become pregnant with a child whose unknown (even to her) father could have been human or any of a number of ape species.

While fled was here, she indicated that we should expect return visits from Giselle Griffin, the free-lance reporter who had been instrumental in tracking down prot's alter ego, Robert Porter, and Giselle's son Gene (named after me!), as well as my intrepid daughter Abby, who accompanied her on the return voyage to K-PAX. She did not, however, specify a date for their arrival.

Fled also informed us that, in the near future, we should expect another set of visitors, the "Bullocks," a rather unforgiving and apparently violent race of beings from an unspecified planet, who were quite displeased with the destructive behavior of Homo sapiens toward our own world, including our malicious treatment of every other species with whom we share it and, for that matter, of one another. She surmised that we would probably have fifteen years to clean up our act before they intervened. Unfortunately, this estimate turned out to be far too generous.

When they arrived, in the fall of 2013, I was dismayed to discover that they, too, came straight to me. Because of my past history with prot and fled, I suppose, I was singled out to deliver their ultimatum – stop the killing – to all human beings everywhere.

Unbeknownst to me, our government was not totally unprepared for the Bullocks' visit. Based on my experience with prot and fled, the Administration had, in fact, come up with a number of contingency plans for dealing with our latest visitors. Ultimately, however, none of that mattered much. Most of the responsibility fell on my own shoulders, and the load was simply too much for me. Maybe it would have been too much for anyone, I don't know. All I know is that I wasn't up to the task.

But even though nothing that occurred during that awful week was my fault, I still feel tremendous guilt for everything that happened. I failed, and failed miserably. The assignment was of such importance that I should have had sense enough to refuse it. But I wasn't smart enough for that. When the President of the United States (not to mention a powerful alien) asks you to do something, it's very difficult to refuse. And now, because of me, the fate of every human being on Earth has been determined, and there's nothing I can do about it. I can't eat, I can't sleep. My wife worries about me constantly, but I no longer care about that, or anything else except for my abject failure to succeed in the mission I was given. Or, for that matter, even to convince the Bullocks to give us more time, another chance. Frankly, I've even contemplated suicide. The United Nations, and many of its member nations, should share some of the blame, I suppose, but perhaps I simply wasn't passionate enough in my speech to the Security Council or clever enough to neutralize the skepticism and intransigence of the world's leaders.

Oh God, how I wish things had been different!

DAY ONE

It all began inauspiciously enough. I was at the grocery store, picking up a few small items my wife had sent me for, when a man I had never seen approached me just as I got to my SUV in the parking lot. I saw immediately that there was something strange about him. He looked like death warmed over and, frankly, he didn't smell too good. Nevertheless, he was clean-shaven, and unusually well-dressed for a trip to the market, sporting a stylish brown suit and a brown and yellow-striped tie. On the other hand, he was barefooted and his voice didn't seem to fit him. He sounded almost like a woman. But an angry, vituperative one.

He asked me whether I was Dr. Brewer. This happens once in a while – a reader sometimes recognizes me and stops to tell me that he enjoyed the K-PAX books (or not, on a couple of occasions). I assumed he was a resident of one of the nearby communities. Despite his odd appearance, and hint of a scowl, I admitted who I was, and prepared for the usual few minutes' chitchat about what the planet K-PAX was like, whether the universe was teeming with life, and all the rest. But that wasn't what he wanted to talk about.

"We're the Bullocks," he said, in his high-pitched, guttural snarl. I froze. All I could think of was "we"? As far as I could tell there was only *him*. Apparently he noticed the blood draining from my face. "Don't worry; we're not going to harm you." I didn't know whether he meant me, or *everyone*. His lip seemed to curl as he said it, and he turned away, apparently to avoid gazing at my revolting human countenance. There was no place to hide or run. If he (or they, or it) was, in fact, from another planet, he would undoubtedly be able to find me no matter where I ran or hid, even if I flew to the moon or Mars or anywhere else.

My next thought was: why the *hell* did I decide to become a psychiatrist, which had led to all this. But I had dealt with two difficult aliens before, and who better for the next one to deal with? In fact, prot and fled might have directed him – them – to me. I finally said, "We can talk at my house. Get in." He climbed awkwardly into the passenger seat and turned to stare at me, apparently having overcome my repugnance.

"The first thing you need to know," he began, as we left the parking lot, barely missing a bicyclist coming the wrong way, "is that the world we come from is far more advanced than is K-PAX, and virtually every other planet in the galaxy."

The cyclist shook his fist at me and shouted, "Watch where you're going, you old fart!"

My passenger ignored him and continued, unruffled, almost in a falsetto monotone, as if he had given this speech many times: "In fact, Bullock is one of the oldest planets in the universe. We don't really look like this, or sound like this. Long ago our physical bodies, which are totally unnecessary for consciousness, began to deteriorate, much like your appendixes, and for the same reason, until there was almost nothing left but our brains and a couple of appendages necessary for providing adequate nutrition. Eventually we learned to control our immediate surroundings using simple electromagnetic commands in order to obtain what we needed. Finally we were able to combine the two – brains and certain mechanical devices – to become what you would probably call 'robots,' except that we controlled our own activities. After a very long time we dispensed with these mechanical devices altogether and became mobile electronic brains and, finally, pure brain waves themselves, though we can occupy any life form we want." He (I could only think of him as a "he") glared at me, apparently to make sure I was still listening, or perhaps understanding what he was saying, though he couldn't resist another curl of the upper lip. "Of course this is a gross simplification of our evolution, which took many billions of years, but it should give you an idea of who we are and what we are capable of. The details are unimportant, but you should know that we can accomplish things you haven't yet dreamed about, and wouldn't comprehend even if you had."

My throat was as dry as ancient parchment, but I managed to squeak, "How do I know you are who you say you are?"

His response was preceded by something like the roar of a lion. Suddenly a huge tree fell across the roadway ahead and, with a brilliant flash of light, exploded and disappeared altogether. *"How many visitors must you encounter before you begin to believe what we tell you?"*

I guessed it was a rhetorical question, so I didn't answer. For a moment I couldn't speak, anyway. I stared at the road where the tree had fallen, but there was nothing there. *Nothing*. Not even a fleck of ash, or anything else to impede our progress. Finally I croaked one of my own. "Why are you telling me all this?"

"Fled sent us to you, 'doctor'. We need someone to convey our message and, with your background, you are as good a representative of your species as any."

It was early October, and already beginning to turn cool, but I was perspiring. "Convey?" I replied apprehensively.

"To deliver our demands in terms others of your species might understand." Again he turned toward me and gazed at me contemptuously. He wasn't snarling anymore, but his eyes were like empty holes, black and staring. I was shivering now, and my flesh was beginning to crawl. He bared his teeth – an attempt to smile? "Besides, as a scientist – of sorts – we thought you might be interested in being involved."

"Involved in what?" I swallowed reflexively. "What is it you're demanding?"

"Your species is known throughout the galaxy as ruthless killers. You will kill anyone, including those of your own kind, to satisfy your lust for death in order to fulfill some psychotic need. That has got to stop. And I don't mean a thousand years from now. I mean *now.*"

"But you come from a planet far away from here. I don't even know where it is. What possible difference could it make to you what we humans do?"

At this point I'm sure prot would have sighed in frustration at my apparent ignorance or stupidity. Fled, too, though more noisily. However, our latest visitor from space simply growled, in another extremely unpleasant sneer, "We have given you a very abbreviated description of our species and how we have evolved. There is far more to it than that. For example, we are not merely individual, isolated beings like you consider yourselves to be, and never have been. We have always been a kind of *society*, on the order of your ants or bees. A few billion years ago we began to tap into the enormous totality of life in the universe, including that of your newly-formed planet. The universe is an enormous network. Everything you do impacts everyone else. You are part of us; you just don't know it yet. Your little lives are merely a miniscule fragment of this totality, which we call "Nediera" (he pronounced it "nay-DEAR-uh"). We think of it as the matrix of the universe. It is the sum of all life everywhere, which itself is like a giant ant colony. When you kill other beings on Earth you cause harm not only to them, but to everyone else in the universe. We can *feel* the anguish, the pain and suffering. "Do you see that cow in the field on your left?"

I admitted that I saw it.

"That cow's life means nothing to you except for a few meals. But to the cow it means *everything.*"

"We're different from cows," I explained. "We have souls."

His response was a kind of gagging noise. "That's a myth created by your multivarious religions. The universe doesn't distinguish between your life and that of any other sentient being. Do you really think you're special in some way? Grow up! You used to think the Earth was the center of the universe, and when you finally realized it wasn't, you thought your sun was at the center of everything. Now that you know that your star and its planets are nothing special, you still cling to the belief that your *species* is the focus of it all. You even make your gods in your own image!" he roared. "This is the *epitome* of arrogance!"

"What about *you?*" I countered. "Surely you consider your species to be superior to ours."

"Are you listening, doctor? Do you think we should hitch you to carts? Use you for medical experiments? Hunt you down and shoot you for 'sport'? Hear us, sapiens: *All life in the universe is equally important!*"

I thought my eardrums might break, but he went on in a softer tone: "You should know also that once you die, you leave Nediera forever. That is why death is such a tragedy, not only for the individual involved, but for the entire colony, the entire universe." He turned to stare pointedly at me again. "Are you getting even a hint of what I'm telling you?" Between the lines, I somehow heard, "*You piece of shit.*"

I shrugged and probably grinned quite stupidly. "Not really."

He stared at me for an eternal second. "You've got a dog. If we were to shoot her in front of you, how would you feel (*you asshole*)?"

I felt myself gasp. Not just at the thought of Flower's death, with perhaps terrible pain, but that this *thing*, whatever it was, could do that to her or to anyone else it wanted to. "Not very good," was my feeble reply.

"Then you understand, at least vaguely, what I'm saying. If, on the other hand, we were to shoot some dog in another of your many countries, you wouldn't feel a thing. You wouldn't even *know* about it. It would mean nothing to you. With us, and the other beings around the universe who have been in existence long enough to have reached our state, it's different. We would know about that other dog. Its pain would be our pain. That is what is happening all the time on this violent planet. The killing is constant: wars among yourselves, the elimination of other humans for reasons of anger, jealousy, or greed, the senseless murdering of other species for food or for your so-called medical research. You even hunt down and kill other beings for *pleasure!*" he seethed. "It hurts constantly, and the incessant distress is more relentless and more terrible than you can possibly imagine." His dead eyes bored into the side of my head. He bawled like the cow we had just passed, and snarled again. "*And we're sick of it.*"

The hairs on the back of my neck stood up. I needed to change the subject, to breathe. To *think*. "Do you have a name? It would help if I could call you something."

"The body we are wearing is called 'Walter.'"

Another shudder. "You killed him?"

He roared again: "Do you see? That's exactly what I've been telling you. No other species would jump to that absurd conclusion."

"Then how did – "

"He was dead when we found him. One of your heart attacks brought on by the constant consumption of your fellow beings."

"Where did you find him?"

He grunted (it was more like a bark) and slapped the dashboard. I jumped a foot in the air. "Does that really matter, doctor (*you dumb prick*)? We're getting off the subject. Time is short. Given the situation, you should try to focus on more important matters, don't you think?"

"Okay, Walter, or whoever you really are, just answer me this: what am I supposed to do to stop people from killing dogs ten thousand miles away?"

"All you have to do is make arrangements to speak to your United Nations Security Council. If they agree to listen to you, the matter would then be taken up by the General Assembly representing all the people of your world."

How did he know about our – "And if they don't?"

"It's over."

I'm sure I gulped quite audibly. "*What's* over?"

"Your species will be eliminated from the Earth."

I could feel my stomach sinking. This simply could not be happening. "And how would I do that?" I asked weakly. "Get permission to talk to the Security Council, I mean?"

I could hear his dead teeth grinding. "When fled was here, your government finally understood – after it was too late, of course – that she should have had a forum. It would be a simple matter to go to your president and ask for such a hearing now. You could tell them some of fled's friends sent you."

"Ask the *President*??"

"Do you have a better idea?"

"But – But I don't *know* the President," I whined.

"Then (*you imbecile*) go back to the people who followed you around when fled was here. They're probably expecting you."

"What is the time frame?"

I could hear him breathing heavily. I wondered how this was possible since he was dead and shouldn't be able to breathe at all. "A week should be enough."

"You want to speak at the United Nations a week from *now*?"

"Ahhhhhh!" he shrieked. "They *told* me you sometimes pretended to be deaf for reasons of your own. No, you idiot, *you* will speak there!" This time I didn't imagine the epithet.

I felt the weight of the whole world drop again onto my sagging shoulders. "You're asking me to present your case to the United Nations?"

He was actually seething now. "Is it possible that you are really as stupid as everyone says? It's not *our* case. It's *your* case."

"But it's *you* who – "

"Try hard to listen to me, sapiens. The entire human race depends on your doing this. Do you care whether your species survives?"

I thought about my grandchildren, who were completely innocent of all this. "Of course I care! But I don't *want* to represent our species at the UN. I'm not very good at public speaking. I don't like it. I don't want the responsibility."

Without a moment's hesitation, and almost in a guttural whisper: "You have no choice."

I felt my respiration rate increase perceptibly. Even speaking at a PTA meeting always made me feel breathless and queasy. When I was working, I had to talk to various groups now and then, but it was about topics I was familiar with and could have recited in my sleep. Now I was being asked to convince the President of the United States that I needed to speak to the United Nations Security Council, and then to actually *do* it. On top of that, I had to sell them on the Bullocks' demands, whatever they were. I was already terrified even though I was still sitting in my familiar old car in my own little neighborhood. Why the hell did my wife have to have a jar of *pickles* all of a sudden? I wished prot had never come here. I wished I had never been born. Why, oh why, did I become a goddamn psychiatrist?"

"A lot of reasons."

"Oh, God, you can read my mind. Like fled could."

"Your feeble mind is as transparent as a glass of water."

"So if I don't need to talk, why are you letting me?"

"You humans need to talk. It organizes your mind. Otherwise your thoughts would be a jumble."

"Then you must know I don't think I can do this."

"Then Homo sapiens will disappear from the face of the Earth. Would you like to reconsider your position?"

"If I said, 'Go to hell!' would you know what I meant?"

"Yes, but it wouldn't get you out of your dilemma, even if there were such a place."

I turned onto Harrison Road. Somehow I felt that if I could just get home, things would be different. At least I would feel safer. But of course there was no place to hide, even there. We drove in silence until I pulled into the driveway. The familiar backyard and the woods behind it suddenly seemed strange, foreign. Even the light looked different, as though darkness were descending. I felt as if I were on the outside looking in, perhaps like a schizophrenic might feel. I turned off the engine. "So you're leaving now? Back to wherever you came from? And I'm on my own on this thing?"

"No, I'll be here for a while. You'll need to know exactly what our demands are, won't you? And if you fail, we've got some work to do." He, or they, seemed to be sneering less than before, as if they had finally gotten used to the revolting appearance of a human being, much as we might slowly become immune to the sight of maggots devouring a corpse. I thought, with a curious sense of false hope, that perhaps the Bullocks were beginning to like us.

"Uh – what kind of work?"

"We'll discuss that later. Make arrangements to speak to your Security Council first. If they refuse, there is no need for further discussion."

"But I'd better not fail, is that it?"

"Only if you don't want to see your grandchildren become the last generation of humans on the Earth."

The brief sense of hope quickly evaporated. I was sick, frozen with fear, not because it looked as though I would have to speak at the United Nations (it was still hard to believe this could happen), or even because it appeared that I was responsible for the fate of the human race, but because I was staring right at the thing almost all of us fear most. And very close up. It was the face of death.

I got out of the car, expecting Walter to follow. But when I looked around, he was gone. For a moment I felt another wave of relief. But of course this, too, was only temporary. The whole conversation flooded back into my mind and I was right back where I was before. Did I imagine it all? No, he – they – were only too real, right down to the scowl. Even Flower knew something was up: she ran out the doggy door and sniffed around the car with intense concentration, as if there were a dead rat in it.

I took the grocery items inside, where Karen was waiting in the kitchen. "You won't believe what just happened," I said. I don't know whether she noticed that I was still shaking.

"Don't be silly. I've met two aliens from the constellation Lyra and traveled from here to the Grand Canyon in a fraction of a second. I'll believe anything you tell me."

"There's another visitor."

Without batting an eye: "Who is it this time?"

"He's calling himself 'Walter' at the moment, but that's probably only provisional. He's currently inhabiting a corpse, unless he's already vacated it."

She actually laughed. "Sounds like an interesting one."

I thought: what is wrong with this woman? "It's not very funny. He wants me to speak to the United Nations."

"*You*?"

"Now you can laugh!"

But she was suddenly quite serious. "What does he want you to speak about?"

"The survival of our species. Except that 'he' is actually 'they.' They're like a colony of ants."

She squinted at me for a moment. "Sweetheart, are you sure you're not imagining all this?"

"I don't think so. You should have heard Walter."

She gazed out the window at the woods behind the kitchen. "And how do you get on the agenda at the United Nations?"

"He – or they – suggested I call in the government."

"You mean Dartmouth and Wang (the government agents who tracked fled's visit)?"

"I suppose I would have to start there, yes."

"Then there's probably not a moment to lose."

"Can I have a hug first?"

"Of course!" She gave me a squeeze and I held tight for a few minutes. "What can I do to help?" she asked.

"I don't know. First I'd better try to get hold of Wang."

"I'll make us some lunch while you do that. Even if you're the most important person in the world, you have to eat."

She was probably joking again, but I pretended not to hear it. Instead, I went to my study to make the call. As my perceptive wife had pointed out: for all we knew, every second counted.

I found Wang's private number lying on the shelf above the phone. I don't know why I had kept it handy – maybe I somehow suspected I would need it again. Of course, I didn't expect him to answer the call himself. But he did – I recognized the annoying voice immediately. He almost seemed to be expecting my call. There was no "Hello," or "How are you?" just "What can I do for you, Dr. Brewer?" even though I hadn't spoken to him in years.

"Houston, we have a problem," I said, trying to lighten up an impossibly serious situation.

"Talk to me."

"We have another visitor."

"I'll be there in five minutes."

"Huh? Where are you?"

The phone clicked.

I went back to the kitchen and told Karen about the call. "Does he eat?" she asked immediately. "Would he like some lunch?"

"I don't know. I'll have to ask him when he gets here."

It was just under (by a few seconds) five minutes when Wang tapped on the door. As always, he showed me his badge before coming into the house. When he sat down in the living room he eyed Flower suspiciously. I reminded him that she was harmless. He nodded without taking his eyes off her.

"Where's your partner in crime?"

"What?"

"Dartmouth."

He gave his head a good scratching, as if wondering whether to reply. "Mr. Dartmouth is in a rest home." Motes of dandruff swam in a beam of sunlight.

"Oh. Well, I hope he's resting well."

He shrugged.

"May I just ask: how did you get here from Washington in five minutes? Not asking for you to divulge any secr – "

"That's classified. Now. Who has been visiting you?"

"He calls himself Walter. But I think he, or maybe it's 'they,' isn't corporeal. I think he's occupying a dead body."

"Yes, we know about that."

"You do??"

"Mr. Aragon disappeared from the funeral home a few hours before you called. That's how we – But never mind that. What does he want?"

"He – or they – want me to give a speech at the United Nations."

Wang stared into space for a brief moment. "That can be done. What does he expect you to talk about?"

"I don't know the details. But he – or they – seem disturbed that we sometimes kill one another, as well as all the other animals on our planet. They can tap into everyone else's pain, or anguish, or something like that. I think they basically want us to stop the killing."

Flower lay down at Wang's feet, as if to comfort him. The feet inched away from her. "That's it?"

"As far as I know."

"And what happens if we don't?"

"They didn't say, exactly. Only that Homo sapiens would disappear from the Earth."

He stared some more. "Did he say when they will return with the details?"

"No."

He stood up. "If he comes back, you have my number. Call me 24/7. Otherwise we'll be in touch. Probably later today." He saluted and started to get up.

"Just one question, Mr. Wang. You already seem to know what I've been telling you. How did – "

"That's not important now. What's important is that we were a bit tardy in recognizing the significance of fled's visit. I took some flak for that, and so did Mr. Dartmouth. That's why he's in – But that's neither here nor there. If not me, someone will let you know what you need to do next." He stood up. "You'll be hearing from us."

Just then Karen came in. "Would you like to join us for lunch?" she asked Wang.

"Thank you, Mrs. Brewer. No time for that." He looked meaningfully back to me. "We'll talk later . . . ." He quickly headed for the front door, Flower following close behind.

I sighed miserably. "Yeah." He hurried out, slamming the door in Flower's face. My wife stared after him. "Doesn't he ever eat?"

"I have no idea."

"Well, I know *you* do, and lunch is ready."

The way things were going, I knew I might not be eating regularly for a while. "Let's go," I said.

"It's not that great," she pointed out. "Just soup."

"It sounds wonderful."

But it wasn't. I wasn't as hungry as I thought I'd be. I kept thinking about those people on death row who get one last glorious meal. Then they can't eat it. Karen, evidently noticing how glum I looked, tried to console me. "Don't worry, sweetie. It can't be as bad as it seems." How unprophetic that turned out to be.

"You know I never liked public speaking," I reminded her. "And now I've got to speak at the United Nations, for God's sake!"

"Maybe they can find somebody else to do it in your place. With something this important, maybe the President himself will want to do it."

"I don't think he can. Walter said it had to be me."

"Maybe. But he wants you to get the world to agree to something, doesn't he? Otherwise, why the UN?"

"I don't even know *that*. He hasn't told me yet what I'm supposed to say. And even if he does, how would I be able to convince the UN to agree on something? They never agree on *anything*!"

"Nevertheless, we don't really know what he wants or how this thing is going to play out. I don't think you should worry about it until it happens."

"Easy for you to say!"

"Not really," she replied glumly.

I looked out the kitchen window at the trees, already turning color, the squirrels gathering acorns for winter, the birds congregating, getting ready to migrate. It was a beautiful scene, reminiscent of dozens of others one sees over a lifetime of more than seven decades. But it's never enough. I wanted to see it thousands and thousands more times. Why is it that we don't notice or appreciate what we have until something comes along to threaten it? Was it all about to end if I failed to perform? It wasn't fair that I should be the only person in the world with the responsibility to save the human race from extinction. There are plenty of books and movies with such a theme, and the hero always does his job, and willingly. But this wasn't fiction. It was really happening. What if I screwed up? What could I possibly say to the UN, even if I had the guts to stand before the whole world and say it? Where was Wang now? Where was Walter? Were they out there somewhere getting ready to pop up and give me orders to jump? It was almost too much to bear.

"Are you going to eat that soup or not?"

I lost it. How in hell could she be so concerned about soup when the world was literally falling apart? I jumped up and stalked out the door and into the woods. Flower, who had been waiting for me to finish, and maybe have the dregs in my bowl, followed me out. As always, she ran after a squirrel and didn't catch it. She has never caught one, though she never gives up trying. It ran up an oak tree and she seemed mystified about where it had gone, as she always is. For some reason this made me laugh. I suddenly realized that no matter what happened, dogs would still chase squirrels and fail to catch them until the end of time. The only question was whether there would be any humans around to see it.

I was in the woods for half an hour or so, meditating and/or praying, things I've never been able to do successfully. As always, nothing came of it. When Flower and I returned to the house, Karen told me there had been a call from the White House. A Mr. Jones, she said. There was a number. "Sure," I responded. "Jones. And no doubt he has a partner named Smith."

"I wouldn't know about that, Gene, but he seemed genuinely eager to talk to you."

I punched the number – a little too vigorously, maybe, judging by the frown on my wife's lovely forehead. It rang once. "Hello, Dr. Brewer," came a surprisingly soft and sympathetic voice. How are you?"

"Just ducky. And you?"

"I am well, thank you. Sir, I won't waste your time. The President and a few other government officials would like to speak to you as soon as possible about a certain matter with which you are quite familiar. May we schedule that conference?"

"You mean a phone conference?"

"Not exactly. The nearest airport to you is Stewart International. Are you familiar with it?"

"Newburgh, right? I've been there once or twice."

"Good. Can you leave immediately? Mr. Wang will pick you up at your home in a few minutes to take you there."

My heart sank, and not for the last time. When you're facing necessary surgery, the only thing to do is get it over with. I took a very deep breath and replied, "How long will I be gone? Will I need a suitcase, or just a toothbrush?"

"Don't worry about that. Everything you need will be taken care of." Oddly, I felt better. Somehow it seemed that the hard part was over. A lot of other people were going to help me deal with the Bullocks. All I had to do now was get on a plane. I glanced at Karen. "May I bring my wife?"

There was a brief pause; evidently no one had thought about that. "Certainly. If you wish . . . ."

"Thank you. And is there anything else I need to know?"

"We'll discuss everything when you get here. The President's plane is already on its way."

"The President's – "

"See you soon, Dr. Brewer."

"Uh – thank you."

"It is we who should be thanking you. And if everything goes well, the entire world will soon be thanking you." He hung up.

I turned to my wife. "Want to go to Washington?"

"Not really."

"Why not?"

"Listen: it looks like you'll be talking to the President. About things that will require your full attention. You don't need any distractions. And you can tell me everything when you get back."

"I don't know when that will be."

"Well, if you're speaking to the UN in a week, you'll probably need to talk to Walter again long before that."

I nodded. "All right, if you're sure. But Jones said it would be all right if you – "

"Tell me about it when you get back."

"You want to go with me to the airport?"

"No, I'll stay here with Flower. Do you think I could call the Siegels?"

Before I could answer, the doorbell rang again. It was Wang. I knew because he showed me his badge. "I would put a hold on any calls," he advised, as if he had heard our conversation.

Karen kissed me good-bye and Flower whined, not knowing what was up. Or maybe she did. I gave her a pat, sighed, and shuffled out the door to Wang's waiting Humvee. Before I got in, I looked around wistfully. From our driveway one can just see the tops of the mountains, alive with color. I grinned bitterly: if the human race is wiped out by Walter and his crew, I wouldn't need the colonoscopy scheduled for next month. A perfectly normal reaction, no doubt. I have read that the first thing some people do when they are told they have cancer is to cancel their dental appointments.

We didn't talk on the way to the airport. In fact, I fell asleep, something I often do after lunch. I had been meaning to see someone about possible food sensitivities, but never got around to it. Now it probably wouldn't matter. As I was drifting off, though, it occurred to me to wonder what I would do if my speech to the UN came right after lunch. If one were offered, I could say, "No, thanks, I'm not hungry." To take my mind off the present situation, I quietly chanted that response several more times.

Before I knew it we were at the airport. Wang drove me to the "Departures" entrance. I had no idea where we would go from there. But there was no need to worry: a youngish (anyone under fifty is "youngish" to me) man opened the door for me when we pulled up to the curb. Behind him, and off to the side, stood a couple of other guys in dark blue suits and red ties. Secret Service, I supposed. Ordinarily I would be overwhelmed by such treatment. But after what had already happened only a couple of hours earlier, it somehow didn't seem either thrilling or weird. It was merely another thing I would have to get used to.

I thanked Wang for the ride. Amazingly, he shook my hand. "We're all depending on you, sir," he said. I didn't know whether he meant everyone at the CIA or the entire world's population.

The last words of advice Karen had given me were, "Relax and enjoy it." I couldn't help but smile. Nothing fazes my wife. Nothing ever has. I wished *she* were flying off to see the President, giving the speech to the world. She would no doubt relax and enjoy it.

It was – you guessed it – Mr. Jones who escorted me into the airport. Surprisingly (to me, at least), he was a genial sort, with a wide smile, shiny teeth, cleft chin, and a firm handshake. He was wearing a tweed sport coat – informally dressy, I would call it. Still under forty, I guessed, though not by much. He reminded me of Arthur Beamish, a former colleague (that's how I remember faces – by comparing them to ones I was already familiar with).

As we proceeded past the ticket counters (I was surprised – no one else was in sight, even the ticket agents) he said, "You have a general idea of why the President wants to see you, Dr. Brewer. Or is it the other way around? In either case, let me ask whether you have any questions at the outset."

I had millions. But I doubted that Jones, or anyone else, would know the answers to most of them. "Well, first, how did Wang get to the house so fast? Where was he?"

He scratched his chin. Perhaps he was thinking about how much he could, or should, tell me. Maybe he was only a low-level spy who hadn't yet mastered the art of guile. On the other hand, it's conceivable that his chin itched. Anyway, his answer seemed forthright enough. "Mr. Wang is our liaison with you. I can tell you now that he's been keeping an eye on you since fled's visit. We wanted to be sure that if she or prot came back, or if you received a visit from anyone else, we would know about it immediately. We don't want to screw this one up – it's far too important." He turned to focus his gaze on me, perhaps to make sure I understood the urgency. He needn't have worried. I was as keyed up as if I had had a thousand cups of coffee. "So we stationed Wang at a location very near you, where he has had one job and one job only: to make sure that, this time, we were in on anything that might happen. You were his only – uh – client during that period."

We proceeded to the gates. For the first time, I took a good look around me. There were cops everywhere, in addition to several more obvious G-men wearing identical blue suits and dark glasses. I suddenly realized that, as Karen surmised, I had become a very important person. It was not an altogether unpleasant feeling.

We breezed through Security, the personnel stepping out of the way as if we were royalty. I don't know where they put the regular passengers, but there were none in evidence. "And where is Mr. – ?"

"Mr. Dartmouth is in a rest home near you."

"So Wang can – ?"

"That's right. He visits him every day."

"And when I called him . . ."

"He's been waiting for that call for a long time, Dr. Brewer. For that matter, so has Mr. Dartmouth. He was delighted when it came. Wang told us it cheered him up enormously."

"And if I hadn't called, would he have known about my visitor?"

"Yes. You might as well know now that we have had you under close surveillance for the past eight years."

"You mean . . . ?"

"Well, no. Not in your house. But in your immediate surroundings, yes. We know when you leave and return, where you've been."

"So you have a bug in my car, as well as around the house."

He shrugged. "Yes."

"I see." I paused to let that sink in. "So you know what Walter sounds like."

"And what he looks like, too."

"You mean my car has a camera in it?"

"No, but there are a couple in the woods and one on your roof behind the satellite dish. And others in the various places you visit regularly."

"Like the shopping center."

"Among other places, yes."

I felt somewhat uncomfortable with this information, but that didn't seem to matter much now. "So I'll be dealing with Dartmouth and Wang again? Or at least Wang?"

"No, his job is done. You'll be dealing with us from now on. You'll probably never see him again."

"Oh happy day."

He frowned at me again, this time a little more sharply. "Dr. Brewer, you do realize the significance of what is going on, don't you, sir?"

"Sorry. Of course I do."

He nodded. We turned down a corridor. I presumed we would be heading for a ramp, but we veered into a stairwell and down and out onto the airport grounds. Straight ahead of us was Air Force One. Beautiful and, with "UNITED STATES OF AMERICA" painted on the side of the fuselage, quite unmistakable. There were a few other planes parked here and there, but none taking off or landing, or even taxiing. A half-dozen of us marched straight toward it. The engines were whining softly, like giant animals purring in anticipation. An ambulance stood nearby – I wondered whether one of the pilots had become ill. As we climbed the steps and went aboard through the executive entrance (I was told), I couldn't help recalling the times I had watched newsreels of Presidents and First Ladies trot up those same steps into the First Aircraft. Until that moment I had been able to deal, more or less, with everything that had happened, even my conversation with Walter. But this seemed so unreal that I honestly thought I would wake up at any moment and find that I had dreamed the whole thing. I was in pretty good shape for my age, but I nevertheless found myself panting before we reached the top step, more with anxiety than exertion, I suspect. That was when I realized that the ambulance was standing by for *me*. I suddenly felt very strange. My life had changed inexorably. It appeared that I was being carried along on a journey to the unknown whether I wanted to go or not. Oddly, though, it seemed like a trip I had taken before, and I almost looked forward to whatever was to come. Once you get into a situation like this, no matter how bizarre, it's everything else – your ordinary mundane activities – that suddenly become unreal.

I had followed Mr. Jones up the stairs and into the plane, where the co-captain greeted me with a cheery salute (though not a handshake, perhaps so that I wouldn't catch any viruses he might harbor). "Welcome aboard, sir." I nodded importantly. We turned right upon entering, just as you would with any ordinary commercial flight. There the similarity ended. Of course, I expected to see rows of seats stretched out before me, as I always have, but we passed through a meeting room of some kind (where I was introduced to a medical doctor named Greaney) and into what was obviously a dining room. Jones indicated where I might sit, and I slipped into a comfortable-looking chair. My host sat down next to me while our armed (I presumed) escorts positioned themselves around the "room," some still standing, at least until takeoff. By then the cabin door had closed and we were already taxiing almost imperceptibly toward a runway. I instinctively fastened my seat belt.

"Comfortable?" Jones asked me. "Have you had lunch? Can we get you anything to drink?"

"Maybe a Coke?"

He lifted a finger and an attendant appeared immediately. "Cokes," Jones told him, and he hurried off, returning in only a moment with two tall glasses fizzing and tinkling with the cola and transparent cubes of ice, served on a handsome tray with the Presidential seal embossed on the surface. I had once spilled a soft drink in-flight, so I took the proffered straw.

"I could get used to this," I said with a feeble smile.

"You'd be surprised how many people say that. Including Presidents and members of the Cabinet, and even the press. On their first trip, at least."

"I suppose so."

We were already rolling down the runway, and those who were standing quickly found seats, though the acceleration and liftoff were so smooth that I hardly felt any change in speed or takeoff angle. I felt a little trepidation, the familiar tingling in my stomach. It wasn't that I was worried about the flight (I, myself, had learned to fly a few years earlier, though I hadn't flown in a while), which Jones told me would take only an hour or so. It was that a whole spectrum of events were rushing forward, indeed accelerating, with me imbedded in them like an insect in amber, and I realized there was no turning back. We were hurtling toward the unknown, just as we were climbing into empty space. I pretended coolness by taking another sip of the fizzy beverage. As we lifted off, Jones told me a bit about the aircraft itself, with its armored windows and defense systems, the various offices on the other side of the plane, the Presidential suite on the upper level. When he had finished this cursory description, he suggested we compare notes.

"I don't have any notes."

After staring at me for a moment he said, "Okay, I'll begin. If I get something wrong, you'll tell me, okay?"

"Fine." I gazed toward the rear of the plane, wondered who or what might be in the rear compartments.

"We know you were visited by a man named Walter, who is, in reality, a corpse." He pulled a picture from his inside jacket pocket. It had been taken in the shopping center parking lot only a few hours before. It seemed like days. "That's him, isn't it?"

And there he was, my worst nightmare. Even in a photo, and a telephoto at that, I could see the eyes, vacant and staring. "Where is he now? The body, I mean."

"Our visitor left him where he found him."

"I think he prefers the royal 'we.'"

"So we heard. I didn't know whether you were comfortable with that."

"I'm not comfortable with any of this."

"Yes, of course. Neither was I. But none of us have much choice in matters like this, sir, wouldn't you say?"

I remember sighing deeply at that point. It wouldn't be my last involuntary bodily function. "Yes, I guess that's true."

"Now, the Bullocks want you to make a speech to the United Nations Security Council, right?"

"That's what he – I mean they – said."

"But you don't know what they want you to speak about."

"No, not exactly. Something about our eagerness to kill each other, I think."

"And that's supposed to happen in a week or so, right?"

"Yes. He said a week. But is that possible? Can arrangements be made with the UN to get something on their calendar that fast? Maybe we should schedule it for sometime next year? By then – "

"Dr. Brewer, let's get something straight. We've learned a few things since your last visitor. The government was a bit slow to react to fled, and frankly we weren't sure at first whether she was really from the planet K-PAX. But we have a different President and a different visitor now. So let's cut to the chase. We believe that anyone who can make a dead body walk and talk, and make a large tree disappear without a trace, is probably who they say they are. And we take what they say very, very seriously. The future of the human race and perhaps everything else on the planet depends on that. We have confidence that you will do whatever is necessary to accommodate the Bullocks' wishes, but we need to be sure we're all on the same page. Understood and agreed to so far?"

"Do I have a choice?"

"No, I'm afraid not."

"Okay," I replied dismally, "what do we do next?"

"The President is waiting for you at the White House, along with the Vice-president, the Cabinet, Congressional leaders of both parties, and a number of diplomats who have made themselves available, mainly to help determine how the Bullocks' demands can best be carried out, if that is, in fact, possible. At a later time some of them will meet with a number of foreign heads of state to inform them and give them a chance to express their views on the situation. There isn't time for that right now."

"What about the military?"

He smiled a bit wearily. "This isn't a movie, sir. It's for real. The military isn't going to attack Walter, or anyone else. We all feel this wouldn't do us the slightest good, and could be extremely counterproductive. Nevertheless, the chairman of the Joint Chiefs of Staff will be there, but only so that the military will be informed, and will not do anything rash, no matter what happens."

I sucked on my straw, vaguely remembering the days when I was a smoker, and even before that, when I sucked my thumb until I was almost three. How odd it is that so many of us can never give up the warmth and comfort of a mother's breast. Or is it? "How long has the government been making plans for the Bullocks' arrival?"

"Ever since fled's departure."

How did you know they would be here so soon? They were supposed – "

"I'll tell you a secret. Some people think our government only reacts to problems that come before it. The fact is, there are contingency plans for many things that might never happen: an asteroid on a collision course with the Earth, a new plague starting in some remote part of the world, nuclear weapons getting into the wrong hands, and so forth. An invasion of any kind, even a friendly one, by alien beings is at the top of the list. *Especially* an invasion by aliens, in view of the fact that we know they are out there, thanks to your two visitors. Now *three* visitors. Maybe even more. A consensus has been reached, both within the government and with other governments, that we need to co-operate with the Bullocks and carry out whatever demands they might make, unless they are impossible for us to comply with. Otherwise the consequences could be disastrous. Are you surprised to learn that the government is on top of these things?"

"Well . . . Yes, I suppose I am. I had the feeling that our government is almost clueless sometimes."

"As I said, what really goes on is not advertised, nor can it be. Some of it is classified, if you will. You'd be surprised what the experts tell us would happen if the public knew about the contingency plans we have in place. Many people would misunderstand our intentions and freak out. A few trusted members of the press know a little of this, but very few."

"So why are you letting me in on the secret?"

"Because of what's happened, you've been put in the 'need to know' category."

"I don't know whether to be proud of this honor, or terrified by it."

"It is what it is."

"So why call me in? You've already decided on what has to be done. There's nothing to do now but wait until I hear from Walter again, is there?"

"Well, sir, there's one factor missing from the equation. That's where you come in."

"What factor?"

"*You*, Dr. Brewer. We need to make sure that you are as well-prepared as possible for your next encounter with Walter, or whoever they happen to be at the time. And for your address to the United Nations."

"What exactly do you mean?"

"We need to make certain that you are in compliance with the general tenets of the overall plan. That you're not going to be a rogue elephant unwilling to co-operate with us, or with Walter. That you have no health or psychological issues that would preclude your speaking at a time certain to the UN. To the world."

"Oh. Yes, I see what you mean. But you have to admit it's not easy to have the survival of the whole world on your shoulders."

"Many others do. Presidents and comparable ministers of state. But they are only human, just as you are. They have grappled with this responsibility at some time or other in their histories and have concluded that they can handle it. Because someone *must* handle it, whatever the situation. I don't know if many people give their leaders enough credit in this regard. There are many who could not deal with the pressure. We want to make sure you are not one of those."

I certainly was one of those. My doubts were sickeningly profound. One last time I tried to think of a way out of my dilemma, but could not. I sucked on the straw, and the last of the Coke climbed noisily up the tube as if it were a death rattle.

"We're descending," Jones advised. "Seat belt fastened?"

"Can I go to the bathroom?"

"Yes, but make it fast." He thumbed to the rear.

The restroom was just in front of a room filled with desks, TV sets and telephones, with more private facilities further back, I presumed. I was tempted to take a look. But nature trumps curiosity. I relieved myself in the beautiful, shiny toilet. But when I turned to wash my hands I saw the reflection of a man with tears running down his cheeks. I remember telling myself to get a grip. I rinsed my face and went back into the "dining room" to confront my unwanted responsibility. Out the window I could see that we were already on final approach.

"Do I get a tour of the President's quarters?" I asked hopefully. "After all, how many chances will I have to ride in Air Force One?"

Jones smiled warmly. "Maybe another time. By the way," he added, "it's only Air Force One when the President is on board."

I barely felt the landing. Before I knew what was happening, the plane rolled to a smooth stop, the engines were shut down, and we climbed down the stairs and into a waiting helicopter, also embossed on the side with "UNITED STATES OF AMERICA," and known familiarly as "Marine One" (but only when the President is inside, presumably). In another minute or two we were flying toward the nation's capital – I could see the Washington monument in the distance. As we buzzed unrelentingly toward it, Jones asked me questions about my past, including my medical and psychological histories. I confessed that I had been a smoker decades ago, though, like many people, I became more concerned with my health when I was in my forties, quit smoking and began a desultory exercise program. I still jog a couple of times a week, and all of my medical exams in recent years have turned up nothing of importance. A stress echocardiogram within the past year and a CT scan a couple of years before that showed nothing ominous. It was comforting to know that even the federal government didn't know any of this, or appeared not to know, though I might have been mistaken about that. In any case, he then turned to my lifelong fear of public speaking.

"Why do you think that is?" he asked me, his eyebrows raised, his pen poised.

"I've asked myself the same question," I replied. "It probably has to do with my insecurity, my feelings of inferiority when I compared myself to my father. He was an authoritative figure who had strong opinions which he rarely questioned. I felt that he wanted to run my life, and I suppose that made me feel incompetent to run it myself. So my dislike of speaking in public is a result of a fear of not being up to the job, to put it in the simplest possible terms. It's basically a fear of laughter and ridicule." I looked him right in the eye. "In my professional opinion," I added, "fear is probably behind much of our personalities, not to mention our religions. It can be both a strong motivator and a powerful inhibitor of much of what we do in life."

He chuckled a little at this analysis. "You sound like a psychiatrist."

"I was, once." I added that most psychiatrists possessed some sort of mental quirk or another, which often motivated their choice of profession.

"I see. So do you think you wouldn't be able to carry it off?"

"Carry what off?"

"Your mission. Speaking to the UN Security Council."

I stared at him. "I honestly don't know what might happen. I don't think I would faint, but I would probably be shaking, and so would my voice."

"I'll tell you another secret. Even presidents and kings have that problem. Especially at critical times like this. The trick is to control your trepidation enough that no one notices. We have people who can help you with that. And one more thing: audiences always pull for a speaker, even if unconsciously, hoping he will do well. They tend to put themselves in his or her place. It's only human nature."

"I'm happy to hear that," I replied. Nevertheless, glancing out the side window at a city full of historically significant buildings, I felt very, very small. I wondered whether presidents and kings ever felt like that.

"On the other hand," he went on, "many people rise to the occasion, and perform quite admirably under very stressful conditions. I've been told that they never felt more confident and happy than when they were thrust into a situation like this. Perhaps you fall into that category."

I noted that we had descended, and were flying between the Lincoln monument and the Capitol building. The sight made me shiver, but whether with awe or terror I wasn't sure. In any case I gawked around at the historic landscape like any ordinary tourist.

Three of the G-men were in the helicopter with us. Two of them were stoically staring out the windows, but who knows what they were thinking. Did they even know what was going on? The other was texting someone. I wondered whether it was the President, or maybe his Chief of Staff or the like. Jones was reading something on his Blackberry. I took a look at his face. His expression was one of serene professionalism, whatever that might mean. Someone who wouldn't be ruffled easily. Whatever it was he did all day, he was obviously good at it. A fairly handsome guy, in an off-kilter kind of way. Otherwise he was rather average-looking, the kind of man you wouldn't notice in a crowd.

I saw that he was wearing a wedding ring. When he clicked shut the phone, I asked him whether he had any children.

"Two," he replied without hesitation, and whipped out a photo kept safe inside his wallet. His wife was attractive, though not strikingly so, and the kids looked absolutely normal. Both boys were wearing soccer uniforms. They looked to be about ten and eight.

"I'm surprised you are being so open and honest with me. Dartmouth and Wang – "

"We're not CIA. I'm a presidential assistant, and these men are Secret Service agents. As you probably know, their responsibility is to the Department of Homeland Security and, ultimately, to the President. You're in good hands, by the way. Their motto is, 'Worthy of Trust and Confidence.'"

"I'm still surprised."

He looked directly at me. As a psychiatrist, I'm supposed to be able to judge certain feelings by a person's facial expressions. What I saw in his was mainly concern, mixed with a hint of sadness. "I'm being honest with you because this is no time for guile. Or politics of any kind. This is about our survival, Dr. Brewer. I can't put it more plainly. Or more strongly. Walter is our only concern right now."

"And after that, you go back to the lying and deceit?"

He stared at me for a moment before breaking into a smile, then a high-pitched, squealing laugh. We both felt a welcome release from the tension. When it stopped, he said, "You may find this hard to believe, sir, but sometimes lying and deceit are necessary in order to run a government."

"Call me Gene."

"Mike," he said, offering me a strong, rough hand, surprisingly toughened by physical work of some sort. I squeezed it for a moment before letting go. Maybe I was holding on to it for support, for reassurance. All I know is that at that point I needed a hand. I wished my wife had decided to come along.

We were already descending to the White House lawn. The well-known home of Presidents was mere yards away. Indeed, it was only another few minutes before we were striding across the well-trimmed grass toward a back entrance. Another pair of Secret Service agents (I presumed) appeared from somewhere and opened the doors. Unsmiling men (and a couple of women) in uniform stood silently, staring straight ahead. Again I wondered whether they knew what was happening or merely assumed I was a visiting VIP.

We followed a young woman carrying a clipboard into a foyer displaying marble busts of various people. One was unmistakably of Abraham Lincoln, I noted. Once more I wanted to cry. Only a hundred and fifty years earlier, he would have been the resident here. A mere grain in the sands of time. Everything was happening so fast! I could feel my heart pounding, my respiration rate increasing. The phalanx proceeded in lock step deep into the building and down a long corridor. I thought briefly about green rooms and blue rooms and Lincoln bedrooms, but there was no time to dwell on such matters. We strode briskly into what I thought was going to be the Oval Office, but it turned out to be the Cabinet Room. It was filled with people, some of whom I recognized immediately. The President, who was sitting at the center of the long, oval table, jumped up to greet me, hand outstretched. My knees almost buckled, but I managed to squeak, "Mr. President."

"Thank you for coming, Dr. Brewer. Before we sit down, I'd like to introduce you to everyone here." We proceeded around the table, where I shook hands with almost all the members of the cabinet (the Secretary of State hadn't yet returned from a visit to the Middle East, and the Vice-President was on his way back from Asia), the Speaker of the House of Representatives and other Congressional leaders, as well as the Chairman of the Joint Chiefs of Staff, and certain other government officials and invited guests, a couple of whom were identified by the title, "Doctor." Were they medical men hovering around the President? Or perhaps they were academic types. There were a few Secret Service people standing along the walls. Perhaps there were other Presidential aides and assistants as well. I caught the eye of Mike Jones, who smiled and nodded reassuringly. After all that, the President waved toward the table. "Please – take this seat." It was the one just to his left. "Coffee? Tea?"

I found myself saying, "I would love a cup of tea." It must have been around four o'clock (I had forgotten my watch), the time my wife and I usually set aside for tea and a nosh, a custom we began after a visit to England a few years ago.

"Herbal, or the real thing?"

"I think I need the real thing." He nodded understandingly, and someone literally ran to fetch it. I took this brief opportunity to look around at the paintings, the bust of George Washington, the numerous draped windows facing the front lawn, the unlit fireplace. Who knew if I would ever be back here again?

The President immediately cleared his throat and began. "Just to bring you up to snuff," he said to me, "we've all been briefed on this morning's events. I can assure you that everyone here is fully aware of the situation, and the focus of our efforts from now until this matter is resolved will be to support you in any way we can." He paused to gaze at me – or perhaps look me over. I think he was waiting for me to respond, to indicate in some way that I had heard him.

"Thank you, Mr. President." What else could I say?

Satisfied that I could hear all right, perhaps, he nodded and bestowed on me his famous smile, up close and personal. "Our first priority, of course, is to determine what these, uh, Bullocks, want to tell us. Or maybe I should say, what they want *you* to tell us – all the citizens of the world – through the United Nations. Apparently they didn't inform you when or where you would be given their demands, if that's what they will be – is that correct?"

"He said nothing about that. Only that he would be back soon. I think he wanted this meeting to happen first. To make sure I had the backing of the government, I guess."

"Yes, we assumed that. And I can tell you now that an appearance at the Security Council has already been tentatively arranged, except for the exact time. This you can convey to 'Walter,' or whoever they happen to be the next time you see them."

Satisfied, myself, in some ass-backward way, I replied, with as much confidence as I could muster, "I'll do that." At least I knew now that I wouldn't be shouldering the responsibility alone.

"The next thing to decide is whether you should stay in Washington until they show themselves again, or return to your home. Do you have any feelings about that?"

At that moment the tea came: a full pot, with a matching porcelain cup and silver spoon, along with ample milk and sugar. An aide poured a little into the cup and waited, apparently for me to indicate whether it was strong enough. When I nodded, she filled the cup and I took a quick, grateful sip. For some reason the only thing that came to mind was, My God! I'm having tea with the President! "Well, Walter didn't indicate where I should be. My guess is that it probably doesn't matter."

He nodded. "We think the same thing. That leaves the question of what you, yourself, would prefer."

"Of course I would like to be home. Unless that would create some kind of difficulty for you."

"Not at all. And that may be where Walter would expect to find you. Of course, we will have to send some people to facilitate communication and to keep a close eye on the situation. I'm sure you understand that we need to be certain there are no misunderstandings between you and the Bullocks, or between you and the various governments of the world. And that there is nothing that might prevent you from delivering their message to the UN. We will be sending you advisors and facilitators and security people, and anyone or anything else we feel you might need in order to accomplish your mission, whatever that may be. There will be daily meetings and briefings. Every detail of your appearance before the Security Council must be worked out to the Nth degree. Is any of this a problem for you?"

"Well, my wife and I were planning a little trip to Vermont next week. But I suppose we could put it off . . . ."

There were ripples of mirth around the room. The President smiled understandingly. "Yes, we would appreciate it if you could do that."

"No problem," I assured him, grinning weakly at my own little joke.

"Now, while everyone is here, do you have any questions for *us*, Dr. Brewer? You might not get a chance like this again before – well, we're calling it 'Message Day.' Or 'M-Day.'"

I glanced around the room. Every single face was turned toward me with anticipation. But my mind was a blank. All I could come up with was, "Does anyone have any suggestions?"

There were smiles and nods of – I don't know – relief, maybe. Relief that I wasn't planning to do anything stupid on my own. I heard someone say, "Just do your best, Doctor."

The President added, "We all understand how difficult this must be for you, sir. Let me just reiterate what you've been told already. All of us – every one of us – is with you. The whole *world* is with you on this. You have been chosen to do something that has never been done before. But we want you to know that when you give that speech at the UN we will all be there with you. If you fail, it merely means that we all share that failure. We all share the responsibility. Do you understand what I'm saying?"

Suddenly I saw something like Walter in my mind's eye. What the President was saying was very much like the way Walter described the Bullocks. A colony of like-minded individuals. All for one and one for all. It suddenly seemed like a very good idea. "Yes, sir, Mr. President, and I'll do my very best."

There was spontaneous applause. I even heard a few cheers. Ordinarily I would have been very gratified by all that. None of it seemed important now. I realized that I hadn't asked for this. But for the first time I thought that maybe I could do it, and for the same reason that others have done what had to be done. Damn the torpedoes, etc. At least that's what I felt at that moment.

The meeting broke up shortly thereafter. Everyone except the Secret Service agents passed along the table shaking hands with the President and with me. "You have my full support." "If you need anything, don't hesitate to ask." And so on.

After almost everyone had gone, the President said, "Walk with me." We (Mike and I and the President's Chief of Staff) strode a little distance and into what was unmistakably the Oval Office next door. Everyone knows what it looks like: the shiny desk with the big windows behind it facing a tree-filled lawn and fountain, lots of comfortable chairs and sofas, huge chandeliers hanging from the ceiling. I realized that the whole world was still oblivious to what was going on here. I felt sorry for everyone out beyond Pennsylvania Avenue.

The President indicated that I should sit. He leaned back against the desk. "I've never met an alien," he confessed, grinning broadly. "Though some people think I *am* one. Tell me what they're like."

"Well, the first one, prot, was like almost anyone. From Earth, I mean. He looked just like one of us. In fact, he explained this by saying that, throughout the galaxy, most species like ours look pretty much like we do. Same for all the plants and animals. Evolution sees to that. He didn't suffer fools gladly, but at the same time he was quite personable. He actually became something of a friend, or even more like a son, to me."

"Yes, I've read your books," he said. "But only recently, I'm afraid. What about fled?"

"Ah. She was entirely different. You've read my book about her, too?" He nodded. "Well, all I can say about fled is that you had to see her to believe her. She looked a lot like a chimpanzee, but was the size of a gorilla. Like prot, though, she spoke perfect English. And you know what I remember most? Her smell."

"What was it like?"

"I don't really know how to describe it. Have you ever stuck your face into a dog's fur?"

The President snorted. "Yes, I have."

"It was something like that, only stronger and wilder. Something like that of an actual chimpanzee, I imagine. But, of course, unique to her own species. Her own planet, maybe."

"Were you afraid of her?"

"Not really. She was loud and boisterous, even a little obnoxious, but I came to like her quite a lot, as I did with prot. In fact, I rather miss them both."

"And Walter?"

"Now that's a different story altogether. *Them* I'm afraid of."

"Why is that?"

"Have you seen the pictures of them?"

He glanced at Jones. "Yes, I have."

"Well, it's worse close-up."

"In what way?"

"Their eyes are . . . Their eyes are *terrifying*. Much more so than in the pictures. Frankly, they looked as if they wanted to kill me. I think I disgusted them, if they're capable of that emotion."

"I see. But aside from that, do you think you can believe what they told you?"

"With absolute certainty. I don't think they're lying, or faking a thing. They're seriously pissed by our continual killing of each other, as if life were meaningless. They don't seem to have any religions, so to them, life is everything. Maybe life is their religion. Anyway, I truly believe the Bullocks could do whatever they want to us. Or to the Earth itself, for that matter."

"That's what we think, too. And the reason we all think that is because of your experience with the earlier visitors from K-PAX." The President thought for a minute. "By the way, do you have any idea where the Bullocks come from? It's not K-PAX, right?"

"No. But he – I'm sorry – *they* never said where their planet is located, only that it's not their first home. The earlier ones have long since become uninhabitable. But I think they were all called 'Bullock.' Or maybe that's what they're using because it's something we can pronounce."

He nodded and mused, "I suppose that could be a glimpse of our own future. If we survive this ordeal, of course. One last question, Dr. B." He smiled as he used the name most of my patients did. "Is there anything else we need to know that hasn't yet come up?" To me he seemed completely in control, almost preternaturally calm in the face of potential disaster. I wished he were giving the speech.

"Do you mean are there any skeletons in my closet?"

"No, nothing as political as that. I meant, is there anything you obtained from prot or fled, or Walter, for that matter, that you haven't mentioned? Or that has occurred to you at some point but no one has asked you about it?"

"You mean some insight into how we might react to the Bullocks? That sort of thing?"

"Yes"

"Well . . ." I hesitated, but there were no longer any secrets worth keeping. I knew that was over for now. "Fled brought a device that sort of read our minds and revealed our thoughts so that we could look into some earlier aspect of our lives. The images could be projected onto a wall or anything else. Like a movie projector. She used it with some of my former patients. And what they had suffered as children was so painful for me that I buried the damn thing in the woods behind the house."

"Do you think you could show us where it is buried, Gene?"

I wasn't sure of that, but I said, "Probably."

"I think we'll need to look into that. Anything else?"

"Well, as you know, I think, Walter can read our minds. So could fled, who could even read the personal history stored there. They know what we are thinking. I don't know what else they can do, but based on what I've seen, the sky's the limit. No pun intended. Even prot and fled were so far advanced compared to us – "

"And Walter is to them as they were to us, is that what you mean?"

I hadn't thought about it that way. Shifting uncomfortably, I nodded. "That's exactly what I mean."

"Then we'd better get busy." He stood up and grabbed my hand. The handshake was firm and prolonged. "After all, they may already be waiting for you at your residence." He turned to Jones. "Mike, see that Dr. Brewer gets safely home, will you?"

"You bet, Mr. President. Are you ready, Gene?"

"I hope so."

"We'll be in close touch, Dr. B." The President scribbled something on a little card, which was otherwise blank. "This is my private number. You can call me anytime night or day without going through my secretary or anyone else."

I stared at the number, wondering how many other people knew it. The Russian and Chinese Prime Ministers? European heads of state? The director of the National Security Administration? Mike was already at the door. I said, "Good-bye, Mr. President. I'll certainly let you know if anything comes up that needs your immediate attention."

"Thank you. Until this is over, I'm not going anywhere," he responded with a sad smile.

Mike and I marched down the corridor to the door through which we had entered the White House only a moment earlier, or so it seemed, and we reversed the helicopter trip back to the big 747 and home.

On the plane I had an opportunity to talk further with my youthful escort. He mentioned some things I might expect in the next few days – briefings and meetings – but we also covered any number of other topics. In fact, I would say I got to know him pretty well. He and his wife had a place in Virginia, and his hands were, in fact, toughened by cutting and hauling firewood. "Very relaxing," he said. "You may remember that President Reagan did the same thing at his California ranch."

Besides a rugged physical appearance, I discovered that Mike possessed an exceptional mind. His memory bordered on the phenomenal: politics, government, sports, history, and even the sciences. He seemed to know everything. It occurred to me that a mind like his could come in very handy in almost any situation, including the present one. I hoped he wouldn't be far away if I needed him for anything. As it turned out, I needn't have worried.

But aside from all that, he was one of the nicest people I've ever met. Calm and level-headed and reassuring. I think he accepted people as they were, and rarely if ever became angry with anyone. On the other hand, one thing I had learned over the years was that no one can tell what is inside another person's head. No *human*, I mean.

The trip from the airport was yet another jaw-dropping experience. It involved a caravan of four identical black limousines; ours was the third. It was equipped with two television sets and several electronic devices, most of which I wasn't familiar with. One of the screens actually displayed our caravan from the air, as seen, presumably from an aircraft flying somewhere overhead. Mike informed me that my new personal physician, Dr. Greaney, rode in the ambulance at the end of the convoy.

When we got back to the house there was a long double-wide trailer perched in the driveway. I asked Mike what it was for, but I already knew the answer. His terminology was "Nerve Center." Inside the mobile complex, he told me, was a tiny medical clinic, surveillance equipment, security headquarters, and a food-handling staff, among other things, including several meeting rooms. I stared at the thing for a moment in disbelief before heading toward the house. "One final thing, Gene," he said. "We're going to have to cordon off the road and station people in the woods around your home. This may inconvenience you a bit, but I'm sure you understand. You're free to call your neighbors and explain everything if you like. For the next week, though, you may find yourself somewhat isolated."

"Can my wife have visitors? She's going to be pretty lonely for the next week."

"I'll see what I can do. But they should be kept to a minimum, for obvious reasons."

I shrugged and went into the house, where Karen was waiting for me with a plate of hot food, which had already been tasted by someone in the trailer. They must have told her that I declined to eat on the plane. "How was your meeting with the President?" she asked me, and we both started to giggle. Soon we were howling. I expected a head to pop up in the kitchen window, but we were left alone for the time being, and we sat down to a nice dinner.

"You know, when I married you," she said, "I knew you were capable of great things. I even imagined sometimes that you would win the Nobel Prize or maybe appear on talk shows or something like that. I wasn't even surprised when your book about prot was made into a big movie and you found yourself doing a cameo. But I can't get over the fact that you just came back from the Oval Office."

"Me, either."

Of course, like any wife, she wanted to know what the President was like.

"Just like he is on television," I told her, but she wanted more. "Well, he's tall, which always makes a person seem more commanding, I suppose, and he has a glorious smile. There's no doubt who's in charge, like there was with the last guy. I think he's pretty deep, too. There are *layers* of personality under his placid exterior." I felt around in my shirt pocket and pulled out the tiny card he had given me. "His private phone number." We giggled again for a while.

"All the kids and grandkids called. Everyone wants to talk to you. Especially your son-in-law."

"Of course Steve would want that. But I suspect he would really prefer to talk to Walter."

"Anyway, I told him you'd call him when you could, like I told everyone else."

"God, I'm tired," I confessed, even though I was still wide awake.

"It's okay. I'll come to bed in a few minutes, after I finish up here." By the time she got there I was already sound asleep. The last thought I had was: How strange life is. You go to the shopping mall for a few little items and end up in the Oval Office . . . .

DAY TWO

If I had any dreams that night, I can't remember them. I've never been able to remember my dreams very clearly, or at least most of them. Some of my former patients could recall lengthy dreams in exquisite detail. It's one of those little mysteries of psychiatry: why some people can and others can't. I used to spend hours wondering about that. Those were wonderful years, years when I was deep in the workings of the mind, the most fascinating subject imaginable. But there was no longer time to dwell on such mundane matters, with the survival of the human race at stake. I needed to keep my aging brain focused on that issue, to the exclusion of everything else. This fact was brought home first thing that morning. I was just climbing out of bed (was the bedroom now under video surveillance?) when the phone rang.

"Good morning, Gene," came a calm, cheerful voice. "This is Mike. Sleep well?"

"No."

He laughed into the phone. "To tell you the truth, I didn't either. But that's part of the job."

"I suppose so."

"I'll be over in a few minutes. Will you be ready?"

I looked at the clock. It was 6:30 A.M. "I just have to get dressed. Do I have time for a shower?"

"Of course. You can have all the time you want, as long as it's under ten minutes. We have a long day ahead of us." I thought I heard a chuckle, but I may have imagined it. There was no longer time for joking.

I found Karen in the kitchen. She had already been up for an hour. But she wasn't making breakfast – she was just sitting there in her bathrobe staring into space. This worried me – she is usually as unperturbed as a sloth. "Are you okay, peach?"

"I didn't sleep at all last night. It finally hit me, I guess."

I gave her a hug. "We'll talk about it later. Mike's coming over in a few minutes."

"What do we do about breakfast? Do I have to take every meal over to the tasters, or do they come here?"

"I don't know. We'll ask him. I'm going to take a quick shower."

When I came back ten minutes later, Mike was there, and so was breakfast. Someone from the Nerve Center kitchen staff had brought it over. It actually didn't look too bad: scrambled eggs and home fries and all the rest. "Are you joining us?" I asked Mike.

"Thanks – ordinarily I'd love to. But you can only have a cup of coffee for now. You have a blood draw in a few minutes. After that you can eat all you want."

I stared at the food while Mike took a generous helping for himself and gobbled it down, explaining that he hadn't had time for a meal the previous evening. Karen declined. "I'll eat with Gene," she explained.

"Is this the pattern?" I asked him. "Will someone be bringing all our meals over?"

"That's about the size of it. Whatever you already have in the house is okay, in a pinch – if you need a snack or something. Otherwise, we'll take care of everything. Even the silverware." He poured himself another cup of coffee from the big carafe and sat back with a sigh. "Now, let's get to work, shall we?"

"Before that happens, should I excuse myself?" Karen asked him.

"Not at all. You're as important as Gene in this situation. But if you have something you need to do, that's fine. You can't leave the house, though, which I'm sure you've already realized."

"Not even with an escort?"

"No, unless it's an emergency of some kind."

She gazed unhappily out the window and nodded. I felt sorry for her – my lovely wife is the active type. She has a whole case full of bowling trophies, for example.

"You can have a few people *here*, though. Family, a couple of close friends. He poured her another cup, then reached over and picked up his clipboard, which he had placed on the fourth kitchen chair. "Okay, I've got today's schedule worked out." He handed one copy to Karen, and one to me. I looked at it, my eyes widening. There were at least a dozen items listed, beginning with a physical, including eye and dental exams. That was followed by a visit with a team of four mental health professionals – two psychiatrists and two psychologists.

"Why do I need a dental exam to talk to an alien?"

"Well, I can imagine a rare instance where you could get a terrific toothache of the sort that might affect your concentration in some way. There shouldn't be any distractions of any kind. Think of yourself as an astronaut."

I've hated the dentist's chair since I was a kid. The smell of mouthwash alone turns my stomach. "But I just saw my dentist a month – "

"Anything can happen in a month."

I shrugged and perused the rest of the list. The exams would take all morning. The afternoon would be spent in meetings with "strategic staff," whoever they were. "Will you be at those meetings?"

"Yes. For the most part, I'm your confidante and your liaison with everyone else. I hope that won't be a problem for you."

"No, not at all. I'm sure it's a dirty job that someone has to do."

He gave me a barely detectable smile before checking his smart phone. "It's time. Are you ready, Dr. B?"

"No."

He shook his head. "Let's go."

I won't bore the reader with the gory details, except to say that it was the most thorough physical I've ever had. The chief physician was the guy who had accompanied Mike and me to Washington and back – Dr. Greaney. I was poked and prodded in places I barely remembered from medical school anatomy classes, asked for blood and urine and saliva samples, had my prostate prodded and squeezed. There was an electrocardiogram and an encephalogram. Nothing I hadn't experienced before. The only difference was that there was no waiting. Pending the results of the blood work, I was as healthy as a horse, my new doctor informed me, adding that "if any problems of any kind come up, even a hangnail, I'll be here." I thanked him and was whisked to the next room.

My glasses were apparently adequate, as was my dental work. I was given thirty minutes for breakfast and told to report back for psychiatric analysis. I complained that I couldn't eat "all I wanted" in half an hour, but Mike merely smiled and grunted, "Welcome to government work."

The Secret Service agents stationed outside the trailer stared straight ahead as if I were invisible. Halfway back to the house, Flower came bounding out the dog door and, like the G-men I had just passed, completely ignored me and started toward a squirrel sitting in the yard. I watched, knowing she would never catch it. But then a strange thing happened. The squirrel didn't move, and I was afraid it was done for. Before I could yell, though, Flower suddenly stopped short and gave it a long, thorough sniff reminiscent of the exam I had just endured in the trailer, before bolting for the house. I heard someone say, "Good morning, doctor." At first I thought it must have come from the woods, or from inside the trailer, but I soon realized it was the squirrel.

"Walter??"

"That's as good a name as any," they growled.

I studied the bushy-tailed rodent carefully, but I couldn't see its mouth move, and I realized it wasn't speaking, but somehow projecting its (their) thoughts into my head. The Secret Service agents stood like a pair of stone statues, saying nothing. I wondered if they were aware that Walter was communicating with me.

"Uh . . . I'm not sure I'm supposed to talk to you yet. There are certain preparations – "

"Your health is adequate for your needs. If it weren't we would have approached someone else."

"Thank you for the expert medical opinion."

"Now comes the mental testing, a process you are quite familiar with."

"That's right. How did – Oh. Right. You know everything."

"Only what is in your mind."

I thought about that. So did they, I presumed. Thought about what I was thinking, I mean. "May I ask you a question?"

They snorted, "You may ask anything relevant."

"Do you know what's in *everyone's* mind? All the people in the whole world?"

He seemed annoyed, but he answered the question. "Not all at the same time. That would be quite a feat even for us. There are limits to everything. Even to the universe itself."

"Can you tell me why you're here *now*? I know it's because of our inherent violence, but that's been ingrained for thousands of years. Since the beginning, probably."

"We all hoped you might evolve at some point, but now it appears that's never going to happen. With your present mindset, you can't even stop your climate from deteriorating. Unless someone intervenes, we've concluded that you will *never* end the killing. It is programmed into your DNA."

"Lions kill!"

"Lions need to kill in order to survive. You don't."

It suddenly occurred to me that Walter wasn't answering my questions with so much malice or contempt as he was earlier. But perhaps this merely reflected the actual Walter's personality when he wasn't occupying a corpse. Or the influence of the squirrel's. It also occurred to me again that maybe I was, in fact, crazy, or at least daydreaming.

"No, you're not dreaming, but we understand why you might think so."

"I'm sure I will have many more questions for you, Walter, but I'm not prepared for that yet. When will I see you again?"

"Maybe never."

"What? You're leaving already? But you haven't – "

"Now that you understand that we can get into your mind, we won't need to physically appear to you again."

"Then why are you doing so now?"

"With your species it's a step-by-step procedure. If we suddenly spoke to you from the inside, you would undoubtedly 'freak out.' Which wouldn't help either of us. That's why we first came to you as a human being."

"I'm freaking out right now."

"You'll get used to it. The worst is over. From now on, we'll be here whenever you need to ask something. Or if we need to tell you something even without your asking."

"No matter where I am?"

"For the time being we'll talk here. Otherwise you might freak out everyone else around you."

I pondered that for a moment before asking a question I didn't want to know the answer to. "So from now on you'll be *residing* in my head?"

"No, doctor, but wherever you are, we'll be nearby."

"As a physical presence, you mean? Like a fly on the wall?"

"Let's just say we will be there in spirit."

Was that a joke? "So you'll always know what I'm thinking, no matter where I am?"

"Only until we leave you seven days from now."

Another unpleasant thought: "Do you know everything I have *always* thought? All my memories? Even things I can't remember any more?"

"No. Only those you are remembering at the present time."

"So you know a meeting with the UN Security Council has already been arranged."

"Of course. We were there when it was discussed."

"You were in the *White House*?"

"Yes."

I felt violated. There would never again be any privacy. As long as the Bullocks were here, my mind would be an open book. Even the bedroom and the bathroom would be under surveillance.

"Don't worry, *doctor* (he uttered this with the familiar disdain). We're not interested in your pathetic sex life, or any of your other bodily functions. Except for the killing."

Somehow this information wasn't much comfort. I looked around and noticed that the agents hadn't moved a muscle. They seemed to be completely ignoring us. I wondered whether their minds were temporarily turned off. Otherwise wouldn't they notice that I was standing in the middle of the backyard talking to a squirrel while they patiently waited for me to go inside? Had their thoughts been jumbled?

"We're wasting time, doctor. Let's try to focus, shall we?"

"I *am* focusing. As you must know, I was merely wondering whether you can put things into our heads. And if that is true, you could be at the United Nations to tell me what to say, couldn't you? And also, if you can read my mind, why don't you know that's what I'm thinking?"

"We can't read your thoughts until you think them, doctor. And we can't put them into your head. Why should we?"

"So if we're talking like this, why aren't the Secret Service guys paying any attention to us?"

"They can't hear our thoughts, doctor."

I shrugged and headed for the door. Walter, or the squirrel, immediately ran into the woods.

My wife was waiting for me in the kitchen. Another breakfast, identical to the previous one, was sitting on the table. "Did they find anything wrong with you?"

"They don't have the results of the blood tests yet, but they think I'm physically capable of saving the world."

"I'm happy to hear that. I just spoke to your granddaughters, and they asked me to tell you that they love you. Of course, they don't know what's – " Suddenly she broke into sobs, which wasn't like her. I found myself becoming angry with Walter, and the government, and anyone else who had put us in this situation. I put my arms around her, tried to comfort her. But how could I be of much help when I was in the same boat as she was? All we could do was hold each other for a while. I felt better, anyway, even if she didn't. Her embraces have always done that for me.

Finally the sobs became sniffles. "You must be hungry," she guessed correctly. "I have to admit I cheated. I already had some scrambled eggs."

I chuckled a bit at that, and she did, too. "Let's eat," I suggested. And we did; we ate everything in front of us. Who knew when our final meal would be?

I decided not to tell her about my latest encounter with Walter, who was presumably nearby, listening to everything we said. I would tell her about them a little at a time. Otherwise she might freak out.

The rest of the morning was taken up with all kinds of psychological exams – memory and logic tests, hand-eye coordination, mirror drawings, and all the rest. I suppose I passed, though I certainly would have done better only a few years earlier. Then the psychiatrists came in. The head man was a Dr. Bernard Schultz. He reminded me of Klaus Villers, the late director of the Manhattan Psychiatric Institute, and his associate, Dr. Feinstein (whose brother is the well-known entertainer, she informed me immediately), looked and sounded like Virginia Goldfarb, the current director of the institute where I was a staff member for most of my career. Both of my ad hoc shrinks were affiliated with New York University.

The details of these discussions are not particularly relevant to the issue at hand. Suffice it to say that they drew out everything they could from my past, some of which I had forgotten about myself. Finally, Schultz asked me, in a thick Austrian accent, whether there was anything else they needed to know. I took a deep breath and told them that Walter could read my mind, and that I could also hear *their* thoughts, at least the ones they wanted me to hear. I suspected that my examiners would think I was a complete nutcase, but they didn't seem surprised to hear this. We ended up chatting amiably about my former practice and their current ones. Both had patients claiming to be from some distant planet or other. I commiserated.

As I was getting ready to leave, I asked them point blank: "Am I crazy or not?"

Schultz looked me in the eye and said, "You're not crazy, doctor. Just unlucky. None of us envy you." An expert on sleep, he asked me before I left whether I had been having any trouble "along those lines." He seemed disappointed when I said I hadn't. "Well, if that happens," he advised me, "we have a lot of new medications for that."

I told him I would let him know.

"Good luck and godspeed," he said, with a certain finality. We all shook hands and I was free to go home again for a brief rest, and lunch if I wanted it, which I didn't, not after the huge breakfast.

Karen wanted me to call my grandchildren, and also our old friends, the Siegels. Instead, I begged off, and Flower and I took a little nap. It was still early afternoon, but I was already exhausted.

The phone rang at 2:15. Mike, of course. "We're all here, Gene. Whenever you're ready." I patted Flower, kissed my wife, and hurried out. Though I was permanently distracted, I managed to note that it was a cool, gray day, the fall colors about as bright as dishwater.

Mike was waiting for me outside the Nerve Center. He shook my hand and smiled warmly, a fruitless attempt to cheer me up and bolster my confidence, I suppose. We went inside and turned in a different direction than we had that morning. "The results of your exams are excellent, so far. For a seventy-four-year-old man, you're in pretty good shape, mentally and physically. If anyone can convince the Security Council to take the Bullocks seriously, you're probably a pretty good choice."

"At the risk of sounding flippant: Hallelujah!"

He snorted. "I think I'm finally getting used to your sense of humor, Dr. B."

"Prot and fled didn't think I had one."

"From their point of view, maybe you don't."

"How's this for a joke?" I described my meeting with Walter that morning. All he said was, "Yes, we suspected they could do that."

"But doesn't that blow your mind? That they can communicate this way? Telegraph their thoughts to me as well as read the ones I'm thinking? Even fled couldn't do that, as far as I know."

"Of course it does, Gene. But so does their being here in the first place, or have you forgotten who they are and why they're here? All this does is confirm that we need to take them very seriously and try to comply with whatever demands they might make. We've probably only seen a tiny bit of what they can do!"

He tapped on a door to Room 4, and we went inside. It was almost like entering another Cabinet Room, though the walls were orange and there were no pictures hanging on them. It was less than half the size, but, like the original, a long table stood in the center of the room, and around it sat more than a dozen individuals, some of whom I had met the previous day in Washington.

Everyone stood up when we entered, and Mike re-introduced me to them as we proceeded around the table. I remembered some of the faces, if not the names: the Secretaries of Defense and Homeland Security, the FBI director, and on the periphery, of course, more Secret Service agents. This time, the Vice-President was in attendance, as well as the Secretary of State, and a couple of United Nations officials. And, of course, sitting in a corner, the ever-present Dr. Greaney. But no military people, as far as I knew. Finally we took our seats on the opposite side of the table facing the door, the VP presiding, Mike and I sitting to his right and left, respectively. At its precise center stood a red telephone, presumably connected to one in the Oval Office.

The Vice-President began: "I don't want to waste anyone's time. But before we begin – " Suddenly he turned to me and asked, "Is Walter here with us?"

I concentrated, waiting for some signal that Walter had heard this, but I didn't sense his presence in the room. "Mr. Vice-President, I honestly don't know. Sometimes he's nearby but chooses not to say anything for some reason."

"Before you got here we were all wondering whether he would come in with you. If he were here it might make things simpler. But I suppose you'll be filling him in later on. Now. The purpose of this meeting is to discuss a schedule for Dr. Brewer and, for that matter, the rest of us." He nodded to a secretary, who passed around the tentative schedule. I glanced at it briefly, presuming I would have a chance to read it later. For the moment, I wanted to listen to everything that was said. But I was surprised to see a summary of the events of the previous day and this morning, the first headed by "DAY ONE," the second by "DAY TWO." I flipped ahead to the last page, "MESSAGE DAY (DAY EIGHT)," which contained only one entry: "DR. BREWER SPEAKS TO THE UNITED NATIONS SECURITY COUNCIL." I executed my usual shudder, which no one seemed to notice.

"If you will turn to DAY TWO," he went on, "you will find that at the end of this meeting we will be breaking up into various task forces. Or sub-committees, if you prefer. Ten, to be exact. These are: 1) The Brewer Speech Task Force. This will be headed by the President's speechwriters, along with a few university professors and others with a general knowledge of United Nations history and protocol, including our UN ambassador and the Secretary of State. Its mission will be to determine what approaches might be more effective than others in addressing the Security Council, which, as you know, is composed of five permanent members: The United States, China, Great Britain, Russia, and France, as well as ten elected member nations. There are a lot of subtleties involved in getting a consensus among this diverse group. Because the speech is the core of our mission, you might say that this is the most important task force of the ten.

"Directly related to this one is the subcommittee on preparing Dr. Brewer to make that speech, or the Coaching Task Force. It will be composed of psychologists, speech therapists, diction and projection coaches, and a couple of throat doctors in case any medical problems arise. We need to make sure that Dr. B is fully prepared for his awesome responsibility." He focused his penetrating blue eyes on me and grinned. I had to admit that he had a way of making one feel at ease. "Incidentally, your physicians and psychologists will also be charged with the task of seeing that you are well-rested and properly nourished and hydrated. It's like a football game: no matter how much talent and preparation you have, you need to be absolutely ready at game time."

He turned back to the list. "The third group is designated the Research and Co-ordination Task Force. Its function will be to obtain information that any of the other subcommittees may require, and to distribute this information to whomever might need it. Its expertise will cover a broad range of subject matter and issues, and will be composed of experts in every imaginable field of human endeavor. As we proceed, questions will probably arise that we can't even think of at this point. But if anyone needs the answer to a question of any kind, this will be the place to go. Or to the Overview Task Force, which I'll get to in a minute.

"Now we come to the more technical aspects of our mission. The fourth subcommittee will cover logistics. That means determining the best means of handling Dr. Brewer's daily activities, including his availability for all potential future meetings and events, as well as any travel arrangements or accommodations that Dr. B might require. Beyond that, it will be this task force's responsibility to make the proper arrangements with the UN on when and where to make him available to the officials comprising its staff or that of any of the member nations involved. And also, of course, his travel to the UN and safe return to his home, as well as that of anyone else deemed to be necessary to accompany him on the trip. This will include the President, of course, and other officials who will need to be present at the time of the speech.

"Which brings us to page 5, the 'Task Force on Security Issues.' This, of course, is a can of worms because it encompasses so many possible risks and dangers. It will be headed jointly by the heads of the FBI, the CIA, and the Joint Chiefs of Staff, who are still in Washington at the moment. In fact, this subcommittee and most of the others will be directed from D.C." The Vice-President swept his arm in a long arc and again produced his famous ear-to-ear smile. "There just isn't room here for everyone! Anyway, we won't be concerned with their duties for now; we'll leave it up to them to make sure no crazy people, domestic or foreign, try to stop Dr. B from carrying out his mission a few days from now. For everyone's information, though, I can tell you that a no-fly zone is already in place above us, as well as check points in a ten-mile circumference around the Brewer household. And, as you are fully aware, Gene, you're being fully protected by the Secret Service as well. Currently, in fact, you have more protection than even the President.

"Any questions so far? Good. Okay, that leaves #6, the Task Force for Foreign Liaison, which, I suppose, speaks for itself. Its function will be to co-ordinate any input from the other heads of state, and vice versa: to keep them informed of our activities. We don't have to worry much about this group – they, too, will operate out of Washington, and we won't hear from them unless difficulties arise. Their first duty, of course, will be to convince the world that Walter is really who he – excuse me – *they* say they are. After that, it should be smooth sailing. At least we hope it will be.

"The seventh group is the Task Force on Media Information, whose function, obviously, will be to co-ordinate any information that isn't of a sensitive nature to the various media outlets. The President's press secretary (the VP grinned and pointed to him – obviously they were on good terms) will be in charge of that one, and I leave it to him to take care of that. He will report to me and the President, of course, but he knows his job and we can be sure he'll do it well." The press secretary nodded a quick thank-you. "He will be working here for now, in a small office down the corridor. When everything is under control, he'll be back in Washington for the duration. I should add that everything that's said in this room will remain here. We want to keep the press and the people informed, but only through the Task Force on Media Information. That goes for Dr. Brewer as well as the rest of us. Otherwise we're going to have a lot of misunderstanding around the country and the world. We don't need that; this isn't business as usual."

"*More* misunderstanding," interjected the Secretary of State. "There is always misunderstanding where communications are involved."

The VP guffawed, as did the Secretary. There was obviously a long history between them as well. But he made no response to the comment. "The next two subcommittees will be working closely together. So far we don't know much about what the aliens want us, as a world population, to do, exactly, but from what Dr. Brewer has told us so far, they seem to be primarily concerned with our violent behavior toward one another. Is that right, Gene?"

I had been sliding down farther and farther in my chair, half-asleep, assuming that the Vice-President, who obviously loved to hold forth, would just keep on talking. I popped completely awake and sat up straighter. "Yes, sir, they seem to be quite annoyed, maybe even angry, with our killing each other. And I would add that they don't seem to care much for our behavior toward everything else on Earth, either. *Any* death seems to bother them a lot. They can somehow feel it, perhaps like an ant knows when another member of the colony has been killed or injured. In fact, he likened the Bullocks to a colony of ants or bees. They claim that all life in the universe is somehow connected. They want *all* the killing stopped. That's really about all I know so far."

"Right. So the next two TFs will deal with the demands of the Bullocks and our response to those demands. The first of these, the Negotiations Task Force, will deal with any possible discussions with Walter – questions we might have in order to clarify their requests, and possible requests of our own. Once we find out exactly what they want, we might be able to reach some kind of mutual agreement on a timetable. That sort of thing. This group will be headed by our Ambassador to the United Nations and, in fact, will be composed primarily of government negotiators, maybe a few others. The details of that haven't been worked out yet. The other, Subcommittee #9, which we're calling the Compliance Task Force, will be concerned with looking into various scenarios, especially how we can work out possible truces around the world in order to reduce any military hostilities, and how soon we can accomplish this. We may have to pull back our own troops here and there. But I won't speculate on any of this now – the TF will be working on that and giving us a report in a couple of days.

"Well. Okay. So those are the bulk of the ten Task Forces we have lined up. The final one we'll call the Overview Committee. This one will co-ordinate the activities of all the others. It will be headed nominally by the President and other government leaders, some of whom, by the way, are on their way to Washington as we speak. Here, in Dr. Brewer's backyard – literally," he added, with the patented grin, "Mike Jones and I will be in charge of the overall co-ordination. So that about covers it. Does anyone have any suggestions for other TFs, or comments on anything we have left out?"

A woman whose name, of course, I had already forgotten, but who sounded like Katharine Hepburn, asked pointedly, "Can we speak to Walter ourselves? Or do we have to wait until he, or they, contact Dr. Brewer?" She seemed to be staring at me with an almost Bullock-like disdain.

All eyes turned to me. "I can't really answer that. So far they have only spoken to *me*. Since they haven't yet told me exactly what they want us to do, I presume they will again."

"How do they contact you exactly?" she demanded.

At Mike's prodding, I told the group about the deceased Walter and about the squirrel, and that now I could speak to them directly, mind to mind. I reminded her also that the Bullocks could actually be present in the very room where we were assembled, listening to the discussion, and we wouldn't know it. There were a couple of gasps, and some looked around nervously. Others seemed dubious.

The obnoxious woman persisted. "Can you ask them?"

I concentrated on the silent question, then asked out loud: "Are you here, Walter?" I felt like an old-time medium trying to communicate with the dead. But if they were, they didn't respond. I shook my head. "I should have tried that before," I apologized, "but I haven't yet come to grips with all this."

The Vice-President spoke up in my defense. "No one is accusing you of failing to do that, Gene." His gaze swiveled slowly around the room. "None of us can know what it's like being in your shoes, facing up to a powerful alien being we know almost nothing about. Any of us would probably find that almost unbearable, and none of us ever met prot or fled. Because of those experiences, you probably did far better than any of us could have. However, her point is well taken. The TF on Negotiations will want to know whether we can contact them, or whether *you* can at any rate, and, if so, when and where this would be done. This, I think, is the first thing we need to determine." Several in the group nodded.

I nodded, too, adding that Walter usually came to me in my backyard. I had already gained a great deal of respect for both the President and the Vice-President, both of whom were extremely competent, it seemed to me, and obviously had the interests of all of us in mind. The latter, if a bit wordy, was nonetheless very good at handling a meeting like this. He was clearly on top of every aspect of a very complex situation.

"Anything else we need to cover before we break up and start the real work?" he asked the group.

The Secretary of State pointed out that perhaps the Bullocks were "occupying" me, as they had done the others, at this very moment. All heads swiveled in my direction. "I suppose that's possible, but I don't think so. I don't feel any different, anyway."

"But you don't know that for sure. Maybe the Bullocks wouldn't affect you in any way even if they were inside your head."

I could only shrug and say, "That's possible, I suppose, though they told me otherwise."

A man who resembled former patient Howie, asked the chair, "What about Dr. Brewer himself? Will any of us be able to contact him whenever the need arises?"

"Good point," said the Vice-President. "For the moment, I think all the TF heads, and probably no one else, except the President and myself, should have access 24/7." He turned back to me. "Does that meet with your approval, Gene?"

"Do I have a choice?" I asked, knowing it was becoming a silly refrain.

For a moment he looked a bit dismayed, but almost immediately the shiny smile filled his countenance as he picked up on my feeble joke. "None of us have much choice in the matter," he murmured. I nodded again, though the comment was probably meant for everyone present.

"Okay, if that's all, we'll adjourn and everyone who is staying here will convene in – uh – fifteen minutes in your respective meeting rooms. Those who are returning to Washington will leave immediately for the helicopters that will take you to the airport. They're waiting at the pads."

As everyone was filing out, I asked the Vice-President, "What pads?"

"We found a suitable field about a quarter-mile down the road. A quick trim and a fast-drying concrete, and now there are two perfectly adequate helicopter pads in place."

"Oh. Probably a good idea under the circumstances," I offered superfluously. He gathered all his papers together without replying. "And is there a task force I should be sitting in on?" I asked him.

Without referring to his notes or papers, he replied, "For now, you will be a member of Task Force #8, the one handling your negotiations with the Bullocks. Later on, of course, you will work with TF #2, which will prepare you for your appearance at the UN, and then #1, rehearsing and polishing the actual speech they come up with. As well as the TF on Media and Information. There will be a time or two when you will need to face the reporters. We'll try to keep that to a minimum, but it can't be avoided. Sound all right to you?"

"To be honest, sir, none of this sounds all right to me. I didn't ask for this, and I don't want it."

This time no smile came. Only a deep frown, which deepened even further and highlighted the worry wrinkles in his forehead. He placed a hand on my shoulder. "All of us wish this could be avoided, Gene, but it can't. No one is more aware than you of the responsibility this whole thing will entail, as well as the importance the entire world attaches to it. You're doing fine. Just keep it up and everything will work out okay. You know why?"

"No. Why?"

"Because it has to."

"I wish I had your confidence."

"Confidence has nothing to do with it. It's a question of doing what has to be done. Of responsibility. I'm a pretty good judge of character, and I know you will accept yours." Then he shook my hand firmly. "Good luck, my friend. After this is over, we'll have a party in the White House. This time your wife will be there. I know mine will." He turned and strode out the door. The VP was pushing seventy by now, almost as old as I was, but he had the energy of a forty-year-old.

By this time no one was left in the meeting room except Mike and myself and two other men. I was an old hand at this now, and I knew they were the omnipresent Secret Service. Anonymous as always, they pretended to ignore me and focused their attention instead on the door. I noted for the first time that there were no windows in the room, and perhaps not in any of the rooms in the Nerve Center.

Mike sidled up to me and patted me on the shoulder as the Vice-President had done. "How are you holding out?"

"Okay, I guess. It's a bit overwhelming for a small potato like me."

He laughed. "No small potato, you. Not anymore. You're more important now than anyone else in the world, including all the people who were in this room. I only have one suggestion for you: don't let yourself get too conceited when this fact sinks in. And it will sink in. Stay modest and humble. The world doesn't want you to start getting grandiose ideas at this point. And neither do you."

I thought about that for a minute. "I see your point, but I'm pretty sure we don't have to worry about that. I may be a giant potato right now, but I know I might blow it. That thought alone will be enough to keep me humble."

"I hope you're wrong about that, but hold that thought anyway." He checked his watch. "We have another ten minutes before the TF8 meeting. Do you want to run over and say hello to your wife?"

"Sure." I lowered my voice. "Are these guys going to be with us from now on?"

"Every minute. Except when you're inside your house. But they and a few others will be all around it. I assure you that no one will be able to get past them, even if they were able to get that far."

"Should I introduce myself?"

"No, they would rather you didn't. There are several reasons for this, but you can take my word for it. In any case, they rotate. There will probably be two different guys next time you show up here. But don't worry; you'll get used to them. After a while you won't even notice them."

"Okay, if you say so. I'll run over and check on Karen. What room do I go to after that? Or did you want to go with me?"

He checked his clipboard. "Room Six. See you there in ten minutes?"

"Fine." I hurried down the corridor and out the only door I knew about. I had shown Mike approximately where the cone was buried, and now I noticed several men with shovels and other devices poking around in the woods. In the backyard I glanced around for squirrels, but none were in evidence. I wondered about that – why a squirrel? Perhaps because one was handy? In any case, I already had a couple of questions for Walter. First, how could I contact them if necessary; and second, would they speak with anyone else?

"The answer to the second question is No, and, to the first: I will be nearby for the next six days."

I felt as though I had received an electric shock. I quickly looked around but there weren't any squirrels in evidence.

"Where – Where are you?" I managed to stammer before looking around to see if the Secret Service agents were listening to us. As always, they stared straight ahead, apparently oblivious.

"Occupying an unused brain cell inside your head. But don't be concerned – we've been somewhere nearby all along. Now that you're used to us, there is no longer a need for an intermediary."

I was sure I had to be completely insane. For one thing, I had known countless mental patients who heard voices inside their heads. Of course no one believed them. (On the other hand, perhaps some of them actually *were* speaking with aliens.) Yet, Walter was right: this was no worse than speaking with a squirrel, and because he came to me in stages, it didn't seem so preposterous as it otherwise might have. Nevertheless, the arrangement was very, very weird, and I could feel my voice shaking as I asked him, "So you were with me during the discussion in the trailer?"

"Of course," they seethed. "Your head was there, wasn't it?"

"But you ignored my question."

"Obviously."

"Why?"

"The others of your 'team' need to get used to the idea, too."

"Ah. I see. And you'll be in my head from now on?"

"As we said earlier, we'll be somewhere nearby. At least until you deliver your speech to the United Nations."

"And after that?"

"We'll return to Bullock for a while."

"For how long?"

"That depends on the result."

I couldn't think of a good response to that. I could barely think at all. "One problem with this means of communication: there's no one to look at. It's quite uncomfortable talking to myself like this. No offense," I quickly added.

"You'll get used to it. And you don't need to move your mouth. We can hear your thoughts perfectly."

"No matter what I'm thinking about?"

"Whatever you're thinking, we'll know about it."

"Does that mean you'll be telling me what to say when I'm in a meeting or a discussion with someone else?"

"No."

"So you're not always inside my head?"

"We've discussed this before, doctor," they roared. "When you need us, we'll be here."

I nodded, but to whom, I hadn't a clue. "And there isn't any way to turn you off? Knowing you're listening could seriously alter my thinking."

"Please pay attention, doctor. You will be able to think as you normally do. The only difference is that we can read your thoughts. But we won't interfere with them in any way. Understand?"

"Not completely. I suppose you know that." I needed to go to the bathroom. "But I suppose you already know that, too."

I thought I heard a sigh. "You're finally beginning to understand. Now why don't you go in and relieve yourself of your liquid waste? We'll 'talk' later."

I found my wife in my study gazing out the living room window, which faces the side of the property away from the trailer. I could see a neighbor's house through the trees, which reminded me of our summer place in the Adirondacks, where the Siegels live nearby. I wished I could have talked all this over with my friend and fellow psychiatrist. Karen was probably thinking the same thing. But for the next week there probably wouldn't be time for any socializing.

The sun had come out, and the oak leaves were flaming yellows and oranges again. It was so beautiful I almost cried. I quickly wiped my eyes in case one of the agents happened to be peering through the window. Karen hadn't yet said anything. "Are you okay, sweetheart?" I asked her.

"I was just thinking about our kids. Do you have time to call any of them?"

"Not now, hon. Maybe tonight. But I don't know when these meetings will be over."

"Can I tell them what's going on?"

"Nobody said not to tell them anything. But you might want to leave out the details for now."

"Like what?"

"Like Walter is probably inside my head right now."

She looked at me as if I were carrying a terrible infection. "How do you know that?"

"They said so. If I think something, they hear it."

"So could fled, remember?"

"Yes, but she wasn't *in* it."

"Can you read theirs?"

"Not for a few billion years, probably."

"If we live that long. Can they read mine, too?"

"Probably. Want me to ask them?"

"I'm not sure I want to hear the answer."

"I know what you mean."

"Are you doing okay? Do you need anything?"

"I have to pee."

"Can't help you with that."

When I returned to the living room I told her I just wished it were over. She commiserated.

I checked my watch. "I've got to get back. How about a hug?"

We held each other tightly for a brief moment, an infinity. As I left the house I called back, "What's for dinner?" I could hear her laugh, which was the intention. I suddenly felt better myself. What everyone says is true: it's better to face something unpleasant with a smile and a loving partner.

I tried to keep my mind blank as I jogged across the lawn to the trailer, where Mike was waiting for me at the door. I told him, "They chose not to answer my question when we were in the meeting room. But they were there. They know everything we're discussing." I declined to tell him for the moment that they were occupying *me*. He would surely have thought I was nuts.

"Not surprised. Actually, that might save time and make things easier."

"No, you don't understand. They can read *everyone's* mind. Have they said anything to *you?*"

"Not as far as I know. For some reason they only want to talk to *you.*"

"Because of prot and fled, you mean."

"Maybe once prot ended up at your hospital, the rest was sort of programmed to follow."

"You mean I've been set up from the beginning? That prot, and then fled, were preparing me for Walter's visit?"

Mike shrugged. "Who knows?"

We came to Room 6, which was just like Room 4 – no windows, etc. – only a little smaller. A hastily penned tag on the door indicated that this was where the Task Force On Communication and Negotiations would meet. The walls of the brightly-lit room were pink, perhaps so that everyone would recognize where he or she was. Maybe all the meeting rooms were color-coded. An attempt at cheerfulness, perhaps?

There were a dozen or so people there, a few of whom had been present at the earlier organizational meeting. Again I was introduced to a very politically correct group: about half were women, two were of African and one of Asian descent. None of the names were familiar. Most, I learned, were ombudsmen or arbitrators, except for a couple of people from think tanks I had never heard of. The President's science advisor was also present, presumably in case any scientific question for the Bullocks needed to be discussed. The entire focus of this group was to come up with questions I might ask Walter so that we, and they, would all be on the same page. Primarily, we needed more information on the Bullocks and what they wanted.

After a few minutes of sober chit-chat, the Ambassador to the United Nations called the meeting to order. She was slim, forceful, a thoroughly competent-looking woman, well-dressed in a powder blue wool suit. Most of the task force, however, were wrinkled and grizzled, suggesting, if nothing else, experience and wisdom. Nevertheless, when the chair spoke, everyone listened. She reeked of dignity and confidence. It seemed to me that nothing would ruffle her.

As the Vice-President had begun the earlier meeting, she passed out printed sheets listing possible questions and concerns for our consideration, as well as Walter's. This is the list as it stood on that afternoon:

POSSIBLE QUESTIONS FOR THE BULLOCKS

- Where is your planet, and how many Bullocks live there?
- Does your planet have a government or governments? If so, do you represent *all* the Bullocks, or only one faction?
- Are you in direct contact with other intelligent beings in the universe? Is there a universal government or governments? If not, by what right do you travel the universe making demands of others?
- Can you tell us more about Nediera and how we can tap into it?
- If you are not corporeal, how did you get to Earth?
- What, exactly, are you demanding of us?
- Is there any margin for compliance? For example, if we meet half your demands within a given period, would we get more time to comply with the rest?
- Would we not eventually evolve toward your general philosophy without coercion?

After everyone had silently pondered the list for a few minutes, the chair pointed out that it was only a tentative one, and it would probably change as we went along. "The first thing we need to know is who or what we are dealing with. Dr. Brewer, would you be so kind as to give us your impressions of Walter, and do you think he would be amenable to reasonable questions or negotiations?"

Everyone turned to scrutinize me. This was the thing I hated most about public speaking: it's like being under a microscope with a thousand eyepieces. By now, however, I had come to realize that my natural reticence was no longer important. That I had to fully participate in my fate, whatever it might be. "Well, from the looks of this list, you already know almost everything I know. But I will say, first, that Walter converses in a straightforward, forceful, no-nonsense manner. There is no mistaking what they mean. Second, they are for real. There is no way they can be anything other than who or what they say they are. Maybe I ought to stop there and ask whether anyone has any questions about that."

No one did. Apparently they had all been briefed on his occupying corpses and squirrels, and obliterating trees.

"In that case, there's something you might not yet know." I took a deep breath and described my encounter with Walter less than an hour earlier, when he had not appeared to me as anything at all, but almost as pure thought. That from now on he would communicate directly with my mind. "We probably won't see a physical manifestation of them again."

I heard little intakes of breath, followed by a moment or two of silence. Someone mentioned my earlier attempt to "speak" with Walter in the larger meeting room. "Could we try again here?"

I looked down at the list and thought hard about the Bullocks and their planet, silently asking where it was and how many beings like them lived there. I waited, but there was no reply from Walter, or anyone else. "I'm not getting an answer."

"Which might mean one of two things," said the chair. "It might mean that they aren't here, or that they simply don't want to answer the question. Do you have any thoughts about that, Dr. Brewer?"

"I suspect they're here, but there's no way to know that. So I guess they just don't want to answer the question." I explained the Bullocks' thoughts about making everyone nervous if they conveyed something to me in public.

The chair quickly replied, "Tell them we won't be shocked by anything they tell you. Or us."

"If he's here, he heard you." Nevertheless, there was still no response. Nor was there one when I tried to communicate this to him silently. But something else occurred to me. "It's possible that they just don't want to bother with irrelevant information. In fact, they once told me that they would answer any 'relevant' questions. They might think we're avoiding the issue by asking any questions at all, unless they pertain to our compliance with their demands. That we're just stalling, in a way. And one other thing (I braced myself for a jolt): they're a nasty old sonofabitch. When they occupied the late Walter's body, they actually sneered at me several times. If they have any opinions on our fate, I would say they would just as soon see us dead and gone."

Again there was a short period of silence. Apparently this was a group who thought before speaking. But someone finally asked, "Do you think they would dispose of us immediately if you asked them a question that they might consider annoying?"

"I really can't answer that. My impression is that they would just ignore it, as they have done already. I don't think asking them a question, even a stupid one, would seal our fate." I paused to see if Walter, or anyone else, would respond to that. "I could be wrong about this, of course," I added weakly.

Someone inquired as to whether I had already asked them a stupid or irrelevant question.

I confessed that I had, on more than one occasion.

"And we're still here."

"So far."

The chair offered a brief summary. "I think we don't have much choice but to proceed like the human beings we are. To try to get as much information as we can and formulate some kind of plan, based on that information, for dealing with the situation we're faced with. In my opinion we should proceed carefully, but go forward confidently, and without delay. Ignorance never solved any problems. Any thoughts on this?"

There was a brief discussion of the dangers involved, but general agreement that a free and open conversation with Walter would be not only worth the risk, but necessary. Once that was settled, the chair quickly moved on. "One other general question before we continue the meeting: if Walter is here at the moment, do you know where they might be, and what form they might have taken?"

"Not exactly. They could be an insect somewhere on the floor. Or even a bacterium. Or," I added pointedly, "they could be occupying any one of our brain cells and we wouldn't even know it." As before, everyone looked around uncomfortably.

Someone asked, "Do they need to occupy something or someone?"

I don't have a clue, but I could ask."

"Do they travel through space on a beam of light?"

"I don't even know that. But I haven't seen any flashlights or mirrors. Maybe they've learned to tap into something else."

A mild reprimand by the chair: "Okay, enough of the speculation. Let's get to work."

For the next two hours we went back and forth, hashing and rehashing some of the items on the proposed question list. When it was over, they had been narrowed down to the following question to be asked of the Bullocks:

What exactly are you demanding of us?

Any further questions depended on the answer to that one. The only other matter left to discuss was how I could contact Walter in order to ask them the question. "I think they'll probably contact *me*," was the only response I could come up with.

Before we adjourned, a man adorned with a huge black beard, who was from a university somewhere in the Midwest (and who looked vaguely like Oliver Sacks), noted that Walter had approached me three times: once in a shopping mall parking lot, and the other two in my own backyard. He suggested it might be wise to hang out in the latter when it became necessary to convey information to them. And, further, that everyone else should avoid the lawn. The consensus was that this was probably a reasonable suggestion.

"But what about the surveillance cameras?" said the woman who had spoken earlier. "Would they object to being watched?"

"There's nothing to watch," I reminded her. "Except me talking to myself."

The meeting adjourned with the admonition that I should call the chairman, or Mike, as soon as possible after making contact with the Bullocks again.

However, the day was far from over, even though it was already late afternoon. I had to attend another subcommittee meeting (TF2, on Brewer Preparation). Same layout, different bunch of "experts," different wall color (blue). I was already exhausted, and barely heard any of the discussion. This group was chaired by a psychologist with a nervous tic, who also happened to have a degree in speech, his specialty. Also in attendance were a comedian and a rabbi, both of whom had had to develop good speaking habits in order to connect with their audiences. The discussion was quite entertaining, I suppose, if you like jokes about giving enemas to people who have died because "it can't hoit." I could have told a few of my own, but I was afraid no one would find them funny. In any case, the upshot was that my fear of public speaking was essentially normal, that the group would plan to begin work on my diction and delivery and "attitude" the following day, the idea being to instill confidence that I could perform well at the United Nations, or anywhere else. I nodded sleepily and the meeting was adjourned.

On the way out of the trailer, Mike offered his usual encouragement. "I think we had some good sessions, don't you, Gene? Accomplished a lot. And tomorrow should be even better, as we start to grapple with what Walter wants from us."

I said nothing except, "So you'll call me again in the morning?"

"No, why don't you have breakfast with your wife and then come back here at, say, seven-thirty?"

"I'm going to sleep like a dead person tonight."

Obviously he didn't get the joke. "I hope so. You'll need all your wits tomorrow. We shook hands and I left the trailer for home, which seemed a million miles away. I hurried across the grass, trying not to think anything, hoping that I wouldn't be waylaid by Walter. I just needed one evening off before all hell broke loose. Before I could get inside, however, Flower came bounding out of the house and flattened herself against my leg. I gave her a good head scratch and body rub, and she zoomed around the yard sniffing for aliens before relieving herself and coming into the house with me.

The Bullocks, apparently, weren't ready to communicate any demands. Maybe they realized I was too tired to hear much of it. At any rate, they didn't bother me again that evening, and Karen and I had a nice dinner, courtesy of, and prepared by, Uncle Sam, including a very good Cabernet Sauvignon. While we were having coffee, and my eyelids were about to close, she handed me a fistful of notes: my son Fred called again, Will called again, daughter Jennifer (in California) called again, two of my grandchildren called, the Siegels and a couple of other friends and neighbors called and, of course, son-in-law Steve, the astronomer, wanted to talk to me. I reflected on children and friendship, noting that at least we wouldn't die alone. Except that Steve, I was sure, only wanted to talk to the aliens. He was almost certainly hoping to pump Walter for any information he could get about the workings of the universe. I didn't think the Bullocks would give a damn about Steve's interests or his career, but I told Karen I would speak to him when I got the chance. By then it was already after nine o'clock, and I had another long day ahead of me. I told her to let everyone know what was going on, in general terms, and I would speak to them all as soon as this was over.

"Can you at least give your grandchildren a ring?"

"Oh, all right, if you'll dial the numbers and hold the phone to my ear."

I gave Flower the last bite of my dessert, and Karen took my hand and led me to my easy chair in the living room. But I was asleep before she could pick up the phone.

I woke up a few hours later, still sitting in my favorite chair, covered by a warm afghan she had crocheted not long after she had retired. It was only two-thirty, but now I was wide awake. Suddenly Flower sat up and looked around. I wondered whether she had heard something. I listened, but heard nothing.

"Hello, doctor. Sleep well?"

The hairs rose from the back of my neck. "Where are you?"

He ignored the question. "Are you ready?"

"For what?"

"It's time to begin your assignment."

"What do you think I've been doing for the last two days?"

"Here is what you will say to your United Nations Security Council: '*We have exactly one year to stop the killing.*'"

My mind started racing. I knew it would be something like that, but now that I had heard it, it didn't seem real. It was like being told that you have an incurable disease and a year to live. It occurred to me that this was an apt comparison for several reasons. But did he mean *all* killing of *anything*? Even bugs and broccoli? Or just the killing of other *humans*? And for how long?

"You should try to relax, doctor. Tension is bad for your physiology. We are not unreasonable beings. Of course we would like to see you stop the killing of anything with a nervous system, but we realize this might be difficult to attain in only a year. So we're going to make it easy on you: exactly one year from the time of your United Nations discussion we expect Homo sapiens to get through one twenty-four-hour period without killing anyone of your own species. Accidents won't count. Do you understand what is expected of you?" they added in a guttural snarl.

I did, or at least I thought I did. But something else bothered me even more. "And what happens if we can't comply with your wishes?"

"You already know the answer to that."

"How will you destroy us?"

"Irrelevant, doctor."

"Yes, I suppose that's true. I'm sorry."

His tone seemed to alter a bit. Or was that wishful thinking on my part? "We accept your apology."

"So if we comply with that demand, we're off the hook?"

"Are you making another joke, doctor?"

"Well, you said we only needed to stop the killing for one day."

"That's merely the first step. If you can't do that, the rest won't matter."

"What's the rest?"

"You will be given another year to stop killing not only yourselves, but all other animal species. For one twenty-four-hour period. Of course, no more humans will be killed during that entire second year as well."

"And is that it?"

There was a pause during which the Bullocks, no doubt, reflected on my level of understanding, and my intelligence in general. They finally replied, without any sneering that I could detect, "After that there will be no more killing of *anyone* for any period of time. Do you understand?"

"I understand. I'm not so sure the rest of the world will."

"That is why we came to you. It's your responsibility to make this clear to your fellow humans. Good luck, doctor."

"My colleagues in the government want me to ask you one other question. Will you answer it?"

"We will answer anything relevant to our demands."

"You won't speak to any of the others who are helping me with this matter?"

"We've already answered that question. You are the chosen one."

"I'm not knowledgeable enough to ask every question we need to ask. If you – "

But I knew the question was irrelevant, and that I would hear no more from Walter that night. I thought about calling the President, but decided that it could wait until morning.

After that, of course, I couldn't sleep. I walked around the house, peered out the windows, gazed at the Nerve Center, dark but probably ablaze with light inside, watched a couple of Secret Service men for a while (they seemed like zombies, as always, though I'm sure they had thoughts of their own), before getting into bed, fully clothed, with Karen. My mind was still racing. I tried to think of a way out of this mess. Could I fake an illness, for example? Probably not after a complete examination had shown I was fit as a fiddle, whatever the hell *that* meant. Why had I taken such damn good care of myself? There was no way out, and I knew it. I lay awake the rest of the night and watched the dawn come up over the autumn splendor.

DAY THREE

Mike called at six-thirty to remind us that he wouldn't join us for breakfast, but would see me in the trailer in an hour.

A shower always makes me feel better, but this time I was so tired it didn't help, and neither did the big breakfast of waffles with fruit and "genuine Vermont" maple syrup. I told Karen about Walter's visit last night, and that they would only talk to *me*, not anyone else, not even the President.

"They came last night? I didn't hear anything."

"They only speak in my head."

She looked dubious, but said, finally, "Prot and fled must have told them they can trust you."

"I wish they hadn't."

"If not you, it would just be someone else. Maybe another person wouldn't have understood what was happening, have the same insight as you."

I couldn't argue with that logic. "There's one more thing. We only have a year to stop the killing."

"Only a year? Can we do that?"

"I don't know."

Since there were a few minutes to spare, I tried to call my grandchildren (Abby and Fred's boys and Will's girls), who, of course, would have no idea who or what the Bullocks were. Unfortunately, Steve answered the first call. He wanted to come over immediately to speak with Walter (there was some noise in the line, and I wondered whether someone was monitoring the call). After arguing with him for several minutes (he couldn't believe that the Bullocks wouldn't want to chat with a cosmologist as renowned as he) I informed him that I had to meet with the Vice-President in a short time (which might have been true), and would call him back that evening. He grumbled for a bit, but finally hung up. I never did get to speak to my grandchildren.

As I was getting ready to go out the door I asked Karen what she planned to do while I was in the trailer. "Probably spend the day on the phone like I did yesterday. I haven't told anyone about the Bullocks, or why they're here, only that we have another visitor from space."

"Probably a good idea. By the way, I haven't had a chance to watch the news. Is anyone reporting on Walter's visit?"

"There was something last night about a rumor of a big space ship landing somewhere in the Northeast, but nothing about the Bullocks."

"It's amazing how the media report everything before they get all the facts." "Let's hope they don't terrify everyone on Earth."

"Why not? Everyone's going to be terrified soon enough anyway."

The phone rang. It was Mike. "Tell him I'm on my way." Flower accompanied me to the trailer, where Mike was waiting. He gave her ears a good scratching. "You look tired," he observed with a frown.

"Me? Or Flower?"

He grinned and gave her a final pat. "She looks fine. It's you I'm worried about."

"I don't know how I'm going to get through the next six days."

"Look at it this way, Gene: six days isn't a very long time. Then your job will be done."

"I hope so." He started to open the door to the Nerve Center. I stopped him. "Before we go in, you should know that the Bullocks came to me last night."

"In the house?"

"Yes. About 2:30."

"What did they say?"

"We have a year to stop the killing."

His eyebrows shot up, but he said nothing. Flower barked at something in the woods and ran off to investigate. The agents, wearing secret little smiles, watched her go. I suspected that almost anything that relieved the boredom would be a welcome sight. I saw that the men with shovels were still carefully digging in the soft earth.

Mike and I went into the trailer and headed for Room 3, where a surprise was waiting. "Mr. President!" A few others were in the room, the same people who were present the day before.

"Hi, Dr. B. How are you? You look tired."

"I'm all right, sir, thank you."

He seemed to be studying my face, as if looking for clues about whether I was still functioning on all my cylinders. "Maybe we could shoot a few hoops this afternoon."

I shrugged.

"Let me tell you a little secret, Gene. When I'm worried about a big speech coming up – to the United Nations, for example – I sometimes need a little help with sleeping the night before."

"I may need something for the next five nights."

He glanced at Mike. "That can be arranged."

"In fact, you have an appointment with your doctors to deal with exactly that," Mike added. I wasn't sure whether or not he was joking – I'm a psychiatrist, and already thoroughly familiar with anxiety medications, including sleep inducers, though I try to avoid them.

"Sit down, Gene. Anything new from Walter?"

I didn't know the protocol, but I sat down even though the President did not. "Walter will answer any relevant questions we might have," I told him and the others, "but only if they come from me."

The President nodded. "At least it's good to know there can be a dialogue. Maybe there's room for negotiation. Not to mention obtaining some useful scientific information from them."

"They didn't say anything about negotiations. I'm not sure they would welcome that."

"Do you think they would be annoyed if you offered a suggestion, or even a plan?"

I thought about that for a moment. Such a strange place I found myself in. An ordinary question like that became magnified a thousand-fold when the survival of everyone on the planet was at stake. I was fully aware that we had to be as careful as humanly possible not to make a mistake, but I gave him the same answer I had given the Task Force on Negotiations the day before. "I could be wrong, Mr. President, but I don't think it would be a disaster."

"Well, at least it doesn't look as if we're dealing with someone who would zap you like the tree that disappeared." I hadn't thought about this potential complication; now I had *that* to worry about. "All right, let's get started, shall we? I'm not here to run this subcommittee, only to listen to what's going on. Is that all right with you?"

"Of course."

He finally sat down, which was a relief. "Good. Madame Chairman, let's get started, shall we?"

"Yes, Mr. President," said the Ambassador. "There were two questions before us when we adjourned yesterday: would the Bullocks speak with anyone else, and what exactly are they demanding of us? The first has been answered. Did they say anything more about the second, Dr. Brewer?"

"Yes, they did." I turned to the President. "I'm sorry, sir. I was going to mention this to you before we came in, but I was shocked to see you here and I forgot."

"No problem, Dr. B. What is it?"

"They are going to give us one year from the time of the UN meeting to stop the killing. I mean, of other human beings. If we can get through one twenty-four hour period by the end of that year without anyone being killed, except accidentally, then we will have another year to stop the killing of all the other animals on the planet for a day."

I would describe the reaction of the Task Force as a classic stunned silence. The President finally murmured, "Well, at least now we know what we're up against."

The chair responded with what everyone else was undoubtedly thinking. "Mr. President, is it possible to meet that demand?"

"The chances are pretty slim, but anything's possible if we can convince the world that the alternative would be unthinkable. Remember nuclear weapons and the Cold War?"

The Ambassador offered this uplifting response: "I personally think it's hopeless."

"Nothing is hopeless," snapped the President. Truth be told, he looked pretty tired himself. "And even if it is, we have to at least try to comply. Posterity, if there is one, deserves our best efforts. And," he added, "maybe doing our best would impress them in some way. Convince them that we're trying as hard as we can. It's conceivable that this could buy us more time."

The President's science advisor asked me, "Does that mean we can kill anyone we want the other 364 days?"

"I don't think that would go over very well, but I suppose it does."

More silence until the chair asked, "Does anyone have a suggestion as to where to begin?"

The President remarked, "Obviously we have to begin immediately to convey this demand to every other country in the world. This would best be accomplished through a preliminary meeting of heads of state. We need to get the world's leaders to speak to this. Maybe the leaders of every country on Earth. This is no time to assert "internal affairs," or "sovereignty." Every country in the world has to be on board, at least in principle, or we may have no chance at all of survival. If we can accomplish something along these lines before Dr. Brewer's speech, it might soften the Bullocks' demands a little."

The chair, and apparently everyone else, concurred. The President wiggled a finger and someone left, presumably to convey that message to the Vice-President, and the Secretary of State. (I learned later that it was for both, as well as the Joint Chiefs of Staff, Congressional leaders, and the entire diplomatic community.)

The Ambassador cleared her throat, looked the President right in the eye, and said, "Mr. President, this raises a sticky issue. If even one country doesn't sign on, wouldn't the rest of the world have to destroy it or its government in order to secure the survival of all the others?"

The President calmly stared back. "Yes, that's a possibility. Let's hope it doesn't come to that." I was overwhelmed by his immediate grasp of the situation, as well as his forthrightness, though I immediately understood the conundrum this raised.

"But what if it does?" she persisted.

The President seemed a bit annoyed by her tenacity, though he was also sympathetic. He suddenly looked ten years older. "We'll deal with that option if and when it arises," he said flatly. No one else spoke up; obviously everyone was trying to come to grips with that terrible possibility.

The chair diplomatically changed the subject. "As for the duties of *this* committee, can anyone suggest a way to approach the Bullocks with a counteroffer of some kind?"

A bearded, elderly man, Professor Something-or-other (who looked like Santa Claus), raised his hand. "We obviously need as much time as possible. Maybe something like ten years would be a more realistic goal. Dr. Brewer, do you think the Bullocks would be receptive to such a suggestion?"

"I don't know."

The Science Advisor said, "I agree that we should try for more time. What if we proposed to reduce the killing by 20% per year for five years? Or 10% over a ten-year period?"

All eyes turned to me again. There was worry and fear in every one of them, including the President's. "I can only ask," I responded lamely.

"Well, we need to negotiate a fairer deal," said the Ambassador. "What they're demanding of us is impossible."

The President spoke. "I think we should assume that some kind of negotiation is feasible. The Bullocks are obviously holding all the cards, but they might trade a few years in order to accomplish their goal. Do you think they might be reasonable about this, Dr. B?"

"Mr. President, I have to say again that I'm in over my head on all this. The Bullocks might be willing to settle for a little less, but my gut feeling is that they would just as soon kill us all and solve the problem that way. They have nothing to gain by giving us more rope."

"How odd," the press secretary observed. "Apparently they find our killing each other abhorrent, yet they seem to be perfectly willing to kill us all to achieve their goal. Have you asked them about this seeming inconsistency, Dr. Brewer?"

"No, I haven't. Not yet."

A red-haired woman, an Assistant Secretary of State named O'Reilly (I learned later) asked, "What if we destroy the Bullocks?"

There was another prolonged silence before the President said, "Not good for three reasons. 1) They would merely send someone else to finish the job, and 2) They would probably not like the idea, which may well shorten our survival time considerably. And 3) How would we do that?"

"I was just thinking out loud," the woman responded brightly. "We need to eliminate all the other possibilities before we decide on a specific course of action."

"Your point is taken," said the President dryly. "Let's move on, shall we?"

"Okay, here is where we stand at the moment," said the chair. "The first step is for Dr. Brewer to approach the Bullocks and sound them out about options."

Something had been bothering me and I raised it. "One more thing, Madame Chairman. In case anyone has forgotten, Walter has probably heard all of this. He could well be present in the room right now."

"Do you have any indication of this, Dr. Brewer?"

"No, but if he already knows about this discussion, and the world hasn't ended, then he may actually be willing to give an inch."

"Has he communicated this to you?" asked the chair.

"Uh – no."

She nodded. "All right, let's get to work,"

The rest of the morning was taken up with determining exactly what concessions we might ask of the Bullocks. A suggestion was also made to ask them to inform us of how and when our species would come to an end if we failed to meet their demands. This would accomplish two things: first, we could better prepare for whatever disaster might befall us, and second, the gory details might help to encourage the world's compliance with their demands.

I pointed out that Walter had already characterized this question as irrelevant, to which it was suggested that I nevertheless try to find out whatever I could about their intentions.

There were also suggestions to pump them about their knowledge of science and medicine and all the other areas of enlightenment, but this was rejected in general because if we failed the primary mission, all that would become moot. Nevertheless, I agreed to ask the Bullocks whether they would divulge such knowledge if we, in fact, succeeded in our goal, because an understanding that this information would be shared with everyone on Earth might also help encourage government leaders to come on board.

Finally, someone asked whether another task force should be set up to give me a tutorial in negotiation. It was decided instead to put that item on the agenda of the Task Force On Brewer Preparation.

As they filed out, everyone, including the President, shook my hand again. "I think everything is going as well as possible, Gene," he assured me. "We're all grateful for your co-operation."

"Thank you, Mr. President."

"I'm going back to Washington. Call me immediately if anything else comes up." He reminded me that "You have my number."

"I will. Thank you, sir, for being here."

He nodded and disappeared out the door. Only Mike and a couple of the Secret Service agents were left behind.

"It will soon be lunchtime, Gene. After that, and a nap if you want it, we'll be meeting again with the Brewer Prep. group. Room 3. Two o'clock. See you then."

For some reason I didn't want to leave him, perhaps because of his uncanny ability to reassure (for the first time, I realized that he reminded me of my son Will in some ways). And maybe the Bullocks wouldn't show up if he were with me in the backyard. I wasn't ready to face Walter again. "I was just wondering: where are all the task force members staying?"

"We commandeered a hotel across from the shopping mall where you found Walter."

"Oh. How ironic."

He nodded in agreement.

"Want to come for lunch, Mike?"

"No, thanks. Maybe next time. Got a lot to do . . . ."

"Okay, sure."

He went back into the Nerve Center, leaving me to deal with the Bullocks alone, should they have anything to tell me. Halfway across the yard, though, I stopped. There was no point in delaying any encounter. Time was critical. I asked Walter point blank whether he had heard the discussion in Room 6. "Of course," came the immediate reply.

"Well, what do you think?"

"About killing everyone in a non-cooperative country? Or whether we'd be willing to soften our demands?"

"Both, damn it."

"Do you remember what prot said about the execution of people who had killed others?"

"I think he said it was an oxymoron."

"So do you think you will score any points for killing everyone in one of your countries so that they can't kill any of their own?"

"Okay, I will pass that on to the President and the others. But what about the negotiations: any chance you could give us more time, for example? A year might not be enough time to convince the whole world not to kill anyone."

"Why do you need more than a year? Is it really possible that you find killing so compelling that you're willing to die for it?"

"Not really. It's just that there are little wars going on somewhere all the time . . . ."

"Then you'll have to stop them."

"I'm not sure that's possible. It takes a certain amount of time for people – Look. You want us to stop the killing, right? If it took ten years, say, or even a hundred, wouldn't your goal be met? Then there would be no more killing."

"Do you have any idea how many people you could kill in a hundred years? How many other animals?"

"Well, what if we come close? What if the killings are reduced by, say, 95%? Would that satisfy you?"

"Not unless 5% of them are accidents."

"So the 100% and the one-year time frame are not negotiable? It doesn't seem fair that we – "

"You're still missing a very important point, doctor. We don't really care whether the human race survives or not. We're willing to give you a year to re-think your 'values,' as you love to call them. Would you prefer that we just came and eliminated the problem without warning? A year is a already a generous compromise, one that will cost any number of lives, not to mention enormous pain and suffering, not only for the individuals involved, but for all the rest of us. The whole universe suffers your thirst for blood! Are we making ourselves clear?"

"One more question. If we fail to comply, you plan to kill us all. How do you explain that contradiction?"

"Who said anything about killing you?"

"But – "

"There are many ways to solve a problem like this."

I could hear myself breathing hard again. "Then how do you plan to solve this one?"

There was no response. I waited, but I soon realized none would be forthcoming.

After greeting my wife and patting my dog, I mumbled something about making a phone call and proceeded to my study. I sat down at the desk, and pulled out the President's phone number. Amazingly, he answered it himself. Judging by the noise, he was probably in Air Force One. "I just spoke to Walter," I told him, "and I thought you'd like to know what he said."

"And that was – ?"

"No negotiations. No margin for error. The one-year deadline is final."

After a brief pause he said, so quietly I almost couldn't hear him over the noise, "Anything else?"

"Yes. I don't think it would be a good idea to bomb the hell out of any country that doesn't want to comply with their demands. It doesn't make sense to them."

"Go on."

"He likened it to capital punishment. It's exactly what they don't want us to be doing."

"What about their killing *us*? Did you ask them about that?"

"He said they weren't planning to kill us. He said there are many ways to solve a 'problem like this.'"

"How are they planning to solve it?"

"I don't know!" I whined.

"Okay. I'll pass all of this on to Mike. He'll notify everyone else."

"Thank you, Mr. President. And I'm sorry to be the bearer of – "

"There's nothing to be sorry for, Dr. B. None of this is your fault. Just keep doing what you're doing. One thing, though: when you're communicating with Walter, do you think you could speak out loud? That way we could all hear what's being discussed."

"Oh. Right. I forgot about that."

"Not a problem."

"Just one thing, though. If I start doing that, he would surely realize why."

"Would that matter?"

"No, probably not."

"Okay, enjoy your lunch as much as possible. I'll try to do the same."

"Thank you, Mr. President. I hope you do."

"Call anytime, Gene. I'm always here."

"You got it, sir." He hung up.

"My God." Karen said, when I returned to the kitchen and told her about the call to the President. "It's actually happening, isn't it?"

"Yes, sweetheart, I'm afraid it is."

"And we only have another year!" Her chin began to quiver.

"Not necessarily. When everyone understands what has to be done in order to save themselves, if not everyone else, it might be possible to stop the killing for a day. And once that's accomplished, it may become a habit. It's just not possible to predict what will happen. The world has never faced anything like this before."

"You're sounding more like a politician every day."

"No need for insults, peach. And there's one good thing, anyway: they aren't planning on killing us."

"What will they do – shuttle us off to a deserted planet?"

"I doubt it. We would just go on with the killing, probably of one another. If there weren't any food, we'd probably become cannibals."

"Or maybe not. You know what I was thinking before you came in?"

"No. What?"

"If everyone were on the same wavelength on all this, we would be more like the Bullocks. We'd become something like a giant colony of ants. Like *they* are."

"Yeah, I thought of that myself. I don't know whether that's a good thing or not, but I think we'd better get used to the idea. Of trying it, anyway."

"I'm scared. Not knowing what's going to happen to us is worse than knowing."

"I'm scared, too."

You want some lunch? They made us a nice fruit salad and – " She broke down sobbing. "I don't think I can do this!"

I tried to comfort her. But I was sobbing, too. Flower began to howl. When there were no more tears, I told her, "When this UN thing is over – maybe this winter – we'll take a nice vacation. Maybe the Caribbean or somewhere."

"I won't hold my breath. You'll probably have to go around making speeches or something for the next year."

"God, I hope not."

"Are you hungry?"

"I wasn't when I came in, but I think I'll have some of that fruit salad . . . ."

Before that could happen, however, the phone rang. It was Mike. "Have you finished your lunch, Gene? We need you back here."

"We were just starting. Can I have five minutes?"

"Make it a fast five. Something came up."

"No nap?"

"No nap."

We gobbled down some lunch. After a quick hug and trip to the bathroom I hurried back to the trailer. Mike was waiting in the main corridor. "The story has been leaked," he told me. There are media people coming. In fact, they're backed up at the barricades. The phones are ringing. In a few minutes the President is going to make a statement." He hustled me into the main conference room, which was packed with people. A television set had been brought in. It seemed to be playing a soap opera of some kind. Despite my best efforts, I found myself watching it while Mike explained, "We don't know who leaked the story, but we knew it would happen sooner or later." He wagged his head. "It nearly always happens whenever there's a sensitive matter that isn't yet public knowledge. God bless the fourth estate, but they're like buzzards on carrion."

I nodded while I tried to determine whether Christine, pregnant with her abusive lover's child, was going to survive her stay in the hospital. She looked okay, though there were beeping monitors everywhere. Suddenly the TV screen went blank for a moment, and a voice said, "We interrupt this program to bring you a message from the President of the United States."

He was sitting at a desk, the American flag to his right. There was a softly whining noise in the background, probably that of Air Force One's engines. His speech was brief and to the point. I found myself studying his demeanor for clues as to how I should behave in the Security Council chamber of the United Nations. After an opening greeting, he said, "Less than an hour ago, one of the cable news networks reported that we have been visited by alien life forms, and that the visitors have made certain demands on human civilization. I am making this announcement to confirm that information. But I state categorically, to everyone listening to this broadcast, that there is no immediate danger, and that every citizen of every nation on Earth should go about his usual business without interruption. I repeat: there is no immediate danger. My administration, as well as the heads of the other branches of government, and leaders form around the world, are dealing with the situation, and we will give you further information as soon as it becomes available. For the present I can only tell you this: a message from the aliens will be delivered to the United Nations Security Council five days from today. Until that time, I assure you once again that there is nothing to be concerned about, and everyone should go about his or her activities as usual."

The President paused for a moment as if to emphasize the importance of his final words, which were: "I am certain that every news and talk program in the country and elsewhere will focus its attention on this matter, and there will undoubtedly be rumors of all sorts filling the airwaves as well as the print media. That is their right and their duty. But I can tell you also that the only official announcements concerning this situation will come either from me or from my press secretary. Statements made by anyone else, regardless of rank, should be considered unconfirmed speculation only. I say again: statements are not to be taken as fact unless confirmed by myself or my press secretary." He paused again to let that sink in, then added, "Thank you for your cooperation, and may God bless the United States of America and all the other countries of this beautiful world."

Suddenly we were back in Christine's hospital room, and it appeared that she and her unborn baby were still alive. Before I could be certain of this, however, someone switched off the TV set. The room was filled with the low buzz of murmurs, but it seemed that everyone present had a meeting somewhere, and they all quickly filed out, still murmuring about who might have leaked the information about the Bullocks. Mike, as always, checked his clipboard, which had felt-tip pen deletions and arrows all over it (he called it his "road map"). "This changes everything, at least for now," he said. "We'll have to schedule a media session. You probably won't have to have any interviews immediately, but we may need to have a press conference sometime before you go to the UN."

"Do I have to do that?"

"If it were anything else, no. But when the survival of the entire world is at stake, it would probably be a good idea to reassure people that you are someone they can trust to take their case to the world's leaders. And that you are, in fact, the only person who can. This won't eliminate people's fears altogether, but knowing who is representing them at the highest levels should calm them down considerably. So a relationship with the news media has now become a priority, and you will need to meet with TF7 right away to get you prepared for any upcoming interviews." Apparently he read the concern in my eyes. "Do you understand why we need to do this Gene? Does it make sense to you?"

I felt terrible, as if I were coming down with a disease of some kind. "Yes, I suppose it does. It's just that everything is happening so goddamn fast . . . ."

For the first time, Mike actually wrapped an arm around my shoulders. "In the short time I've gotten to know you, Dr. B, I've learned that once your mind is focused on a problem, you proceed to deal with it quickly and forcefully. This one is no different."

I have to admit: that kind of encouragement helps anyone. "If you say so, Mike. All right – bring it on."

"Good. Let's get to Meeting Room 5."

To take my mind off my dilemma, I tried to guess what color the walls would be. When we went in (I was wrong – the walls were green) I was greeted by the President's press secretary. Apparently he was chairing this hastily drawn-up session. We shook hands and sat down on the same side of the usual long table (I wondered whether they moved it from room to room for these meetings). The others were mostly new to me, though I recognized a few familiar faces from the television news programs. Their voices were a bit different, however, as if they had been enhanced for their telecasts. I realized immediately that they had been summoned earlier, as if Mike and the others were expecting something like this.

"You all know why we're here," the press secretary began. "For your information, Dr. Brewer, this meeting is to inform you not about what to say in any interviews that might be necessary, but what *not* to say. It's the first rule of doing any interview, especially for government officials and politicians. The second one is: tell the truth. There were snickers, and even a couple of horse laughs. "All right," said the chair, "tell the truth *whenever possible*. He turned and looked me in the eye. "This is one of those times. There is no reason for lying to the public, and no point to it. It could be dangerous and counter-productive The people need to know from you, rather than their elected representatives, including even the President, that we have been visited, and that our visitors have made certain demands that must be met. Once people are convinced there is hope, no matter how small this hope may be, that we can get ourselves out of this situation, they will generally want to do whatever is required to accomplish that goal. And this is something we need to emphasize to all the people of the world: that if we try our utmost to comply, there is hope that we will all survive this thing and maybe even come out far better for it."

"I understand. So is someone going to write a speech for me to deliver to the media?"

A highly respected newscaster across the table, someone I seemed to know intimately from merely watching him read the news almost every evening, answered the question. "Unfortunately, Dr. Brewer, it's not going to be that easy. You'll probably have to answer some questions from reporters, and maybe even appear on a talk show – something like that. We haven't yet decided which is the best approach. That is one of the purposes of this committee. After talking with you, we'll try to determine which will work best for everyone concerned, including yourself."

"You want to see which strategy I'll be able to handle."

"In a word: yes. But, for what it's worth, I like your question; it suggests that you can think on your feet. Or on your derriere, as the case may be." This brought a few chuckles from the subcommittee, including one or two from me.

"So you're going to prepare me to handle some kind of interview. Like the candidates in a Presidential debate are prepped."

"Exactly."

The chair asked, "Did you ever compete in a debate in college? High school?"

"No, sorry. I was pre-med. No time for games."

There were feeble grins all around. Apparently many in the group had done this, and to them it wasn't a game.

"In that case, there's no time to waste," the chair soberly asserted. "Shall we begin?"

Mike, who was sitting next to me, slid a pad and pen toward me. The press secretary explained that those present would bombard me with questions that a wily reporter or newscaster would be expected to ask. And, for the next hour or so, that is exactly what happened. After each fumbling answer, I was advised to give my response in a different way, and I repeated the answers any number of times, until I finally started getting fuzzyheaded from my attempts to focus intently on what I was hearing and what I was saying. I started to stumble on the simplest questions, including some I had answered before. That's when I asked Mike for a break. His unwelcome answer was another question: "Can you hold out for another fifteen or twenty minutes?"

I glared at him, but I understood groggily that I needed to practice giving answers while I was tired, even exhausted. I held out until I was giving such convoluted answers that *everyone* needed a break. "Nice job, Gene," Mike said, and the members of the task force nodded in agreement. I, on the other hand, could barely remember my own name.

After a fifteen-minute bathroom break, and some welcome coffee, we began the process all over again: same questions, same answers, until I could have answered them in my sleep, which, indeed, I might be called upon to do. Most of the questions centered around Walter – how I could be sure they were from another planet, how did I know they had the power to eliminate the human race from the Earth (if, unfortunately, it came to that), how confident was I that they *would* carry out that program (i.e., was it just a scare tactic?). I began to understand that the main point of my meeting with reporters, whenever that might be scheduled, was to convince them and, by extension, the general public, that they could 1) believe that Walter actually existed, and was not a figment of my imagination, and 2) believe that the Bullocks were far more powerful than the total military capability of the entire world's forces. This would be no small achievement: unless virtually the entire population of the Earth bought into our response to the Bullocks' threats, nothing we did to try to appease them would be sufficient.

Then the focus shifted to related questions, such as: what did the Bullocks look like, was I afraid of them and why, and how was my family taking all of this? In addition, there were technical details to be worked out – for example, whether I should stand or sit during the questioning. It was felt that a stronger tone would be set if I were to stand – behind a lectern, probably – but if the questioning went on for hours, which might happen because of the seriousness of the matter, would I become too tired to continue? Someone suggested that the media session should take place first thing in the morning, when I would be fresher. The issue was left undecided, but it was unanimously agreed that we should reconvene the next day and rehearse all the questions again non-stop to see how long I could go on at the lectern.

At the end of the discussion I was actually given a brief round of applause, probably more for encouragement than anything else. And I certainly was exhausted, even though it was only mid-afternoon. Mike suggested I go home for a brief visit with my wife, and maybe take a short nap, before continuing the afternoon meetings, which would have to be condensed because of the time lost in preparing for the media onslaught. I gratefully complied.

I nodded to the SS agents on my way out the door, but they didn't return the greeting. Crossing the backyard, still trying to get the cobwebs out of my head, I heard Walter ask me something. I was devastated – for a few hours I had almost forgotten about the Bullocks except as a topic for questions, not the reality of it all. Remembering to speak out loud, as the President (and Mike) had requested, I said, "What? Sorry, I wasn't listening."

With less animosity than usual, they said, "I have visited much of your planet. Your story of the garden of Eden is true – what a beautiful place your world would be without Homo sapiens and your clamorous cities to ruin it."

"Thank you."

"For your information, also, you and your advisors shouldn't worry so much about your performance in front of a group of reporters. The only thing that matters is that your fellow humans get the message. Whether you bumble or stutter is unimportant."

"It's not that simple, Walter. We're not ants. Every one of our species has a mind of his or her own. We have to convince every person in the world, or at least all of the world's leaders, that you are who you say you are, and that you can, and will, do what you say you are going to do."

"What would convince your people to take us seriously? Would another demonstration help?" There was no snarl, it was simply a suggestive question.

"Uh – what kind of demonstration are we talking about? You wouldn't 'eliminate' any of us, like we were so many trees, on national television, would you?"

There was no response to that appeal.

"Walter?"

Apparently he was gone for the day. Planning a convincing demonstration, perhaps. Or visiting Antarctica, for all I knew. But I was so tired I didn't give a damn where he was. When I went inside, Karen pointed out that I looked like shit. I told her I needed a nap. "The bedroom is that way," she reminded me, and I slept like a dead person for almost an hour. When I awoke, I felt a little better, but not much. I gave my wife a peck on the cheek and slogged back to the trailer, telling myself over and over again how beautiful the fall colors were, how beautiful, how beautiful, so that the Bullocks wouldn't hear me say or think anything else. Nevertheless, I noticed that the guys with shovels were still poking around in the woods. It occurred to me that maybe Walter had beat them to it.

Mike was, of course, waiting for me just outside the door of the Nerve Center. "You heard what the Bullocks said?"

"No. Did they say something to you?"

"Did you hear what I said to *them*?"

"No, we didn't. Did you forget to talk out loud?"

This was puzzling. "I'm sure I spoke out loud. Maybe they have some way of neutralizing my spoken words."

"I'll see that someone looks into that. In the meantime, please fill me in."

"They're afraid we might not get the message unless they give us another demonstration of their – uh – capability."

"Did they say when or where this would take place?"

"No."

"Maybe you can get that information from them later on. Otherwise, all we can do is wait. By the way," Mike confided, "there has been a change of plans."

"Bully for that," I snapped. I didn't even ask what plans were changed. It seemed I would be carried along with whatever happened, like a log in a fast-moving river, and I wouldn't have a thing to say about it. Unless, of course, I refused to cooperate . . . .

He ignored my irritation. "The news conference has been arranged for six o'clock. We need to get you sharpened up a bit more for that."

"It's going to be *today*?? Where?"

"In Washington. You'll be meeting the President at the White House at 5:30. We leave here in an hour."

"Oh, God. I need to tell – "

"Don't worry about that. We'll send someone over to tell Karen where you are."

"Why the rush?"

"All hell is breaking loose. More and more networks and local affiliates are spilling the story. Some of which is inaccurate. We need to quell that, or the whole world could implode before you even get to the UN."

I could feel my shoulders slumping. "Well, at least I had a little nap."

"Let me tell you something, Gene. It won't be nearly as bad as you think. In fact, you'll probably enjoy it – believe it or not. Like a party or a dinner you didn't want to go to but you enjoyed after you got there."

"Even if Walter knocks off a few reporters to prove their authenticity?"

"Did he say he was going to do that?"

"Not exactly."

"Well, we don't have time to worry about something that might or might not happen and that we can't do anything about anyway, right? Okay, let's go. We only have time for a brief run-through. They're waiting for you."

The same people as before were in the conference room. Or almost the same – who could remember them all under conditions like these? And the procedure was much like before, except that, as the press secretary put it, "This will just be a kind of dress rehearsal of the questions you will almost certainly be asked by the press later this afternoon. Nothing too intense – we've already covered almost everything. But we'd like you to stand there at the lectern. Would you prefer a jacket when you're in the press room at the White House?"

I thought about that for a moment. Having worn coats and ties all my professional life, I had come to hate them and had barely worn one since my retirement. But I indicated that I would probably feel more comfortable in them for the unwelcome briefing. Something to do with authority and confidence, I suppose, as well as familiarity. "Good decision," said the chair. You should *feel* like you're on top of things. Mike, give Dr. Brewer your jacket for a while, will you?" I was impressed by this attention to detail, and I did feel better with it on. I began to imagine myself standing in the White House briefing room fielding the same questions I was rehearsing in Room 5. The main purpose of this "warm-up" was to make the setting seem more comfortable, and it did. As for the questions, I was reminded for the umpteenth time that I had nothing to worry about as long as I simply told the truth.

Everything went well enough. I was less tired than I had been earlier, and was beginning to feel that I actually knew what I was talking about. The only new questions were about what I planned to say to the UN Security Council (still to be determined) and whether I was developing any sort of familiarity or friendship with the Bullocks. I repeated that a certain familiarity was beginning to set in, and that Walter seemed to be softening their attitude toward us, at least a little. Several of the committee members advised me to say, instead, that I was "working on that."

Someone had run to the house to tell Karen what was going on and to retrieve my favorite jacket, and we were on our way in the usual vehicles to the makeshift helipads. Mike and I were joined in the helicopter by the press secretary and the Vice-President, who was cheerful, even optimistic, as he apparently always is, no matter what the situation. None of us spoke about the Bullocks on the way to the airport. In fact, we talked about everything else but them. Family reminiscences and the like. The VP is a good storyteller as well as a strong voice over the noise of the "chopper," as he called it, and he had us actually laughing a few times, something there had been little of in the past couple of days. Despite the good cheer, however, no one discussed any personal plans for the future.

With the Vice-President on board, we were flying to D.C. on Air Force Two (Dr. Greaney was already on board). It was laid out a little differently from the earlier plane, but still quite comfortable, even cozy, and we had some tea and little cakes as soon as we were airborne. After that, the VP fell asleep (he snores). "Does he do this all the time?" I asked Mike.

"Whenever he can. That's why he has so much energy the rest of the time."

I told him about a former patient of mine, "Rip van Winkle," who fell asleep even during intercourse.

"I don't think the Vice-President does that," he mused.

"Fall asleep? Or intercourse?" I asked. Even Mike's high-pitched giggling didn't wake the Vice-President.

Thinking about one of my patients led me to reminisce about my entire life and career, and raised again the question I have asked myself all my adult life: *Why the hell did I decide to become a psychiatrist?* Why does anyone decided to do *anything*? Because everything that happened before led to that decision. We often hear the query, "What would you do differently if you could? Even with the benefit of hindsight, I suspect that most of us would do everything pretty much the same way. Prot, in fact, once told me that we are all just vessels of thinking chemicals, and our responses to any situation, given the particular test tubes we found ourselves in at the time, were virtually automatic reactions.

I suddenly realized that the press secretary was speaking to me, advising me how to handle the conference. During the remainder of the trip he gave me a number of tips, the most significant of which was: "Don't ever get angry. No matter what they ask you, no matter how stupid or pushy the question is, don't get angry."

I told him I would do my best.

The next thing I knew we were on Marine Two making our way to the White House lawn. By this time – we were late – it was already nearly six o'clock, and we were hustled to the Oval Office, where we were all warmly greeted, as always, by the President, who joked that I was becoming a familiar figure there, and maybe I would like to have an office of my own down the hall. I managed to counter his joke with, "No, thanks. I'm perfectly content with this one."

The President chuckled for a moment, but there was no more time to waste. He quickly proceeded to brief me on what to expect in the press room. "I will make a short background presentation and introduce you. At that point you will replace me at the podium. From then on it should be a piece of cake. Your crew in the Nerve Center has prepared you well, and you will field questions for an hour or so. I'm sorry you had to come here for this, but it's better than having everyone involved travel to upstate New York on short notice. Any questions before we go in?"

"I guess not."

"One more thing: we have the video of Walter in the form he first approached you, as well as the disappearing tree, already set up in the briefing room. Just ask for them at the appropriate time."

Suddenly I remembered what they (Walter) smelled like. It made me nauseated again. "Okay," I sighed.

The President gave me a quizzical look. "Are you okay, Dr. B?"

"Yes, I'm okay."

"Good. Everyone ready?"

No one admitted otherwise, and we all marched briskly down the red carpet and into the press room, the President on my left, the Vice-President on my right, Mike and a few others trailing along behind.

The briefing room was about as I expected, having seen television coverage of many a press conference, though it was somewhat smaller than I had imagined (I suspect it would hold several dozen people at most), and I expected there to be more bright lights than there were. The President strode to the podium, and the din suddenly died, as if someone had flipped a switch.

"Good evening, everyone," he began. "I think all of you know by now that the Earth has been visited again by an alien, or aliens, this time from a planet called Bullock. Spelled B-u-l-l-o-c-k. These visitors, unlike those from the planet K-PAX, are a co-operative, linked society sharing an intellectual capability which is, I can assure you, quite superior to our own. They have come with a message for the people of Earth, and their message is that we must stop killing one another. It was delivered to Dr. Gene Brewer, formerly of the Manhattan Psychiatric Institute, who is with us here today. Since Dr. Brewer is the only person who has been in direct contact with this alien race, we thought it prudent that he be here to answer any questions you might have about the Bullocks, what they are demanding of us, and what the time frame for our compliance is." The President turned to me, winked surreptitiously, shook my hand, and said, "Dr. B, the podium is yours."

And here I was, standing before sixty or more reporters from newspapers, magazines, television and electronic media networks, and God knows how many people watching at home. Two days ago I would have been scared out of my mind to be standing there, but by now it all seemed like a stroll in the park.

From a pocket I pulled out some notes I had jotted down on the trip, dropped them on the podium, and briefly summarized the events to date. There is no need to repeat those remarks here, except to say that the story of the talking squirrel elicited a few smirks. I confessed that I could hear the Bullocks inside my own head now, without a "middle man" of any kind.

At that point some of those in attendance exchanged looks of disbelief.

"I know what you're thinking," I said. "And I'm not crazy. Or at least I don't think I am. I'm going to show you a short video of the Bullocks' completely obliterating a tree, leaving no trace of it whatsoever, not even a speck of dust. I personally witnessed that and it is documented. If anyone here can explain to me how this is possible, then I'll admit I'm crazy and we can all go home." I nodded to the President and the video, showing "Walter" getting into my car, and the elimination of the tree, and all the rest.

The reporters sat silently, and it appeared they were beginning to accept the possibility that the Bullocks were, in fact, somewhere on planet Earth and were probably who they said they were.

Someone asked, "No disrespect, Dr. Brewer, but everything you've told us is your own interpretation of the alleged events of an alien visit. The disappearing tree could be the result of a camera trick, and no one else has spoken with these beings but you. Is that correct, sir?"

"Well, that's true, of course, but – "

"And this 'Walter' could have been an actor playing a role, isn't that true?"

"No! That's *not* true! They are here, whether you believe it or not!" I had already forgotten the press secretary's admonition not to get angry regardless of the tone of the questions asked. I glanced at the President. All he could do was offer assurance that the corpse in the film had been identified as a Walter Aragon, of Hartford, Connecticut, who had passed away two days before the video was taken.

Someone pointed out that there were also photos of "Bigfoot" and the "Loch Ness monster."

I replied, feebly, that the Bullocks inferred that there would soon be a more convincing demonstration of what they were capable of.

"Any idea what that might be?"

"They didn't say." I'm afraid my dander was still showing.

A familiar-looking newscaster asked where the Bullocks were right now.

"I don't know. Probably in this room somewhere."

Everyone looked around, examining the walls, the ceiling, each other. "We don't see them, sir – do you?"

I answered, calmly I hoped, that I didn't either. "They could be taking the form of a dust mite on the floor. Or maybe one of your liver cells, for all I know."

There were a few more smirks. Another familiar face, host of a Sunday morning discussion show, asked, "Are they saying anything to you right now?"

"No, they aren't telling me anything at the moment. Except for my initial contact with Walter, the communications have only come to me in my home or backyard." Some of the reporters were still looking around the room, more with curiosity than trepidation.

"What do the Bullocks sound like?"

"Like a whiny old woman." There were still more titters. A couple of the attendees looked at their watches. There was even a yawn or two.

"I would remind all of you that prot and fled were demonstrably here. There is no doubt about that. Neither of these, or Walter, are figments of my imagination." I was beginning to hyperventilate.

The President returned to the microphone. "Look," he said. "The government has ample evidence that Dr. Brewer's first visitor, prot, could travel at, or faster, than the speed of light, and that fled returned to K-PAX with nearly a hundred thousand apes and monkeys, plus an indeterminate number of humans. Those are facts. You have my word on that. This press conference was called not to defend Dr. B's credibility, but because someone leaked the information about the Bullocks' visit. The Administration wanted to get out in front of this thing and to assure the American people that their government is on top of it." He calmly stepped aside and I returned to the microphone.

A tall man I had seen on some news program or other, and who resembled Alex, a former resident at MPI, asked, "Why are the Bullocks here?"

"They brought certain demands, and they expect us to comply with them."

When the man followed up with: "Can you tell us what they are demanding of us?" the room quieted down a little. Even if they didn't believe me, at least I had their attention. Everyone likes a good story whether it's true or not.

"First, they want me to deliver a message to the United Nations Security Council next Saturday. After that we will have one year to comply with their demands, which are these: By the end of that year there shall be no killing of any human beings for at least a twenty four-hour period, except for accidental deaths. If that can be accomplished, we will be given another year in which to stop the killing of any other animal on Earth for at least one day."

"Are you saying we can kill anyone we want as long as no one kills anyone during a single twenty-four-hour period?"

"That's what they said."

"That doesn't make any sense. Are you sure you heard it right?"

I quelled another surge of anger. "Very sure."

Fortunately, someone changed the topic. "Sir, what happens after the two years? If we can comply with the Bullocks' demands, will we be allowed to return to our normal lives, even if a few people are killed?"

Oddly, no one at the Nerve Center had asked precisely that question. "I don't know. But I'm pretty sure they will want us to continue without – "

"Pardon me for interrupting, Gene," said the President, "but I don't think we want to get into that kind of speculation at this point. Our immediate concern right now is to figure out a way to comply with that first year's demands. If we can't do that, everything else becomes moot."

There was a long pause before someone asked, "Mr. President, how will they know whether we have complied? Will they be around from now on, spying on us?"

The President referred the question back to me. "I don't know that, either," I admitted. "But they're already here observing us. Walter – the Bullocks – have told me they have recently visited much of our planet. They like what they've seen, by the way. Except for the human element."

"Well, what happens if we don't, or can't, comply with these demands?"

"Human beings will disappear from the Earth," I said.

There was another pause while this fact was digested. Even though there were cameras present (only two or three – I hadn't realized that the networks shared film footage of such events), there was furious scribbling on little notepads. A tiny woman followed up with: "How do these – uh – Bullocks propose to accomplish this?"

"They haven't yet told me exactly what will happen to us."

"Do you mean we will all just *vanish*? Like that tree in the road?"

"I don't know. But I can tell you this, and maybe I should have mentioned this earlier: they are a very old civilization, so old that they have outlived the suns that originally warmed their planet. They have somehow tapped into a universal consciousness that we didn't even know existed. I suspect they can do things we can't even imagine might be possible. I suppose this is pure speculation, but yes, I think they could make us all disappear, if that's what they want to do. I suspect that the Bullocks could eliminate the entire population of the world in a matter of seconds. Realizing for the first time, perhaps, what I was saying, I actually felt my shoulders slump. "Of course it might take a little longer than that . . . ."

A younger woman (she reminded me of Laura Chang, a former colleague) in the back of the room raised her hand, and I nodded warily to her. "Isn't there an inconsistency here? If they are so opposed to killing, how can they justify killing seven billion people?"

"I don't think they plan to *kill* us per se. I don't know – maybe we'll be transported to another planet. Or to another dimension, for all I know. As I said, they haven't told me exactly what they have in mind for us."

A portly man in a beautiful blue suit asked, in a nasal Midwestern accent, "What does Walter say about our religions? Do they believe in the same God that we do?"

"Walter says there *is* no God. That's why a death is so tragic."

There was a period of silence while that information was digested. The young woman in the back smiled and said, "The Bullocks just lost their credibility with that one."

I retorted that they'd probably get it back after the demonstration they're planning. The smile disappeared.

The familiar news anchor asked, "When did you say this demonstration will take place?"

"As I said before, I don't know. Probably soon."

A woman with a German accent lifted a hand, but didn't wait for recognition. "I'd like to direct this question to the President if I may. Mr. President, it seems to me that Dr. Brewer doesn't really know much about these Bullocks' plans or what we really need to do to meet their demands. We're not even sure they're for real. Is the government holding anything back?"

Reluctantly I stepped aside, and the President returned to the podium. Essentially ignoring the questioner, he looked directly into the eyes of the cameras. "As you know, the story was already leaked last night or early this morning. We don't know who leaked it, but that's unimportant now. Dr. Brewer and I didn't plan to have this press conference prematurely, and we don't yet know much about the Bullocks or their intentions. We are here to reassure the people of the world that there is absolutely no need for immediate concern. We have all been asked to do something that is theoretically possible to accomplish, and if we all work together, we should be able to pull it off. I'm not saying this will be easy, and no one should be led to think it will be. But people need to go about their daily lives for the next year without thinking the world is going to come to an end. This will require some restraint on the part of the news media, and maybe even some encouragement. There will be some who will push the panic button, and I can see certain potential headlines now, such as: ALIENS PLAN TO DESTROY US IF DEMANDS NOT MET, or some such thing. That is exactly what we *don't* want to convey to the world's population. We need to suggest possibilities. Give people hope. A panic on the order of a global epidemic or the like would make our task virtually impossible to accomplish. Headlines like the one I just mentioned would be a self-fulfilling prophecy. Is there anyone here who would disagree with this assessment?"

"No, Mr. President, but those are the facts, are they not? If these aliens *are* in our midst, as you and Dr. Brewer claim, they plan to eliminate us in some way if their demands aren't met. Isn't this what you're saying?"

"As far as we know, this is true. Nevertheless, we need to remember, and to emphasize to your readers and viewers, that this can be avoided, and that we must cooperate with the Bullocks, to every extent possible, to see that it doesn't happen. We can do this, but we need to begin *now*. For this reason, today I am ordering a moratorium on capital punishment in every state, and I'm going to ask the Secretary of Defense to begin rapidly scaling down all ongoing military operations, including drone strikes. I'm also going to convene a meeting of all the governors of the various states to assess all police activity within their jurisdictions to see what can be done to urge officers to use restraint at all times, regardless of the circumstances. We will also be working with world leaders to ask for similar restrictions in their respective countries."

The President paused for only a moment, and I could almost *feel* him organizing his thoughts. "We are all in this together, folks. Everyone in the world. *Everyone*. This is what the American people need to hear. We trust that you will make the effort to assure the people that we are all working on this problem and that, together, we can accomplish our mission. Yes, call it a mission. A year doesn't give us much time, but if we work hard, it may be sufficient time. We have an entire year to get our message to the people and to make sure everyone understands what is at stake and what it will take to achieve this goal. But first, you all need to convince yourselves that there is hope and that we can work together to make that hope a reality. You are the first line of defense against the naysayers and the doubters who will try to undermine our objective. I'm personally asking you to help us with this. If we can avoid a potential disaster, the entire world will be in your debt.

"Now I'm going to give the microphone back to Dr. Brewer, who will answer any additional questions you might have about the Bullocks and how we can deal with them through him."

There was a round of applause. For a moment I thought it was for me, but I quickly realized it was for the President's eloquent appeal for calm and restraint in the face of a possible threat to human life on planet Earth.

The remaining questions were almost trivial, or repeats and clarifications of what had already been said. Someone again wanted to know when we could expect Walter's "demonstration." He confessed there was still a great deal of doubt in his mind about the whole thing. All I could do was shrug my shoulders.

The President tried to bail me out again. "The Bullocks came here two days ago. We simply haven't had time to dig that deeply into the problem. We were forced to hold this press conference prematurely. We should be able to answer all your questions more completely in the next few days." Perhaps he had noticed that I was becoming visibly tired. In any case, someone stepped up and said, "Thank you Mr. President, and thank you, Dr. Brewer." At that point the room erupted in noise and confusion, and most of the members of the press core rushed out to do what they were compelled to do.

On the way out the door between the gold drapes, the President shook my hand. "Very well done, Dr. B. For a first press conference, you did an admirable job."

"You mean there are going to be others?"

He chuckled and said, "Who can predict the future?"

With that we returned to the Oval Office, where I was asked if I'd like anything to eat or drink. "Rye on the rocks?" I replied, requesting our usual before-dinner cocktail. The President waved a finger at someone, and said, "For everyone." The drinks came in a matter of minutes, and I could sense the relaxation creep into every soul in that room. As soon as our stomachs were warmed, we talked, unbelievably, about the chances of the Knicks in the upcoming season. "I'm always hopeful, Mr. President."

"So am I," he responded. "Of course, I *have* to be."

"Thank you for bailing me out back there," I said. "You set the right tone, and I feel better about what might happen. I think everyone does."

"I hope we were able to get our message across," he replied. "I underestimated the degree of skepticism we would encounter. Let's hope that Walter's upcoming demonstration will quell that doubt."

"And that no one will be hurt by it," I added.

"Amen to that," he said gravely. "Do you have any sense whatever of what they have in mind?"

"None at all, Mr. President."

He nodded. "At least the secret is out," he said, "and we can concentrate on the main problem we're all facing. Tomorrow morning we get back on schedule. A lot more work to do."

We finished our drinks, and the Vice-President, Mike, and I, along with our usual entourage, returned to the helicopter, whose rotor was already slowly turning. I saw the famous historical structures shining in their respective spotlights as we returned once again to the airport and the flight home. I know we had an elegant dinner aboard Air Force Two, though I can't remember what I ate. I fell asleep immediately afterward while the VP and the indefatigable Mike were discussing the morrow's schedule.

It was nearly eleven o'clock when I got in the door. Karen was waiting up for me. Actually, she was sleeping in the living room chair, but she came awake when she heard me come in, running to greet me as I sagged to the sofa. "You were wonderful," she assured me.

"It's funny. I was terrified when we came into the press room, but once I got to the podium I was fine, even though I couldn't answer many of the questions. I think I could get used to fame. It's too bad it had to come under such awful circumstances."

I was still feeling pretty good when we went to bed, and didn't go to sleep right away, though my lovely wife soon drifted off.

"Good evening, doctor."

The leaves are beautiful, the leaves are –

"Yes, we know. You've already mentioned that."

"What do you want, Walter?"

"You have questions for me."

"Well, yes, I guess I do. But I don't know if you will want to answer them."

"What are they?"

"You know about the press conference."

"Yes."

"Were you there?"

"Of course."

"Then you must know a lot of people don't believe you exist, and that the most important question that came up concerned your demonstration. You didn't tell me what you're planning and when it is going to happen."

"Very soon."

"Very?"

"Anything else?"

"What about killings that are justified?"

"There are no justified killings."

"But surely there are cases of self-defense, for exam – "

"The universe honors someone who doesn't kill far more than one who kills to save himself."

"Not on Earth."

"That's part of your self-centeredness. You're going to have to rethink the logic of that."

I understood immediately that this was going to be a problem, but I let it go for the time being. "There was a question about what happens after the two trial years, if I may call them that. I presume that if we meet your goal we will have to restrain ourselves from killing anyone for a while?"

"Did you think this was a one-time thing, doctor? Nediera is forever!"

"And there is no leeway? No margin for error?"

"How many times must we explain our terms?"

"And if we fail to – "

"Then you will cease to be a burden on the universe."

I knew there wouldn't be much room for compromise, but I asked the question anyway: "Is any negotiation possible? You want the killing stopped, and we might be able to do that, but maybe not in a year. We have become who we are over a period of 100,000 years or more. One year to change our entire makeup is asking too much. We might be able to satisfy the universe and make everyone happy, but it might take a little longer than you're demanding. For example, we might be able to reduce the killing by 10% a year for the next decade. Is that something you can work with?"

There was a pause, which rarely happened with the Bullocks. I wondered whether they had gone. I was almost asleep when they said, "No."

At the risk of instant annihilation I said, "Isn't there *any* room for negotiation? I don't think you're being fair."

"Is ending the life – the only one it will ever have – of any being *fair*?"

"What if you kill only the killers? *That* would be fair, wouldn't it?"

In a roar I hadn't heard for a while: "Can't you understand a simple universal truth? It's a disease of your DNA. You're *all* potential killers!"

After another period of silence, they said in a low voice, "Here's something fair: If there are no guns shown on your television sets anytime in the next twenty-four hours, we'll let you off that hook."

I screamed, "I've already told you: We can't change overnight!"

Was that a laugh I heard? Whatever it was, I didn't hear it again that night. Nevertheless, I thought that perhaps some progress had been made. Or maybe I had made everything even worse. But I had done all I could for one day. I had gotten through a Presidential press conference, stood up to the Bullocks, and my conscience was clear. For once I slept like a baby.

DAY FOUR

I woke up feeling better than I had in days. For the first time, I felt as though I might be able to complete the mission that was thrust upon me. I had, after all, (with the President's help) answered questions from the national news media, as well as several foreign correspondents. It seemed to me that the speech to the United Nations Security Council couldn't be much worse. I had only to tell them why the Bullocks had come and what they wanted from us, something that was becoming as familiar as the back of my hand. Then I remembered that the existence of human life on Earth might depend on how well I conveyed that message, and my confidence quickly dissipated and I became moody again. My annoyance was not alleviated in the slightest with the news that son-in-law Steve was on the phone and wouldn't take no for an answer.

Reluctantly I picked up the bedroom extension. "Hello, Steve. How's it going?"

"Ah saw your press conference last night, and Ah came up with an idea. Right now you're surrounded by a bunch of politicians that don't know shit from Shinola. You need to have a scientist along when you're talkin' to the Bullocks. Someone who can speak their language."

"Steve, it doesn't work that way. There's no shortage of scientists here."

"Do they go home with you? Hang out in your backyard?"

"Well, no, but – "

"There you go. What if Ah come over and stay for a while?"

"I don't think that would be a good idea, Steve. The Bullocks might not like it if a stranger suddenly appeared."

"So introduce me."

Karen was waving at me from the doorway. "Got to go now, Steve. I'll talk to you later."

"What about that introduction?"

"All right, all right. I'll think about it."

"Is that a promise?"

"Yes, dammit, it's a promise."

"Can you call back tonight? Even if you don't want to talk to me, your grandson would like to say hello." Before I could ask which one, he hung up.

Karen said, "Mike is here."

Still wearing my pajamas, I went with her to the kitchen. For some reason I remembered that fled had first appeared at the kitchen door, then ate a bowl of dried beans at the table. How I longed for those simple days when there was only a normal alien to deal with, and no demands imposed. Yet, it was fled who warned us that the Bullocks were coming. Stupidly, we had virtually ignored her. Even *I* hadn't taken her seriously. "Hello, Mike. Do I have time for breakfast and a shower? Or is the sky falling again?"

"Breakfast is on its way. You don't smell so bad – maybe you could skip the shower."

"Very funny. Anyway, what's the urgency?"

"We've found the cone-shaped device you buried several years ago. It's in the trailer, and the scientists are trying to analyze it. But it's a lot more than you thought it was."

I was so sickened when I saw the patients' mind readings (elicited by fled) projected by the cone that I hadn't explored the damn thing any further before burying it. It hadn't occurred to me at the time that there might be something else there. "What else is on it?"

"The K-PAXians have visited thousands of worlds, and there are videos and holograms from some of those. And that barely scratches the surface. There are evolutionary charts for these sample planets. Including ours."

"Really? How far back does it go?"

"To the beginning."

"You mean K-PAXians were here millions of years ago?"

He shrugged.

"Anyway, what's so great about that? Don't we already know how we evolved?"

"Not exactly. It describes several of our ancestors, and what happened to them, including the Neanderthals and a lot of others."

"What happened to them?"

"Every single species eliminated the one that came before."

"Oh."

"It's a wonder the Bullocks weren't here a long time ago," Karen said.

Mike replied, "Maybe they were, but were hoping we'd evolve again."

"So the cone's about evolution?" I asked him.

Mike shook his head. "It's a lot more than that. But I'll let Dr. Uttley tell you about it."

"Who's Dr. Uttley?"

"He's a physicist and a chemist and a few other things. Has four Ph.D.'s. He's in charge of the team that's trying to decipher the thing."

"Where is it now?"

"It's over in the trailer, but it will soon be on its way to Washington. We thought you might like to take a look at it before they whisk it away."

I told him about Steve, that he wanted to be in on all this.

"Maybe he'd like to be part of Dr. Uttley's team. They can use all the help they can get."

"He wants to be more directly involved. He wants to talk to Walter."

"That would be up to Walter, don't you think?"

"Maybe they wouldn't care if he hangs around. Walter speaks to me with the G-men around. Unless they don't hear us for some reason."

"None of them have reported hearing anything, anyway. And the surveillance cameras haven't shown us much."

Karen reminded him that the Secret Service people wouldn't be able to hear my thoughts.

"But I was speaking out loud!" I pointed out. At least some of the time."

"Are you sure?" She turned to Mike. "Have the cameras shown Gene speaking to Walter?"

"Not really."

Someone (a G-woman?) brought in breakfast. We ate in silence – all of us were probably thinking his or her own thoughts about the Bullocks, my communications with them, the cone, and the days ahead.

After that I hurriedly changed clothes, kissed my wife, and Mike and I were out the door. As we left, I called out, "Have a nice day!" She didn't laugh.

On the way to the trailer Mike asked me whether the Bullocks had said anything during the night.

"He said the demonstration would come 'very soon.'" I nodded to the agents on the morning shift, who nodded back, a first for me. I thought: perhaps they're human after all. And, of course, potential killers.

We went to Meeting Room 6 (I knew that because the walls were pink). It was filled with people watching a morning news program. A newscaster was on a New York street interviewing passersby about what they thought about the "invasion" of the Bullocks. The answers covered the entire spectrum of logic and emotion. One man advised "blasting the aliens to smithereens," while others suggested prayer, diplomacy, cooperation. Some felt that Walter was the devil incarnate (I had to chuckle at this, since the Bullocks were far from "incarnate"), while others "had long known this was going to happen." Still others declared that it was "time we paid for our reckless disregard for the sanctity of life." A member of some political group or other called it "a liberal plot to take away our firearms and curtail our military might." Some wanted to know where the government was "hiding the aliens." Many people, however, were weeping. Suddenly I understood the President's eagerness to hold the press conference before the whole process could be overtaken by rumors. Even though there was still some confusion about what had happened and what to expect, at least the basic story that people were grappling with was correct. They weren't really worried about an invasion of body snatchers or the like. I only hoped that when the public fully absorbed what was at stake, support for compliance with Walter's demands would merge into something more uniform and co-operative.

Someone turned off the set, and I found myself in another meeting of the Task Force on Negotiations with the Bullocks. I could report to Steve that there were, in fact, a couple of astronomers (including a guy from SETI, the Search for Extraterrestrial Intelligence), a physicist and a mathematician, and even a philosopher or two, among the negotiators. As before, it was headed by the UN Ambassador. At this particular meeting the Vice-President was again in attendance.

After all the introductions and re-introductions, the chair summarized where we stood at that moment, ending with: "The Bullocks apparently still aren't giving us much room either for negotiation or error. Is that right, Dr. Brewer?"

"I would say that a better description would be *no* room for error. They want us to stop all the killing, period. Not 95% of it, or 98%, but *all* of it. They don't even want to hear reasonable questions about how we might comply with their demands without totally destroying our identity as human beings. But I can also say this: when I spoke with Walter last evening, I asked them whether they might consider something like a decrease of 10% per year over the next decade. Before they said no, they hesitated for a couple of seconds. It was almost as if they were computing the results of – "

"Maybe they're a computer!" the math professor interrupted with some enthusiasm.

The chair asked whether it mattered. Someone said it might, pointing out that computers can be flummoxed if they are overwhelmed, or are asked questions they don't understand. There was silence for a moment while everyone pondered that remote possibility.

The young physicist, who reminded me of my grandson Rain, opined that if the Bullocks were, in fact, a highly-advanced computer, they were probably still too smart to be "flummoxed' by the likes of us.

"Maybe some of you can work on that," I went on, a little testily, perhaps. "But the point I was making is that there might be an opening for negotiation if we can come up with a reasonable alternative they would find acceptable. After they said the 10% thing was unacceptable, I told them they were being unfair because we can't change overnight, maybe no species can."

"What was their response to that?"

"I think it might have been laughter."

A logician, an acknowledged genius who was not affiliated with a university but preferred to work alone, offered this: "One plus one equals two." While everyone was trying to decide what the hell that might mean, she explained, "If you can show that one death is better than two, even the Bullocks might agree that would be permissible."

"And whose two deaths are we talking about?" the chair calmly asked her.

"As I understand it," the logician went on brightly, "the Bullocks aren't requiring us to stop all the killing immediately, only that we stop it for one twenty-four-hour period during the next year. One day is only $1/365^{th}$ of a year. But if we kill only 99% of the current total during that one-year period, more lives would be saved than they are demanding. Isn't that right, Dr. Brewer?"

I confirmed that this was my understanding.

"And even if we are able to comply with their demands, we could kill as many people as we wanted for the next twelve months and still be in compliance with their wishes, right?"

I couldn't find anything wrong with her logic. "But after year one, there would have to be no killing whatsoever of our fellow humans. Are you suggesting that we indulge our blood lust for one last orgy of killing?"

There were murmurs around the room. The Vice-President stated that he didn't like the sound of that. "They must know that we'd figure this out and offer something less as a counter-proposal. Anyway, there's a catch: If we fart around with the numbers like this, that itself might not go over very well with the Bullocks, as Dr. B has suggested. Maybe it's our earnest attempt to comply with their demands that really counts."

'I agree with Dr. Brewer and the Vice-President," said the chair. "Nevertheless, we need to buy as much time as possible. If it's not possible to eliminate all the killing in one twenty-four-hour period, it's over. The question then becomes: is there a more reasonable goal we can propose?"

"I agree with that assessment," said the physicist. "I personally think that no killing in one twenty-four-hour period will be impossible to achieve within a year. Maybe at a later time, if we get that far. If there is any room at all for negotiation, maybe we should try to get the Bullocks to agree on something that's to our mutual benefit. Maybe Barbara has a point," he added, nodding to the logician. "Maybe they would settle for something more reasonable the first year as long as the number of lives lost is significantly less then they're demanding."

The Secretary of State, who had come in late, raised his bushy eyebrows. "Gene?"

"Sir, I just don't know," I replied. "All I can do is ask."

"Of course there's still the question of all the animal killing."

"One of the older diplomats reiterated, "If we don't meet their initial demand in the year one, all the rest is irrelevant. I suggest we focus on that."

The Vice-President said, "Not necessarily. If there are negotiations, they might be more impressed by our thinking about the lives of the other species we share this planet than with just ourselves. After all, the number of animals we kill every year is far greater than the number of people, and to the Bullocks they seem just as important as us."

"Your point is well-taken," said the chair. "And perhaps we ought to get some wheels turning there. Convince more people to consider becoming vegetarians. But the question remains, will Walter work with us on *anything* we might suggest?"

There was further discussion on this topic, but I didn't hear much of it. I was speaking with Walter. "Let me save you some time, doctor," they said in their familiar nasty tone. "We are not impressed with your attempts to obfuscate, delay, and modify. You seem to be more interested in how little you can do to comply with our demand, rather than the demand itself."

"But if we kill thousands less than you're asking for, that's good, isn't it? All those people – and the other animals – will stay in Nediera!" I was so dumbfounded that they were communicating with me in the presence of everyone else that I forgot again to speak aloud. And I noticed a fly walking around on the ceiling – could that be Walter? I surreptitiously looked around for a flyswatter before quickly realizing that squashing it might not be a wise move.

If they heard these thoughts, they chose to ignore them. "What you should be discussing is not how to outsmart us in order to 'buy' some time. It's not for sale. What you should be focusing on is how to stop *all* the killing as soon as possible."

I'm sure I said this out loud: "But Walter, I don't think you understand – "

"We're fed up with this discussion," Walter roared. "So here's the new deal: you cut back the killing by 20% of the current rate every year for the next five years, and we'll let you continue as a species. Same for the other animals beginning in year two. Do you accept these terms?"

"Yes!" I blurted out without thinking. "But why did you – "

"The fact is, the terms really don't matter. We're absolutely certain you can't stop the killing for one day, or even cut it back by twenty per cent over a year." I could almost see them sneering, their rotten teeth exposed. "This discussion is over."

I said, loudly, "Walter?"

The buzzing around me ceased immediately. "He's here?" asked the chair.

"Yes, and with new conditions. Didn't you hear them? I think they're final, and I'm sorry, but I went ahead and accepted them."

There was some murmured chatter about inexperienced negotiators before the chair asked, "What are they?"

I noted that I had everyone's full attention, something I was beginning to get used to and somehow enjoy.

"They say they will accept a 20% reduction in the killing every year for five years."

The chattering started up again: How did I know that was final? Same for the animals? Why didn't we hear any of the discussion with Walter? Etc. Of course I had no answers to any of it. The mathematician finally asked me, "Is that 20% of the current rate, or 20% of the deaths in the previous year?"

"I think they said 20% of the current rate for five years. That would make it 100% at the end of that period," I added drily.

"Can you get him down to 10%?"

I was becoming almost as irritated as Walter. "I don't think they are looking for another compromise. They said they're 'fed up' with our trying to outwit them."

"So you think 20% is the best we can do."

"Yes, I do."

"Might as well be 100%," someone ventured, perhaps prophetically.

"I don't agree," said the chair. "I think it's a fair compromise under the circumstances. At least there's a *chance* we can make that number."

A man who reminded me of Chuck, and later identified as a logistics expert, suggested, "We need to get some hard data on how many people are killed every year. This may seem premature, but we wouldn't want to miss the quota by three or four people. I think it's roughly half-a-million per year, but this isn't something we can guess at."

"A good point, Sandy," said the chair. "Will you look into that? As well as the number of animals we kill every year?" She jotted this down in a little notebook.

Someone else pointed out that there are other subtleties we ought to consider as well. "For example, didn't the Bullocks say that accidents wouldn't count as part of the total?"

I thought this might be another wrong turn, and I said so. "I think what they really want to see is a commitment to maximizing the numbers and to leave the minutiae to them."

"But – "

I went on. "I think we should try for 100% *now*. That way they'll know that our intentions are genuine."

The chair spoke up forcefully. "Dr. B is right. Let's accept the 20% figure, accidents or not, and try to beat it. I was impressed by her grasp of the problem. "Okay," she continued, "if there's no further discussion, the chair will accept a motion to report the figures to the President and to the other TFs, and to dissolve this one."

"So moved," said the Vice-President.

"Second," added the Secretary of State.

The motion passed, though there were scattered loud "Nays."

"The meeting stands adjourned."

Before anyone stood up, however, an ethicist ventured, "I still think we ought to try to get someone else involved in the discussions with Walter. No offense to Dr. Brewer, but if the Bullocks are so intelligent and wise, they surely know there are some serious ethical questions that pertain to their demands and what they plan to do if these aren't met. We need to respectfully request that they speak with others more experienced in these matters."

"I would agree with that idea," said the chair of the task force that no longer existed, "except that Walter seems to prefer talking with Dr. Brewer. I suspect that if he wants to talk to someone else, he'll let Dr. B know. Besides, if we bring in others, a religious leader, for instance, all the other clerics on the planet will want to get into the act."

"Same for every other discipline."

I reminded the now-defunct subcommittee that if anyone had a question, I would put it to Walter, but it better be about how we can best satisfy their wishes, not how we can cloud or postpone complying with their demands. Or even to suggest that they are unfair. "I think their patience is wearing thin."

"Can you at least ask them how we can overcome the resistance we're going to encounter? Regardless of the terms, a lot of people aren't going to buy into it."

"I think they would consider a question like that." I pondered it for a moment, but there was no response from Walter. "But they're not saying anything about it at the moment."

No one had any further comments, and everyone started to drift out. Before anyone got very far, however, the chair shouted above the din, "I think we ought to express our thanks and congratulations to Dr. Brewer for what he has accomplished so far. This cannot have been easy for him."

There was a scattering of applause. I looked around and nodded awkwardly.

As Mike and I were leaving, I strongly felt the presence of the Bullocks, and when we had reached the main corridor I nudged Mike's arm and asked Walter out loud whether they had heard everything that had been said.

"Of course."

I pointed to my head and mouthed that answer to Mike. After taking a deep breath, I asked aloud, "Walter, we need help. Will you teach us how best to end the killing before it's too late?" Mike remained motionless, but seemed to be giving us his rapt attention.

"Fled brought you prot's nine suggestions for the survival of your species. You chose to ignore them. You'll find the answers to your questions on the cone."

"Where? How do we find it?"

No response.

"Walter?" I repeated.

Only silence.

"They're gone," I said.

"Who's gone?"

"Walter."

"They were here? Is that why you were pointing to your head?"

I stared at him in disbelief. How could he have missed something as important as this? "Didn't you hear me talking to him?"

"No."

It occurred to me that maybe the Bullocks were able to stop time, or shield our conversation in some way whenever we spoke. "He said the answer to our dilemma is on the cone."

Mike nodded vigorously. "I'll pass that information along to Dr. Uttley. Maybe his group can intensify their efforts." He suggested I forget about the Bullocks for a while and go home and have a nice lunch.

"Forget about them??" I said, with almost a Walter-like sneer. "How can I forget about them?" I left the trailer mumbling, to any alien beings who might be listening, about the difficulty of complying with their demands, not to mention the difficulty of dealing with my own species, and of life in general. Is it this difficult for everyone who existed anywhere in the cosmos? It occurred to me that it probably is, but the Bullocks opted not to confirm this suspicion.

On the way back to the house I kicked myself for not pressing them to speak with more knowledgeable individuals than I on a variety of levels. On the other hand, it probably wouldn't have done any good. Maybe, I thought, they were through playing around. After all, their demands were crystal clear.

When I got inside, Karen was waiting for me with the mobile phone, demanding I talk to as many of my children and grandchildren as I could before the food came from headquarters, or wherever it originated (for all I knew they ordered everything in). Anyway, I called Will, our youngest, first, because he was the only one I hadn't spoken to recently (aside from Abby, of course, who, as far as I knew, was still on K-PAX). Besides, I missed our weekly chat about his patients at MPI. Unfortunately, he was with one of them, but the receptionist told me she would ask him to call me as soon as he was finished with his session. Immediately she was in tears, and wished me good luck in dealing with the aliens. How weird it was to hear that! A few years ago only crazy people had dealings with beings from space. For me, at least, it was now quite commonplace, and I could hardly imagine not having one or more of them around.

Then I called Fred, who was at a rehearsal for a new off-Broadway play he was directing. We chatted briefly about his life. It was good to know that his career was coming along nicely, and that in his mid-forties he was on schedule to direct his first Broadway show next year (if there *were* a next year). Also that his wife and son were well, etc., etc. At the end of our little talk (Freddy was always on his own wavelength and we never converse for very long), he, too, wished me luck, and offered to help if there was anything he could do. I thanked him and told him I would let him know (it was Fred, in fact, who had helped me bring Robert Porter out of his catatonic state some years earlier).

Finally there was Jennifer in California, knee-deep in testing another new AIDS vaccine. Even though we both knew that Homo sapiens might not have much time left on Earth she spent the whole conversation talking about a cure for that awful disease. It's amazing how life goes on even when a potential catastrophe is at hand. But she closed with, "Good luck, Dad. All my patients are pulling for you!" How cheering it was to hear that!

Lunch came as I was hanging up, but we were only halfway through it when Mike called. "I hope you enjoyed your meal," he said, knowing we hadn't, "but I think you'd better get back here as soon as you can."

"What's up?"

"I'll tell you when you get here."

I swallowed a mouthful of grilled cheese and tomato sandwich, stuffed my mouth with salad, patted my wife on the head, and headed for the trailer. Again, thank God, no word from the Bullocks. When I got to the trailer Mike was waiting just inside the door with a man wearing a white coat. He was the famous Dr. (x4) Uttley, a computer scientist who headed one of the major technological companies. As we proceeded to the far end of the corridor, Dr. Utt, as he preferred to be called, felt the need to inform us that he was an adopted Vietnamese. Nevertheless, he spoke English without a trace of an accent. "I was only two when I got here," he explained, almost apologetically.

We entered a tiny room (Room 1), about the size of my study, which contained a small table and a few folding chairs. The walls were stark white. Sitting on the table was the cone-shaped device I had hoped never to see again, clean and shiny once more.

"You've already watched the projections of the thoughts of some of your former patients, right?" he said.

"Yes, and I hope I don't have to watch them again."

"And also a greeting from prot and your daughter Abby, as well as Giselle and her husband and children on K-PAX."

"Yes, fled showed me that when she first arrived on Earth."

"What you apparently didn't realize is that there is far more on this instrument than the things you've seen."

"It never occurred to me to look for anything else. I was so appalled by what I saw in the minds of my patients that I – "

"Exactly. But take a look at this." I noticed then that the device was resting on a circular sheet of plastic of some kind, with dozens, maybe hundreds, of compass directions delineated on the sheet. He switched off the overhead light and turned the device to face a certain direction, about 190 degrees, just west of due south. On the opposite wall (where a kind of curved screen had been set up) there suddenly appeared a white light. Dr. Uttley drifted effortlessly into his ponderous lecture voice. "Now bear in mind that the K-PAXians have been around for several billion years longer than we have. Not as long as the Bullocks, but far longer than us. So maybe they have a general-issue format that they put on all these devices. But some if it is specific for Earth. What you're going to see next will probably blow your mind." He turned the device a fraction of a degree further around the circle. When he stopped, a beautiful picture of a bright red apple appeared on the screen.

I was puzzled for a moment until the camera, or whatever it was, began to move in. As it got closer and closer to the apple's skin I could see movement. Closer and closer, and we were inside the skin, and there were molecules of various sorts, presumably carbohydrates and proteins and, of course water: the two hydrogens forming an angle with the oxygen atom were unmistakable. And then we closed in on the oxygen atom. In a matter of seconds we passed through the cloud layer of electrons and entered a vast blackness, where we stayed for several seconds. In the distance appeared the nucleus with its distinct protons and neutrons (they weren't so distinct, actually – they sort of merged together to make a whole. I had seen animated, computerized versions of this sort of thing before, but this seemed to be the real thing. We all gaped in awe as we dove into the nucleus itself, and suddenly there were tiny, bright units of three, moving around each other at high speed. The quarks grew bigger and bigger until the camera, or whatever it was, closed in on one of them. The bright spark faded again into utter blackness. We waited, expecting to see nothing more, but suddenly a whole universe appeared, and we moved rapidly through the galaxies, coming to rest on a solar system, then an Earthlike planet, closing fast on a continent surrounded by water, and finally ending up focusing on an apple, where the movement came to a stop.

"What does it all mean?" I asked dumbly.

Dr. Utt, almost unable to speak, whispered, "It means there is no end to space. It goes on forever. Some of us have believed this for a long time, but we've never actually had any evidence for it."

"So it's 'turtles all the way down,'" I mumbled, gazing uncomprehendingly at the apple. Suddenly I thought of Steve. "My son-in-law is a scientist, and he believes in something called string theory."

"Apparently that theory is wrong."

"He's not going to like that."

"Too bad." Uttley gazed lovingly at the apple for a moment before crooning, "Shall we move on?" Another short turn of the cone and there appeared a pastoral scene, vegetation of all kinds and various small animals, including a variety of insects, which changed rapidly as time passed, and the animals grew bigger. The time-lapse "photography" continued, and various other creatures appeared and disappeared, until finally some easily-recognizable dinosaurs showed up. Eventually there was a flash of light followed by something like a huge dust storm, and they, too, finally disappeared. Other kinds of animals became evident, and there was movement, and birth, and death, and then came the apes, and other hominids, which quickly became humanoid and, unmistakably, Homo sapiens appeared on the scene. Small groups became tribes, and these became villages, and finally towns and cities, and farms and factories. We all watched in frank fascination – I wondered whether Dr. Utt and Mike were thinking the same thing I was: how long would we humans last before we also disappeared, like so many of our predecessors – as the cities and the buildings and factories became bigger and bigger. Sometimes there were periods when the various structures were destroyed by war or natural disaster, but always they were rebuilt and grew.

At some point I realized that we had already passed the present time, and I became very much afraid for our species, but more and more time passed and man-made things became less and less recognizable, and even the people changed somewhat: they had become smaller and uniformly bald, even the women. The only constant was that there were more and more of us and fewer and fewer of every other species. Spacecraft began leaving the Earth for unknown destinations (though most people were left behind), until the Earth itself was engulfed in flames, presumably because the sun had expanded to a great size. Finally the burning ended, and there was only a blackened, waterless rock – no Earth, no people, no *anything*.

I could feel my voice shaking as I observed that at least we weren't going to die out in a year or two.

"I wouldn't count on that," said Dr. Utt. "I think this depiction merely represents a hypothetical future, one of many possibilities."

I could feel my shoulders drop. I thought I had just been led to believe that we would go on and on until the end of time. "But doesn't this video thing mean that they think we're going to survive well into the future?"

"Not necessarily. The fact is, there are several more scenarios implanted in the device. In none of them is the outcome as good as this one. Would you like to see some of the others?"

"Do they show how the Bullocks will destroy the human race?"

"No. We think they depict the most likely outcomes if we were left to evolve on our own. Besides, this was probably produced some time ago, long before the Bullocks' arrival."

"I think I'll pass on that."

Mike nudged me, and I told Dr. Utt what Walter had said about the key to our survival being on the cone. He stared at me for a moment. "Then it probably involves our DNA. Something like 40% of this thing appears to be a description of how every human gene works, what would happen if any of them were mutated in any number of ways. The information in it would fill a library.

It would take a supercomputer just to organize and catalog it, let alone figure everything out."

"You mean it tells us how to manipulate our DNA?"

"Yes, that's what we think. But not right away, of course. The scientists who are working on this have years, maybe decades, or even centuries, of analyzing to do."

"We may not have centuries, or even decades. We may only have a year."

"In that case, we'd better get started as soon as possible. I'm only here because we thought you should have a look at it before we took it away. It's technically yours, after all, though fled probably meant it for all of us."

"I don't care what you do with it, just as long as you find the key to our survival somewhere on the damn thing."

Dr. Utt went on dreamily, as if I hadn't said anything. "There are many other things depicted on this incredible device. There are mathematical formulas which no one understands, strange music scores, pictures and descriptions of what may be medical devices, and so on. Chemistry and biology texts which mankind probably won't produce for centuries. There are mind probes, if we can call them that, of various species inhabiting the Earth. Anthropologists are going to be beside themselves."

"How nice," I responded a bit sarcastically. "But – "

"I wasn't sure I should mention this, Dr. Brewer, but, as I said – uh – fled probed the minds of several of the people and animals she met while she was on Earth. One of them was yours."

"I don't want to see it!" I shrieked.

"Okay, okay," Dr. Utt said sympathetically. "But we thought you should know."

"Thank you! Now I know!"

Mike sighed as Dr. Uttley went on. "And many more things we haven't even looked at. It's a universal encyclopedia! *Everything* is on there. It may even have a primer for light travel, if we can figure out how to read it. We've only had a day or so to analyze it."

"But prot wouldn't tell me how that's done. Neither would fled."

"The emphasis here is, 'if we can figure out how to read it.' He shook his head in awe. "We probably won't be able to understand light travel until we're ready to use it responsibly. But this thing will vastly increase our knowledge and understanding of all the sciences, and everything else. Right now it's too much to comprehend, let alone really appreciate." The voice of the lecturer was replaced by that of a whimpering old man. "I'm not sure we can interpret much of it in only a year. We'd need a Rosetta Stone."

I bowed my head. When I looked up, they were both staring at me. I knew what they were thinking. I said, "We're probably too late. I shouldn't have buried the damn thing eight years ago, should I?" Mike and Dr. Utt bowed their heads, too.

"Okay, I think we're finished here," said Mike.

Dr. Uttley cradled the cone-shaped device in his arms, as if it were a newborn baby, and headed for the door. "There are a couple dozen people in white coats who are impatiently waiting for this thing."

Before he could leave, however, I blurted out, "It may well be too late for us to get much use out of this," I said. "Fled must have known this. I wonder why she gave it to us *now*?"

Dr. Utt stopped as if he had run into a wall. For a moment he said nothing, then turned back to me. "As you said, the key to our survival may be on here, if we only knew what it is and where to look."

"Maybe the Bullocks would be willing to tell us that much," I said hopefully.

"There's something else, too," Mike added. "There's so much useful information on the cone that no reasonable human would want to take a chance on losing this opportunity, even if it means we have to stop killing each other."

"Not everyone on Earth is reasonable," I reminded him.

He shrugged. "Perhaps that's where you come in, Gene. All you have to do is to convince the rest of the world that this tremendous knowledge would be of more value to us than all the killing."

Dr. Uttley nodded impatiently before running out the door. I wished I could have followed him. This was an aspect of my dilemma that I had frankly not thought about. It's bad enough that I had to make a speech to the principal representatives of all the world's people, but to *convince them to be reasonable* was something else entirely. No matter what I told them it might not be enough. I felt like some mental patients must feel, those who are suffering from an acute inferiority complex, who know they can't succeed no matter what they do or how hard they try.

Mike must have sensed my renewed feelings of uncertainty and doubt. "We have you scheduled with the psychological support group tomorrow, Gene. Maybe we should move it up a little?"

"Is there a backup for me in case I can't do it? If I get sick or something?"

Mike sighed deeply. "We've been over this before, Dr. B. There would be no point in a backup. For whatever reason, the Bullocks came to you, and you alone. Not even the President can do this."

"Somehow that doesn't increase my confidence."

"It's just something you'll have to deal with. And you know that everyone involved has faith in you and will do everything possible to help you through this ordeal."

"What else have we got scheduled that I don't know about?"

"Have you seen today's *New York Times*?"

"No."

"The world seems to be going through the classic stages related to dying. Right now it's in denial. Despite what I just told you, a lot of people are questioning your authority, even your veracity. Some are wondering why a retired psychiatrist with no leadership or political experience has been called upon to speak for them. Even though there's credible evidence to the contrary, they are wondering whether you are faking the whole thing for some reason. Maybe to get attention. Some people even think you might be crazy. We may have to have another press conference, or something like it. The President is still deciding how best to handle this."

"But after denial comes anger. What does that mean in this context?"

"It may mean that someone will try to kill you or a member of your family."

I froze again.

"But don't worry; you're under maximum security watch. There is no more reason to worry about your assassination than that of the President himself."

I remembered all the Presidents who have been assassinated, or almost so, over the years. "How comforting."

"I'm going to tell you a secret, Gene. Every President initially worries about the possibility of assassination, even before he is elected. But my study of history and getting to know a couple of Presidents tells me that there is so much to do that this feeling quickly fades." He patted my arm, as if I were a little boy. "It's simply not going to happen."

"What about the rest of my family?"

"We haven't told you this yet, but they're all being protected by our security forces. Mainly Secret Service but also plainclothes FBI and local police. We're throwing everything we have into your security and that of your family. Right now no one in the world is more important than you. You're all safer than the Pope. (I recalled the assassination attempts on various Popes.) Besides that, it would be very difficult for anyone to determine who your family is and to assess their comings and goings before the Security Council meets. It's only a few days from now. After that, the whole situation will change."

I wondered whether to tell Karen that our kids and our grandchildren were under threat, no matter how minimal. "Okay, I'll take your word for that. But I'll still worry about it."

"Fair enough. Now why don't you go back and say hello to your wife. Have a cup of tea or something, and we'll reconvene in half an hour."

Still dazed by what I had seen and heard, I stumbled past the guards, neither of whom I recognized. Both ignored me. I got halfway across the yard before I heard Walter's voice. I had almost forgotten about them. "You haven't seen the best part."

"Huh?" I remembered to speak out loud. "The best part of what?"

"Your Jones was right. The K-PAXians want you to know what's in store for you if you are able to give up your endless lust for blood. The universe is so vast and so full of wondrous things that if you get a taste of it you might be persuaded to re-think your self-centeredness in order to see more of it. It's like behaving so that you will get a good Christmas present."

"You know about Christmas?"

"We know everything there is to know about you. All your comforting myths."

"Yes, of course. But why are you telling me this? I had the feeling you'd just as soon we were gone."

"We've seen a lot of your world in the past few days. Despite all your faults, you do have some virtues." I waited, but there was no further elaboration; I thought they had disappeared again. It suddenly occurred to me that the Bullocks might be convinced that our newly-discovered "virtues" might make us worth sparing. But if they heard this, they chose to ignore it. Instead, they said, "Want to go for a ride?"

I froze. "A ride to where?"

"Around the galaxy."

I had very mixed feelings about that – I desperately wanted a cup of tea, for one thing. And to see my beautiful wife, get some reassurance that everything would turn out okay. "Uh – "

"The cone has some representative depictions. Would you like to see the real thing? Believe us when we say that you won't regret it."

Should I trust the reassurances of an alien? "I only have half an hour . . . ."

"Don't worry about that. Here we go!"

The next thing I knew I was looking at the Earth from somewhere in the vicinity of the moon. The only thing I could think to say was, "Oh, shit!"

Walter snorted, "If that's what you wish to call it."

As all the astronauts know, the sight was breathtaking. I actually found myself tearing up at the beauty I saw and felt. The Earth is, in fact, a rich brown and a deep, beautiful blue, with puffy white clouds hovering over parts of it. It reminded me of my favorite marble, a shooter I had as a kid. How I wished I could be back there! I stared and stared at planet Earth, thinking of the myriad life forms occupying our small, lovely world. I couldn't get enough of it. Yet, I knew that a huge part of that life force might soon disappear. Namely, us. Then there would be no one to see this sight ever again. Or, at least, no Homo sapiens. My tears gushed from my eyes and fell onto my shirt.

"If that doesn't make you want to stop the killing, what would?" Walter asked.

"I've never killed anyone in my life!" I yelled, though (I assumed) there were no sound waves to carry the message.

"You've never eaten a hamburger? Swatted a fly?"

"Well – "

"It's part of your violent nature," he barked. "It's time for you to *evolve*."

Suddenly I realized that I was somehow hanging in empty space! How could tears be falling from my face? How could I be *breathing* in a vacuum? How could I even *be* here?

I heard Walter's high-pitched voice: "When will you realize that we learned how to overcome these obstacles long ago? You have a unique opportunity here. Why not just relax and enjoy it?"

My muscles refused to unclench. "Easy for you to say."

"And for you in a few million years, if you are willing to end the murder and mayhem, of course."

The next thing I knew we were hovering above a planet (or moon?) quite unlike our own. As on Earth, the sky was blue, and the vegetation green, but the landscape was absolutely flat and I could see for hundreds of miles, perhaps, and there was no sign of a human being anywhere – no cities, no buildings, no man-made objects of any kind. Instead, the wide-open fields were scattered with animals of many kinds, and birds (or the equivalent) many and varied, flying from tree to tall tree in pairs or flocks. The most noticeable feature, however, was the abundance of flowers of all sizes and colors, as well as the flitting of millions and millions of insects. It was a strangely calming and pleasing sight (though I couldn't hear any buzzing). The sun was brighter than ours, and it moved across the sky at several times our sun's rate of speed (actually, of course, the speed of the rotating Earth). It looked like a hot summer day on our own planet. My muscles finally began to unwind. I gawked at everything going on below, and in a while that yellow-orange sun set, while another one, bigger, and redder in color, rose on the other side of the horizon. "As you may have guessed, we show you this to demonstrate that life exists on countless planets, some like your own, most not. This one is typical for those with climates similar to that of Earth."

"Where are the humans?"

"There aren't any. Nor are there on most other planets or moons."

"They never evolved?"

"Is that so hard for you to imagine? Homo sapiens has arisen on very few planets. And on those that have, most destroyed themselves before they could eliminate everything around them."

"You mean *you* destroyed them?"

"That was not necessary in most cases. Wars, overpopulation, destruction of the environment, man-made diseases, and so on. In the cases where we had to step in, the sapiens, or sapiens-like beings, were virtually the only species left on their planets before the end came. You know how people are."

"But it isn't always that way, is it?"

"Not always. Would you like to see an example of a successful human-populated system?"

Before I could blink an eye we were somewhere else. This time it looked considerably cooler (thought I couldn't feel anything). As promised, there were people engaged in various activities. They were wearing coats of various colors, which didn't seem to be made from skins or furs. Perhaps they were sewn together from plant materials. Some appeared to be quite elderly, yet still very active. None of them appeared to notice me (of course they wouldn't notice Walter). But the part I could see resembled a countryside on Earth, rather than a cityscape. The vegetation was quite different, however. Sparser, I would say, and more rugged. There were various animals in the trees – not birds, more like mice. The colors of the vegetation were a little unusual, especially the shimmering blues and yellows of the trees and grasses. "Where are we?"

"A planet circling what you call Betelgeuse. One of the stars of the "Orion" constellation. But this is only a small fraction of the place. Let's do a flyover." And fly we did, at the speed of a jet plane or the like, from an altitude of perhaps a thousand feet. There were mountainous areas where I saw no humanoids at all (it was surely colder, and the air might have been too thin), tropical areas, deserts, and huge lakes containing God-knows-what creatures – but no apparent oceans like those on Earth. Dotting the planet were a great many small fields planted in various crops, apparently. There were a variety of small animals, but no fences of any kind. Most of these regions contained structures that looked like Indian pueblos, but there were no actual towns or cities *anywhere*. On this world the sky was greenish and the sun a brilliant blue, but smaller than ours, and evidently a little farther away.

"Are you getting the idea?"

"What idea?"

There was a brief pause, apparently long enough for them to get over a fit of pique related to my stupidity. "Have you noticed how peaceful this place is?"

"You mean they never kill *anything* in order to survive?"

"Only the plants. You like it here?"

I had to admit that I did. "And this is what Earth should be like?"

"Only if you want to survive. Now to complete your education, we're going to see a somewhat different planet, one that you may find more familiar." The next thing I knew we were obviously somewhere else. There were people, or people-like beings here, too, but of a different sort. There were cities and towns, too, but most of these had been destroyed or abandoned. In most places there was no sign of any living thing at all, plant or animal, except for groups of men and women (I supposed) and their various war machines. Highly advanced devices, I would judge, for all the good it did to the possessors, since both, or all, sides, had access to the same kinds of equipment.

"I suppose you're going to tell me that this is what our world is coming to."

"At the rate you're going, this will happen in just a few more years. When your ideologies become a bit more polarized or you start running out of certain resources you think you can't live without."

"So why haven't you come to destroy this race?"

"We waited too long, and it happened too fast. Even if they survive this latest conflict, this world is no longer habitable for them. And believe it or not, after they have gone, most of the other animals will come back. And we'll restore the ones who can't. It will be a paradise again some day, much like the other planets you saw."

"But why can't you just leave *us* alone like you have these people, to live or die on our own?"

"Look around you. Is that what you would prefer to ending the killing?"

"How can I convince you that a political solution to a problem like this takes – "

"Killing isn't a political problem. It's a human problem."

"You people don't give an inch, do you?"

"We're not 'people.'"

"Can you just tell me how many of these three kinds of worlds there are in the galaxy? I mean – "

"The first planet we saw is the predominant type of the inhabited worlds – no human-like species. On many, the dominant species are insects. On others, various other animals. There are some, by the way, that harbor only microorganisms! Of course they aren't 'micro' from their point of view. The second category – the planets with humanoids – comprise the remaining inhabited planets in our galaxy. Out of these, nearly all the human-like beings evolved into warriors. Only a few figure it out in time to survive themselves. Does that answer your question?"

"I suppose so," I replied sourly.

"One last trip and then we'll take you home."

"Where are we going? Is there another kind of planet? One without any kind of life at all, maybe?"

"Of course. There are many of those. But that's not where we're going." Almost immediately, it seemed (though it could have been years on Earth, for all I knew), we were zooming across the surface of a planet I had never seen, but which nevertheless seemed familiar. The sky was a lavender color, there were few trees, little water anywhere, and several purple moons dotted the sky. A huge red sun lay close to the horizon, but its light wasn't strong enough to brighten the landscape much. A few small elephant-like creatures roamed the fields of grass and grains of some kind, as well as an abundance of cows and what appeared to be a variety of apes. Birds filled the lavender sky.

Suddenly we slowed down, and sitting or lying below us were several people, who also looked familiar. Of course I recognized my daughter Abby, and the boy must have been little Gene (who wasn't so little anymore). Prot was there, too, as well as a couple of my former patients. "Abby!" I called out.

"She can't hear you," Walter said.

"What? I don't understand. Is this all just a dream?"

"No. It's real. But we traveled here in a – Well, that would be impossible for you to understand. Let's just say it's a different dimension. We can see everything, but to them we are invisible."

"Is that why we can't hear them?"

"You can't hear, feel, smell, or taste anything, but light is different from sound and all the rest. It transcends dimension."

"I'll take your word for that. But this *is* K-PAX, isn't it?"

"Do you know of anything else like it? And by the way, our travels have taken no time at all. When we get back to Earth, it will be the same moment as when we left."

"No time – But that's not possible, is it?"

He roared in obvious exasperation. "Of course it's possible! Haven't you learned *anything*? Do you still doubt that there are things in the universe that you don't understand?"

"Uh, no. Not really."

"We've brought you here so that you can see that prot and K-PAX actually exist. They weren't figments of your imagination."

I watched as Gene chased some sort of animal around and around, and vice versa. Even the creature seemed to be laughing. I looked at Abby, who was eating a purple fruit or vegetable and smiling happily. In fact, I had never seen her so happy when she was on Earth. Again, the tears started to flow.

Walter ignored my blubbering. "Now there is one last thing to show you before we return . . . ."

Suddenly I found myself in a bedroom. Sitting on the floor was a child, about four, who was making something with a set of Tinker Toys. The boy seemed vaguely familiar, but I couldn't identify him. After a few seconds of this the scene shifted to what appeared to be someone's backyard, and the same boy, now six or seven, was riding a tricycle around it as fast as he could go. Again I tried to identify the boy and, when I couldn't, I took a closer look at the setting, which seemed very familiar. And then I understood: it was my own backyard as a child, and the boy was me.

Another minute or so and the scene again shifted to a later time, and I was on a hospital visit with my father. The patient was an older man, very old, in fact, and it seemed to me that he was probably near the end of his life. My father spoke to him, acted as though the visit was routine. They chatted about the Yankees. The man smiled as they discussed yesterday's game, which the Yanks had won 10-3. Dad smiled, too, and so did I. I was about eleven then, and already a fan. When I mentioned the home run by Yogi Berra, the old man held out his hand for me to shake. He smelled bad, and I didn't want to take it, but Dad nodded to me and I did. It was rough and leathery (I remembered), and he held it for a long time, as if holding on to his youth. Or life in general. Until now I had, of course, forgotten that scene, but it all came back very clearly. I think the guy died a few days later. It's countless incidents like this that make up a life, I thought, like pages in a book.

The scene once again became our backyard. Older now, I was playing basketball with a few of the neighbor kids. My younger self shot and missed. I felt a peculiar mixture of disappointment and elation. And something else, too. Awe and wonder that I was actually revisiting my own past.

"Do we see a glimmer of hope?"

"You mean – "

"Once you begin to accept the fact that you humans know nothing, and with a different mindset you could know everything, you'll finally be on the path to your salvation – if you want to put it in terms you can vaguely understand."

As usual, I didn't understand, not even vaguely. It occurred to me that the Bullocks weren't very different from what we might call "God." In fact, talking with the Bullocks felt almost like praying. "Walter – can you do *anything?*"

"Certainly not. Only what is possible."

"And all the things we've just done are therefore possible."

"Obviously."

I went for the basket and lost the ball. "I didn't think time travel was possible."

"It isn't. Not in the way you mean. You can't interact with yourself in the past. You can't kill Hitler, which is something most human beings would dearly love to do. You can't even communicate with anyone. Try to imagine the havoc if you could. Again, you're invisible to any other beings. Call it a law of nature."

I thought about that for a minute before asking the obvious, not really wanting to know the answer: "Have we been visited by humans from the future?"

"That would be entirely possible if you *have* a future." He paused, apparently to let that sink in. "But if you were being visited by future Earth beings, you would never know it."

"But if they did visit us, they could watch us no matter what we're doing?"

"As we said before, sapiens, future beings, whether from Earth or from distant places, are not titillated by your sexual contortions any more than are you by the propagation of your insects or worms."

"If we can visit the past, can we also visit the future?"

"The laws of the universe preclude this. Even if they did not, are you sure you would want to visit your future?"

"What about the present?"

"No. But you can visit the immediate past, as long as it's on a different time page."

"Time page?"

"Time is like the pages in a book. Each page is a quantum of time. You can travel at will back through the pages of time and return to the time page you left. All of this is on the cone."

"I don't think I can take much more of this."

"You're ready to return?"

"Yes."

The next thing I knew we were standing in my own backyard, and the leaves were quite unchanged and still beautiful. Or at least *I* was standing there. I don't know where Walter was.

I went into the house, where Karen and Flower were waiting for me. "I need to call the President," I said breathlessly.

"Why? What happened?"

When I told her what I experienced on the way from the trailer, she just stared at me as if I were crazy. "What's the matter – don't you believe me?" I asked her.

"Of course I believe you. But I wouldn't mention this to the President or anyone else."

"Why not?"

"Because *they'll* think you're crazy."

"But it really happened! I can still see it. It was incredible!"

"Gene, listen. What if the public found out that you are claiming that you went to all those planets, and traveled back in time to your own childhood? What would *you* think if someone reported this? I've heard you denigrate people who claim they've been taken aboard a space ship and examined by aliens. Or anything else of that nature."

"But this really happened!"

"Did it, sweetheart?"

I pondered that for a moment, wondering whether it was possible that – "Well, I *think* it happened. I'm almost *sure* it did."

"Yes, but who would believe it? What about your credibility when you go to the UN?"

"Okay, yes, I see what you mean. Maybe I shouldn't go on a talk show and broadcast this. But I think I should tell the President, at least."

"Maybe you should see what Mike says about it."

"All right. I'll call him." I picked up the phone but put it down again before I could punch in the number. "But don't you see? If the Bullocks can come here and make trees disappear, make an entire species disappear, probably, then maybe they can do the things I experienced, even if we don't understand how they do it."

"Tell that to Mike."

Flower sidled up to me while I was redialing. I scratched her ears and she plopped down for more. "*You* believe me, don't you, old girl?"

She stared blankly at me.

Mike came on. "Yes, Gene?"

"Walter took me for a ride."

"Can you get back here right away?"

"I'll be right there."

Karen smiled understandingly. She always smiles, and always understands. "Will you be late for dinner?"

"I have no idea. I don't even know where I'll *be!*" I shouted as I ran out the door.

The same bunch I had left a short time before were sitting around the long table eating sandwiches. A place had been made for me, but I declined the food. I just wasn't hungry anymore. Nevertheless, someone slid a bowl of fruit toward me. I took an orange and began to peel it.

"Tell us what happened after you left," Mike prodded.

Before I had finished peeling, I had recounted in detail everything I had experienced only moments before. During my discourse, there wasn't a sound in the room. Someone occasionally took another bite of his lunch, but, for the most part, no one even moved.

"We need to call the President," observed a man who resembled my former colleague Arthur Beamish so much that I had to look twice.

"And everyone else," a man whose name I have forgotten, added.

"You mean you believe me?"

"Of course we believe you, Gene," Mike assured me. "A week ago we might not have. But now . . ."

The Vice-President noted that Walter appeared to answer some of the questions I had put to him during the trip (or whatever it was), "even though they didn't appear to be relevant to ending the killing. Does this mean they've had a change of heart? Are they softening their position? Maybe now they'll talk about other things, and maybe to someone else?"

"I don't think they *have* a heart. But yes, maybe they have. They mentioned that they think we might have some virtues."

"Did they say *what* virtues?"

"No."

"Can you ask them? Perhaps we could build on those."

"I've discovered that it does no good to try to contact the Bullocks about anything. When they want something, they will come to me. If and when that happens again, I'll ask them what virtues we have. If I can remember to," I added.

"Arthur Beamish" asked, "Is there any other reason they might have changed their attitude toward us?"

"I don't know. Maybe it's because I asked them to help us."

"And that's why they escorted you around the galaxy?"

"I think it was supposed to be an example of what we can look forward to if we come out of this alive. I believe it was the kind of incentive we talked about earlier regarding what we might find on the cone. In fact, they mentioned that device again." There were grunts and nods all around.

The Vice-President asked, "Should we advise the President to call another press conference or to make a statement of some kind to the general public?"

The ever-present Barbara wondered aloud, "Should we even mention this to anyone? If people don't believe this really happened, it may be counterproductive."

The Secretary of State almost snorted, "How else can we convey the incentive the Bullocks are supplying us with?"

"It might be counterproductive," she repeated. "Even though there's some evidence to the contrary, a lot of people are going to think Dr. Brewer is imagining this whole thing."

The Vice-President observed that if the Bullocks were to come forward and demonstrate their authenticity in an unmistakable manner, no one would doubt Dr. B's veracity. "What are they waiting for?" he wondered

"Any comments on that, Dr. B?" asked the Ambassador. "Did they say anything about the promised demonstration?"

"Not during this episode, no."

No one had any other comments or questions for me, and there was no further discussion on the matter. Mike continued: "Given what's happened, I don't think we'll proceed with the regular schedule of events for today. Barring objection, we'll give Dr. B the rest of the day off. The President may call you at home later, Gene, but in the meantime we'll take care of getting this information to him."

Now I was hungry. "Barring objection, I'm going to take the rest of this beautiful orange home and have lunch with my wife."

There were none.

For the moment the whole matter was out of my hands, and we enjoyed an almost relaxing lunch, followed by a leisurely nap. Later that afternoon, I called Steve back and told him, after he had sworn not to divulge any of the details to anyone else, about my voyage to the stars. I could almost see his tongue hanging out, dripping with saliva, as if anticipating a thick steak. "Ah'd give my eyeteeth to talk to them for five lousy minutes," he whined.

I mentioned that the Bullocks only wanted to talk to me, but if he had a question – "

"Their loss," he stated sourly before hanging up. I didn't even have a chance to tell him what was on the cone.

Later, Will returned my call. He talked about a couple of his patients, more to take my mind off the present situation than anything else, I think. He advised me to have a couple of stiff ones before dinner. "I can't wait until next week, when you'll be free of this thing," he said. "Then maybe we can get back to normal."

"For another year, maybe," I reminded him.

"At least we can try to enjoy whatever time we have left."

"Which we should be doing regardless."

"I wonder if the Bullocks enjoy their time?"

"Who knows?"

After he had hung up I had a serious pang of sadness and regret that my own father had died at an early age, and that we might have been having a similar conversation – though under very different circumstances, I would hope. In that case I would have been Will, my father me. Dad would have handled the whole thing much better than I was doing, I'm sure. He was far more confident and outgoing than I, and probably a better doctor as well. I wished we could all revisit the best parts of our past. Walter could probably show us how, and the information might be present on the cone as well, if only we could decipher it. But this kind of speculation only served to increase my general guilt for burying the damn thing. If I had turned it over to Dartmouth and Wang instead of trying to get rid of it, could we have avoided a visit from Walter in the first place?

The President called that evening. There was a time not so long ago that I would have been flabbergasted, but now it seemed like a chat with an old friend. After the usual "How are you?" and "Fine, how are *you*?" he asked whether I had heard from the Bullocks lately. We both had a good laugh. It's amazing how some people are able to put others at ease, even under such crucial circumstances.

"Nothing in the last few hours," I confessed.

"Okay, here's what we think. If it were anything else, we'd probably keep what happened under wraps for a while. So as not to complicate matters. But this is a once-in-a-lifetime thing – once in our entire history, for that matter – when we need to be completely forthright with the world's people. We need to keep everyone on the same page. The support must be there for this to succeed.

"But no matter how we convey this information, a lot of people are not going to believe the things you have experienced. It *is* pretty far-fetched, after all, and our advisors here have only one question for you: do you have any evidence at all for what happened on your 'voyages' earlier today? Anything like a disappearing tree or the like? Maybe you picked up a souvenir or something like that?"

"No, Mr. President. As I told the committee members, this all happened in a wink of time. According to Walter, in fact, there was no passage of time at all. And we couldn't interact physically with anyone or anything in any of the places we visited. To anyone we encountered we were completely invisible."

"Yes, I was informed of that. I just wanted to confirm it. And Walter didn't tell you anything about how they are able to accomplish these things, did they?"

"Sorry, no."

"Okay, I would suggest you jot down a record of everything you saw, every detail you can think of. This might help to convince others that these things really happened as you said they did."

"I'll try to do that, sir. But what happens next?"

"I was coming to that. We want you to make another TV appearance in the morning. Can you be ready to leave by 7:00 A.M.?"

It was here that I caught myself groaning. Rather loudly, apparently, because the President apologized and said, "Please bear with us, Gene. This will soon be over. And it may be the most important press conference that ever took place in the history of the human race."

"I'll try to be ready."

"I knew you would be. Until then, good-night, my friend, and pleasant dreams."

I had an extra rye on the rocks before dinner, and another one afterward, and was sound asleep the minute we got into our nice, warm bed.

DAY FIVE

I got up in the middle of the night to go to the bathroom – another reason not to like broccoli (the drinks may also have had something to do with it). After that I went to the kitchen for some water, looked out the window, shocked as always by the huge trailer with the ever-present guards out front, looming in the glare of the backyard light. It seemed so unreal that I wondered whether I was imagining it. But I could also feel the presence of something else. "Walter, are you here?"

"Where else would we be?"

"Back where you came from would be nice."

His reply, "Our deepest apologies," reeked of cynicism. "However, we're going to be here for a little while yet."

Once again I was breathing hard, and my ears were ringing. Things were happening that I couldn't control, a situation I have always hated, that we all hate and fear to one degree or another. That's why we panic when we feel a sudden chest pain or the like. I was having a hard time determining where I was, *when* it was. Somehow I had lost all track of time and place. How was this possible? I felt myself sighing as I resigned myself to my situation, like a horse that has just been broken after a long struggle. "Can you tell me what you've got planned for me today?"

"That's up to your government friends. We don't care what you do today, or any other day. Only the eighth day matters. We've been watching some of your television stations, reading your newspapers. The odds against your success at the United Nations are astronomical. You sapiens care about a dozen short-term desires more than your own long-term survival. It has always been this way and will be so until you evolve into a species less self-centered and violent."

For some reason that statement, uttered so arrogantly, if matter-of-factly, peeved me. Who did these – these *ants*! – think they were, to come here and tell us to "evolve"? "When the hell are you going to demonstrate to the world that you can do what you say you can?" I screeched, with a very Walter-like scowl.

"You'll get your demonstration very soon now."

"You said that before!" I shouted internally.

He disappeared immediately, of course, but I felt nauseated as I went back to bed, unable even to finish the water. I turned over and watched the numbers on the digital clock cleverly lose or gain a little red bar. It's amazing how slowly time passes when you watch it, and how quickly when you don't. Either way, though, it moves relentlessly, and you eventually end up at the same place. Unless you're a Bullock, of course, and can probably manipulate it any way you want. I wondered whether they could, in fact, stop the movement of time at will? Apparently, since they can stop or even reverse it when they saunter through the galaxy. But then they become invisible and unable to interact with their surroundings. As Heisenberg said, there are limits, though not the ones he imagined.

Speculation aside, the Bullocks had promised a convincing demonstration of their power, one, presumably, that many people could witness. I hoped it would come before my re-grilling by the world's press. Maybe then there wouldn't be any doubt in anyone's mind that what I was telling them was the truth.

I must have dozed off, because the clock suddenly said 6:45 (the alarm was supposed to go off at 6:00, when I would have an hour to get ready for another trip to Washington). I jumped up and headed for the shower, quite annoyed with my wife for re-setting or turning off the alarm. But before I could get out the bedroom door she came in with a tray. "I thought you might like something nice before you run off to the see the powers that be," she said sweetly. "I called Mike and everything has been delayed an hour." I remembered again how much I loved her. It seemed as if a great load had been lifted from my shoulders, if only for sixty minutes. We enjoyed a quiet breakfast and, after a leisurely shower, I was ready for anything.

At eight o'clock to the minute there was a tapping on the back door. "Come in," I yelled, and Mike appeared.

Instead of the usual cheery "'good morning," he said, rather breathlessly, I thought, "Have you been watching the news?"

"No. Is something happening?"

"I'll tell you about it on the way. You might want to turn on 'Good Morning America,' or something, Mrs. B."

I kissed my wife and we were off to the waiting limousine, one of the usual four or five, adorned with ambulance. On the way to the helipads, Mike turned on the car's television monitor and we watched in silence as the horrible scenes were repeated over and over and over. First the Taj Mahal disappeared. Then the great pyramid at Giza, followed by the Eiffel Tower. And finally the almost-finished Freedom Tower in New York. It was just like the tree, only on a gigantic scale. Police had cordoned off all four areas, and no one was allowed on the sites themselves. Behind the ropes, onlookers stood with mouths gaping, like so many fish out of water. The newscasters seemed to be beside themselves. All I could think of was how horrible it must have been for those who had been inside these famous edifices. It was like hearing about a passenger plane going down. Then I realized it was merely a taste of what would probably happen to all of us in the near future.

"Keep watching," Mike said, turning up the sound. Suddenly the Taj Mahal reappeared, then the pyramid, the Eiffel Tower, and finally, the Freedom Tower. It was as if they had never disappeared. The people coming out were being interviewed, along with others who had merely witnessed what had happened. It was almost impossible to believe, but apparently not a single person (perhaps not even a fly) had been injured in the demonstration. Most were surprised by all the fuss that was going on. For them, time had simply stood still for the twenty minutes they had been missing. They didn't even know they had been gone. Indeed, a few mentioned that their watches and cell phones were precisely twenty minutes behind those who were left behind.

Mike and I watched silently as these events unfolded. It was almost impossible to comprehend what had happened. At last he said what I was thinking: "There can no longer be any doubt about the veracity of your story, Gene."

I only hoped he was right. I was beginning to wonder myself whether I had imagined everything. Over and over the huge edifices disappeared and reappeared, interspersed with breathless interviews, as more and more people recounted their stories of coming out and finding that they were the center of attention, for reasons they didn't understand. To them nothing had happened. By this time we had reached the airport and were soon ensconced on Air Force Zero, or whatever it was without the President on board. The only passengers were Mike and I, Dr. Greaney, and the Secret Service. Everyone else had stayed behind; there was work to be done.

This was my chance to visit the President's quarters upstairs. Mike reluctantly agreed, and I took a good look at the suite, with the bedclothes actually turned down for occupancy. I was tempted to use the bathroom, but decided against it. I took a good look at the furnishings, however, and the linens and even the walls so that I would be able to describe them to my wife.

Otherwise, the trip was becoming almost routine. The only difference was that it was a rainy day and the visibility was limited, so all the monuments looked gray and lifeless. With no one to see and appreciate them, would they just crumble, one grain of marble at a time? Or would they, like the great pyramids, remain virtually intact for the next 5,000 years?

The President welcomed me to the Oval Office without his usual beaming grin. His only comment was, "I guess we're in as deep as it can get now. Do you have any questions, Dr. B, before we proceed to the briefing room?"

I knew immediately what to ask. "Should I tell the press about my trip to the other planets and my own past, or will they think I'm crazy?"

"I hear what you're saying, Gene. But at this point I don't think we should hold anything back. After today's demonstration it seems perfectly logical to me that the Bullocks can take trips through time and space like we might go for a Sunday drive. Okay, are you ready? Let's go."

We strode down the familiar red carpet and into the briefing room, where the atmosphere was entirely different from the last time. The air of cynicism and doubt had vanished, and all the reporters were at full attention, waiting almost breathlessly for what we had to say.

The President took the podium and asked a rhetorical question: "Is there anyone here who hasn't seen the footage shown on virtually every television channel of what happened early this morning?" Of course there was no one who had not. "If there was any doubt before, there can be none now that we have been visited by an alien life form so powerful that we have no choice but to listen to what they have to say and try to comply with whatever demands they are making. The combined military forces of the entire world could not do what you have seen today. And what the Bullocks' intentions were in this little demonstration – 'little' to them, perhaps – was to show us that they are fully capable of eliminating us, or any other species, from the face of the Earth.

"Right now our scientists don't know where the planet Bullock is in our galaxy. Now, for reasons of their own, the Bullocks have chosen to communicate their wishes through a single human, a psychiatrist who treated and became friends with another alien, whom many of you may remember reading about in Dr. Brewer's book, *K-PAX*. Some of you may also have seen the film. It is probably that visit, and one by another K-PAXian called fled, that led the Bullocks to take their demands to Dr. Gene Brewer. You've met him before in a recent press conference, so he is familiar to all of you. If there's anyone on the planet who knows the answers to your questions, it would be him. If there are questions he can't answer, then there's no one in the world who can. Dr. Brewer, will you come to the microphone, please?"

And there I was, front and center again, looking as if I knew something when, in fact, I knew nothing. Hands shot up everywhere. I pointed to someone at random.

It was another of the anchors I had seen on the evening news countless times. "Dr. Brewer," he said, "I think all of us owe you an apology for doubting your veracity, and maybe even your sanity, the last time you were here. But the possible sudden end of the human race is a lot to wrap your head around in one sitting."

"I understand perfectly. Sometimes I doubt my veracity, and even my sanity, myself." The room filled with laughter, which, if nothing else, relieved the tension a little.

"If I may proceed, then: do you have any further information on what the Bullocks will do to the human race if we cannot – or refuse – to comply with their demands?"

"I can't tell you exactly what they will do. All I know for sure is that we will all disappear from the face of the Earth – maybe much like the structures and the people inside them did in the video recordings we have all seen this morning. I don't know where we might end up – maybe nowhere at all. Wherever it is, I don't think any of us will be returning to this planet."

I pointed to another familiar face. He looked a little like George Clooney. Maybe it *was* George Clooney who asked, "Do you know more precisely at this point what they want from us?"

"Since the previous press conference I attended, they have modified their demands somewhat. Now they're saying they will be satisfied with a 20% reduction in the killing of our fellow human beings every year until we have stopped it altogether within the next five years. Same for the animals whom we share the planet with, beginning next year. But bear in mind that if we don't reach the 20% goal in year one, the rest is irrelevant."

"Is that negotiable at all?"

"I think the negotiations are over."

"If we reduce it by 20% the first year and 30% the second, would it mean that we could do 10% the third?"

"I don't know. Probably. But I think Wal – the Bullocks would say: just do it and stop quibbling about the numbers."

A French reporter who identified himself as representing *La Monde*: "Dr. Brewer, can you tell us something about what these Bullocks are like?"

"I have no idea what they look like. They are not corporeal; they can assume the shape of anyone or anything they want: people, animals – even a chair, maybe. Without something to occupy, they may not look like anything. I think they may be pure energy, perhaps in the form of brain waves of some kind.

"Also, they are not really individuals, but behave like a colony of ants or bees. When you talk to one of them, you're talking to everyone in that community. It's also true that they might be in this room right now." At the first press conference, the reporters looked around in mock trepidation when I said that. This time the fear was real. Some even gasped.

"But you would never know it unless they chose to make their presence felt. I apologize if I said some of this earlier. I'm a little tired, and I, too, have a hard time getting my head around this." Some were still gawking around, tugging at their ties, straightening skirts.

"Perhaps I should also mention here what happened to me yesterday . . . ." I glanced at the President, who nodded vigorously. "Before Walter's demonstration, I suspect most of you would have thought I was crazy for saying this, but what you saw on the monitors a few minutes ago pales in comparison to an experience I had a few hours earlier." I went on to describe in some detail my travels through the galaxy and back in time, all within the blink of an eye. "Also, you should know that we have in our possession a cone-shaped device which apparently describes how we, ourselves, can accomplish these feats, as well as everything there is to know about our DNA and what every gene does, plus a great deal of other information that, on our own, we might not come up with for thousands of years. I mention this only because everyone around the world should know that if we can survive the next year, or the next decade, we can learn to make the Earth the paradise it once was. Just imagine, if you can, the cures for every known disease, travel through the galaxy at the speed of light or faster, and a million other things we don't know now."

One of the reporters asked whether I had traveled into the future.

"The Bullocks told me that this is not possible. Nor would we want to even if we could. But the important point is that we can determine what that future will be like by our actions today and for the next few years."

"If someone can travel back to the present from some future time, where are they?"

"They may be here, but we can't see them. I'm not sure why. I think they're in a different dimension."

Another familiar-looking television reporter asked whether the Bullocks had destroyed any other planets.

"Apparently they don't destroy planets. Only their humanoid inhabitants."

"Have they told you how we can best comply with their wishes?"

"They said we need to evolve."

"How do we do that?"

"They said the answer to all these questions are on the cone."

"But that won't help us now, will it?"

"No. The first part – stopping the killing – we will have to do on our own."

At this point the President suggested that I take only one more question. "We have a lot of work to do," he explained.

In answer to the final question, I informed those present (and watching on television) that with the support of all the governments of the world I would be presenting the Bullocks' demands at a meeting of the United Nations Security Council on Saturday. "Until then," I said, "I hope to have the support and encouragement of everyone here and all those watching this news conference. I'll need all the help I can get."

"Thank you, Dr. Brewer. Thank you, Mr. President." This time there was a round of applause before everyone hurried out.

In the Oval Office, the President, as always, shook my hand and commended my performance. "Now get going," he said with a warm smile. "We only have three more days to get you ready to face the world."

Over lunch on the flight home, I asked Mike whether he thought the average person was beginning to accept the fact that we have a problem.

"The newspaper and television reporters are interviewing people right and left, Gene. The fact is, people are still confused. Most know there's a serious problem that affects everyone on Earth, but they still don't want to believe it."

"I don't want to believe it, either."

"But it is true, isn't it, Gene?"

"Unless I'm dreaming."

"Then I'm dreaming, too."

"Why does everyone say that? If you're just a part of my dream, you'd say that anyway, wouldn't you?"

"But *I* know I'm not dreaming!"

"You'd say *that*, too!"

Back at the Nerve Center, Mike said something that had obviously been on his mind the whole trip: "Listen. Are you *sure* about what happened to you yesterday? That it wasn't all a dream?"

"Ninety-nine percent."

"Go have a cup of tea with your wife. After that, we'd better have a talk with Dr. Schultz."

I literally ran across the yard to the house, where Karen greeted me with, "You were wonderful!" We had a nice talk over tea and cookies, courtesy of Uncle Sam. I still had some time before I was supposed to see my shrink, so I asked Karen if she'd like to go for a walk around the yard, maybe a little hike on our quarter-mile trail in the woods. "That would be great. I haven't been out of the house much since all this began."

"I haven't either, except for a few trips to the White House . . ." That joke was becoming all too familiar, but we laughed like fools anyway.

Flower happily accompanied us. Before we entered the woods I nodded to the government men, who nodded back solemnly, and one of them followed us in. "Do they ever smile?" my perceptive wife wanted to know.

"I've never seen it." The colors of the leaves seemed to be even stronger and brighter than they were a couple of days ago. I wondered where Walter was and whether they enjoyed such beautiful scenery on the latest planet Bullock.

When we got into the trees I took in a lungful of the wonderful aroma of fallen and decaying leaves. "This certainly brings up memories," I told her. "Remember when we used to jump into piles of leaves that your dad had raked up?"

She chortled. "We scattered them all back where they were before. It made him so mad!"

I could see him now, almost as if we were there, fuming that he had to do it all over again. But I could tell that he really didn't mind. He was a good father, and he loved to see his daughter happy and smiling. So did I. We were pre-adolescents at the time (Karen and I were neighbors from the day she was born), but it seemed like only yesterday. I watched as her dad picked up the rake and, shaking his head, began again to pile the brown, crinkly leaves into mounds. I could smell them, hear their sharp rustling, see the bright red of the rake's tines shining in the sun. I started to jump into the first pile, but Karen held me back. She knew that her dad wouldn't be so lenient the second time. She took my hand and we went into her house to play Monopoly.

As she was throwing the dice I realized that Walter must be playing his own game, sending me back to the past for his own amusement, though they weren't whispering in my ear as they did on our other "journeys." "Where are you, Walter?" I silently asked them. No response. "C'mon, Walter," I pleaded. "This isn't funny! Why are you sending me to the past? What am I supposed to see?"

Karen landed on Pennsylvania Avenue, pondered her options for a moment, and bought it. It didn't escape my attention that she also owned Broadway and Park Place. I gazed into her pretty, smiling face as she counted out the money. "Your turn," she said, handing me the dice.

"Please, Walter," I begged. "Take me back to the present!" If they heard me they didn't respond. I was beginning to feel a bit alarmed even though I knew what was happening, had experienced something like it before. But what if the Bullocks decided to leave me here? "Why are you doing this, Walter?"

My youthful me took the dice and made a big production of shaking them in his (my) closed hand, but what number turned up I haven't a clue because I suddenly found myself walking in the woods with my wife. I could feel my heart pounding and I told myself to take my blood pressure when we got back to the house.

"I don't know what time it is," she said, "but it must be about time for your meeting with your psychiatrist."

"Probably," I panted, and we turned around and headed back. I asked her whether she remembered a day, when we were ten or eleven, that her father admonished us for wrecking his leaf piles, and then going into the house to play Monopoly.

"That could have been anytime," she said. "There were leaves every year. And we played a lot of Monopoly."

"I didn't even like Monopoly very much. Did you?"

"Not really. I just liked being close to you. Smelling your clothes, your breath."

"Me, too. You were so pretty."

"You were cute, too. It was like having a puppy."

"You mean I was playful?"

"More like ungainly . . . ."

"I still am!"

"Sometimes."

"You're still pretty, anyway."

"Thank you. And you're still cute."

"Thank you, too." I gave her a quick smack on the lips. "Do you suppose there's a camera somewhere watching us?"

"I wouldn't be a bit surprised."

"Doesn't that bother you?"

"Not really. They're not going to see anything they haven't seen before."

The agents were standing exactly where we left them, though they seemed a little different. Maybe another shift had started. Mike was waiting in the yard.

"Have a nice walk?" he asked.

"Lovely," Karen replied.

"Ready, Gene?"

"I suppose so." I gave my wife a serious kiss and headed for the trailer with Mike. She stood, smiling her lovely smile, watching us leave. I didn't want to go in, but Mike led me to the makeshift medical clinic, where he left me to fend for myself. The comfortable chair and the chief psychiatrist were the same as before. I glanced around the room, my eyes alighting on the bench with all the now-dormant equipment ready in case something were to happen to me. "We understand that something's bothering you," said my colleague, the pill-pushing Dr. Schultz. "Do you want to talk about it?"

"It's more than I can handle," I confessed. "I not sure I can go through with it."

"Tell me what the worst of it seems to be."

"At first, it was the pressure of representing the human race in a challenge to our survival. But I seem to have dealt with that, gotten used to it. I'm even beginning not to mind the meetings with the President and the press conferences and all the rest." I waited for him to comment, but he merely stared at me and said nothing. "Now it's more about what is real and what is not. I just found myself taking a trip to the past. I didn't even ask to do that, but somehow I was there." Schultz again said nothing. "Am I going crazy?" I prodded.

Like a ventriloquist's dummy, he suddenly started to speak. "I don't think so. You have to keep in mind that you're in a unique situation that no human being has ever been in before. And you're dealing with an all-powerful alien, almost godlike in their capabilities. *No one* could possibly deal with a situation like that. My advice to you is to accept whatever happens and handle it in the best manner you can, with the help of all your advisors, of course. That's all anyone can do, and all anyone could reasonably expect from you. Remember this: if you fail, there is probably no one else in the world who could have done better. I suggest that you carry on and try not to worry about success or failure."

I thought: what kind of quack is this? I knew all that, but it didn't do much for my feelings of inadequacy and loss of control. I remembered all the similar advice I had given to my patients over the decades. How they must have hated me! My fatuous advice had probably made things even worse for many of them. Now, in addition to everything else, I had to try to forget the inadequacy of my life's work. "But why did they send me back to the past?"

"That's exactly my point, Gene," he replied fatuously. "I don't know. You just have to go with it and move on."

"Should I ask the Bullocks why they sent me back?"

"Sure. Ask them, if you want."

"You don't think it would make matters worse?"

"It hasn't so far, has it?" He glanced at his watch, something I've always tried to avoid with my patients. It always seemed to signal impatience, a non-caring attitude.

"Thank you, Dr. Schultz," I murmured. "I'll try to do my best."

I could see the wheels turning in his head – whether to continue the discussion or let me go out and face my responsibility without further comment. Finally he nodded and said (big surprise!), "Do you need something for your anxiety? Something to help you sleep?"

Who hired this guy? I'm a psychiatrist, for God's sake. "No, thanks. I have some meds I can take."

He nodded in obvious disappointment. "Fine. Good luck. I'll be here anytime you need me."

"Thanks again. I don't think I'll give you any more trouble."

"No trouble. How's the wife and family?"

No need to patronize, doctor. "Fine, fine. How's yours?"

"I don't have a wife. Or a family."

"Do you want to talk about it?" I joked. He didn't laugh, but I think he might have welcomed the opportunity to discuss his personal problems.

Mike, of course, was waiting for me outside the door. "Feeling better?"

"Yes," I lied. "Dr. Schultz was very helpful."

"Good." By now it was late afternoon and, I supposed, there wasn't much time left for meetings. I was wrong. "We think we ought to get started as soon as possible on the matter of preparing you for your speech to the Security Council," he informed me.

"Before dinner??"

"We'll have dinner in the meeting room if necessary. Shall we go?"

He started walking; I meekly followed. "Where are we going?"

"We're going to meet with TF1 – the task force on the speech you're going to give – for the remainder of this afternoon, and evening if necessary. Unless something else comes up, today and tomorrow will be spent on the speech itself.

Obviously this is the most important part of the whole process. And we'll take as much time as you need to get it right. Sound okay to you?"

"Fine." All I could think of was: I wonder what color the walls will be? I began to feel the usual cold, clammy feeling, as if I were in bed with Walter. Where are you, Walter, you old – How odd, I thought as always, how stupid. I was more concerned about standing before the United Nations Security Council than with the disappearance of human beings from the Earth. That made no sense at all. I needed to get a grip. "Yeah," I added. "Great."

Mike looked hard at me. "Remember how worried you were about the press conferences? You've been through two of them now, and once you got into them, you actually seemed to enjoy being there."

"I wouldn't go that far, Mike," I replied, lamely, almost ashamed that I had apparently seemed so nonplussed throughout those ordeals. "Anyway, answering a few questions from reporters, with the President as backup, is nothing compared to convincing the representatives of the entire world that all the killing should be stopped. I wouldn't even know where to begin."

"That's where we come in. We have experts who deal with this sort of thing all the time. Put yourself in their hands. Let them help you. It won't be as bad as you think."

If that were the case, why was I feeling so strange, both physically and mentally? It was almost as if I were someone else watching what was happening from the outside. Maybe this was what dissociative identity disorder was like. Some alter egos know that they are not the actual person who harbors them. How bizarre the mind is! No matter what disorder you might imagine, there is someone in the world with that very condition. Was I trying to dissociate myself from myself so I wouldn't have to face my responsibilities, as so many mental patients do? Hold on, Dr. B. Stay calm.

On our way down the short corridor, I asked myself again how I had gotten to this point. I thought of my first encounter with prot, and how I had erroneously assumed that he was merely a psychotic mental patient. But before we got to the meeting room, and without any sense of time or movement, I realized that I was back on K-PAX. How the hell – Well, there was nothing I could do about it. Schultz had advised me to go with it. Walter? Did you send me here? If you did, why? But there was no response from the Bullocks, or anyone else. I decided to make the best of it. Presumably they would soon send me back to Earth, where I would find myself exactly where I was, walking down a short corridor with Mike, about to enter the Task Force 1 meeting room. For now, though, I was somewhere on K-PAX.

I seemed to be hovering, if that's how to describe it. It was as if I were dreaming. Most of us have had that experience – I wasn't flying, exactly, but able to move around above the surface. I floated here and there, able to go anywhere I wanted. The big red sun was in the sky, so the ambience was a bit brighter (and redder) than before, as it would be on Earth perhaps not long after sunset. There weren't any people (human or otherwise) around that I could see, only myriad animals, some familiar-looking and others I couldn't begin to identify. Of course they couldn't see or hear me, so I could approach any of them for a closer look. Curiously, some of them seemed to have faces that were almost human in nature. (Prot had informed me that we're more similar to the animals on our planet than many of us would like to believe.) I reached out to touch one of them, but of course I could not, and he or she didn't notice me. This is all very interesting, I thought, but why am I here? "Walter?"

No response.

I was beginning to feel a bit of trepidation. How the hell was I supposed to get back to Earth? "Walter!" I shouted helplessly. But the Bullocks either weren't around, or they were ignoring me. I tried to calm myself again, and I looked around for some kind of reassurance. It came in the form of a small copse of trees in the distance. Prot had told me that there wasn't enough water on his planet to support many of them – no rivers, no lakes, no oceans. Not even any rain. The only water was underground. Enough to allow the growth of a number of plants, whose moisture then supported the animal life. But K-PAX was nine billion years old – hadn't the inhabitants figured out how to make water? By the fusion of hydrogen and oxygen, perhaps? If so, there weren't any big water-producing factories anywhere on the horizon.

I caught a glimpse of the huge red sun again. Could this be a red giant, slowly swelling up to eventually engulf its planets, much like our sun will swallow us, in another four or five billion years? K-PAX was already old; how much longer could it have? Though it was thinly populated, it was far bigger than the Earth, about the size of Neptune, prot had said. What would happen to all its inhabitants when the red giant began to lap at its "shores"? I suddenly felt very sad, even though this probably wouldn't happen for millions of years. And for the Earth as well, whose human inhabitants might have far less than that. The K-PAXians presumably could go somewhere else. So, probably, could some, or even all, humans get off the earth before it was burned to a cinder. But not if the sun exploded a year from now, the equivalent of what was going to happen if we didn't heed the Bullocks' warnings. Surely if I explained that to the United Nations they would listen. How could they not?

Easy. There would surely be holdouts around the world whose ideology was unconcerned with the well-being of the human race, but only of their own principles and desires. Some of these don't even care about their own personal survival, let alone that of anyone else. Even many Americans consider war to be a "necessary evil," trumping all other considerations when our "way of life" is at stake. How can I, or anyone at the UN, convince any of these people otherwise?

I wanted to find Abby. Or prot or fled or Giselle. Anyone I was familiar with, anyone I *knew*. But the planet was gigantic, and no one stayed in one place for long. How could I hope to find them? I started toward those scrawny little trees in the distance and found myself stumbling toward Meeting Room Two and the task force charged with preparing me to face the United Nations Security Council. Before we got there, I heard someone say, "Enjoy your trip?"

I glanced quickly at Mike, but of course it wasn't him. "Walter?"

"Who else?"

"Why did you send me to K-PAX?"

"We sent you nowhere. It was your own idea."

I felt as if I had been electrocuted. "But I didn't ask to go there. I wasn't even thinking about K-PAX. At least not consciously. How could – "

"Perhaps you wanted to get away from something unpleasant. This seems to be a very human response to dealing with a problem."

"But I don't know how to *do* that. I can't travel to another planet!"

"Of course you can. You just did. Anyone can do it."

"*HOW?*"

"The explanation is on the cone. How many times must we tell you? *Everything* is there!"

"But I can't read the cone. No one can!"

"You have deciphered the part of it that deals with space and time travel."

"When did that happen?"

"When we went for a ride."

"But you didn't tell me how – "

"Once you've done it, it's like riding a bicycle, is it not?"

"I don't understand. Do you mean I can go anywhere I want??"

"Anywhere."

"And anytime in the past?"

"Anytime."

"But dammit, Walter," I shouted. "I don't know how to do it!"

"Gene?"

"Huh?"

"You were talking to Walter, weren't you?"

"Yes. But now he's gone again."

"Can you tell me what you were talking about?" Mike asked sympathetically.

"About space and time travel."

"Did he tell you anything you didn't already know?"

"Only that I could go anywhere I want to. But – " I shrugged.

We came to the Meeting Room 2 (the walls were yellow), where I was welcomed by the chair of the Task Force on the UN Security Council Speech, who introduced himself as the President's chief speechwriter.

Normally I would have been intimidated by him, as would most other Americans. But I was becoming so used to meeting important people, indeed the top people in the government, that I merely nodded and shook his hand matter-of-factly.

He frowned and asked how I was doing.

"About as well as I could have expected."

He smiled, seemingly satisfied with that non-committal answer. "Are you ready for the final phase of this thing?"

"No."

Everyone chuckled, though the chortles sounded forced, nervous. We all knew the "final phase of this thing" might be the final phase for everyone on Earth. But apparently there wasn't any time to waste. He quickly introduced the others in the room (except for the Secret Service agents), who included, of course, the Vice-President and Secretary of State, both of whom greeted me warmly. "Let's get started, shall we?" said the head speechwriter, indicating where I should sit. Chairs scraped, people thumped into them, and the meeting began.

The first part of the session was devoted to questions about my experience in a number of areas: public speaking (I was given a bye on that one, having spoken to the world through two high-profile press conferences), debate, negotiation, history, world geography. By now I knew something about the art of negotiation, particularly with Walter, but not, of course, with world leaders. As for history and geography, I, like most Americans, was compelled to regret that I had wasted my life watching football games and the like when I could have been doing something more important. I was given a book of maps and two thin primers: one about the United Nations, which I was advised to read "as soon as convenient," and the other a brief history of the world. I was pointedly informed that I would be tutored more fully in these subjects "if there's time." Then, with a big sigh, the chair finally got to the crux of the issue, the purpose for this and the other task forces, maybe the purpose of all our lives: what I would be saying to the Security Council on Saturday.

After that, the meeting was turned over to a "special guest," a former President renowned for his speechmaking ability. I didn't know much about his diplomatic skills, but it dawned on me that he had probably spent much of his career pleading with the leaders of the nations of the world, as well as the United States Congress, for moderation, reason, and good sense. Indeed, he had achieved many successes, and if anyone knew how to convince the world of something it was probably him. I only wished Walter had approached the ex-President instead of me.

"Now, Dr. Brewer," he began, "the most important advice I can give you at the outset is to remain calm during your presentation to the Security Council. No matter what you're thinking, no matter if you are interrupted or even sneered at, no matter what happens, you will need to remain perfectly calm. It is always best to speak in measured tones, and at a low level. You will have a microphone, and fluent translators, so you can speak in a normal tone of voice. If you feel any emotion, it should not show in your voice or your countenance.

"For the most part you will be reading your speech from a plain piece of paper, but you should look up occasionally to the five member representatives of the most powerful nations on Earth. Briefly. A second or two. You don't stare at anyone. It's fine to be nervous, but at the same time you must appear confident and knowledgeable, even if your mind happens to wander or go blank." Before I could ask how my mind could wander under such circumstances, he shrugged and said, "It happens." Several in the room nodded. He quickly went on. "It's okay to have a tiny smile on your lips, but there will be no humorous remarks, nor will you express any anger or frustration or scowling of any kind. You will be sitting, and this will reduce the tension you might experience by standing. It would be stupid of me to advise you to completely relax. Under the circumstances, that would be impossible.

"Of course this all comes under the heading of preliminary advice. We will go over all these things again and again, and we will practice and practice, but you should have all this in mind at the outset. We will have plenty of time to work on your presentation. In fact, that is about all we'll be doing for the next two days. The other task forces will take care of the other matters. From now on, the only thing all of us in this room will be thinking about, and working on, is your speech. This is true not only because it is probably the most important one of your life, or perhaps anyone's life, but because with familiarity comes confidence. It's like Carnegie Hall: practice makes perfect, or as nearly perfect as we, and you, can get it."

Without another word he turned the meeting over to the head speechwriter/chairman, who asked, "Dr. Brewer, do you have any questions at this point?"

"Yeah. How do I get out of this?"

More titters, though not from the chair. "Anyone else have a comment or question?" he asked solemnly.

A former Secretary of State, who had spoken at the United Nations many times, suggested, "Perhaps it would be worthwhile to give Dr. Brewer a collection of speeches made to the Security Council? With video if possible?"

"Point well taken," the chair agreed, nodding to someone at the end of the table. "Anything else?"

"Perhaps we should give Dr. Brewer a chance to read the material and think about all this a bit before we proceed?" the Vice-President suggested.

"Fine," said the speechwriter. "But let's take a little time to go into some of the issues first. Here is what we know so far." He gazed at Mike and me before proceeding. "Please correct me if I'm wrong about any of this." He looked down at a little brown notebook lying on the table in front of him. "Briefly, a race of aliens called the Bullocks have sent a representative, or representatives, to the Earth to demand that we stop killing each other." He looked up for a moment and interjected thoughtfully, "Not such a bad idea, I might add – under different circumstances, of course. But we only have a year to accomplish the first phase of this program. The good news is that we only have to stop 20% of the killing in the next twelve months.

"I've been informed that the total number of fatalities due to war, civil or otherwise, atrocities, protests, executions, gun violence, and all the rest, currently amounts to approximately 650,000 human lives every year. Twenty per cent of this number would amount to about 130,000 fewer killings worldwide. I personally think this is a reachable goal. Does anyone here think otherwise?"

If anyone did, he or she said nothing to contest this optimistic assessment. Walter, regardless of his expressed view on the subject, likewise had no comment.

"The bad news is that we need to end at least 20% more of it by the end of the second year, and to begin to curtail the killing, during that same time period, of all the other animal species that inhabit the Earth." He glanced at me. "This means we all have to start becoming vegetarians, and to put an end to practices such as hunting and fishing, and animal-based research, and so on, and we'd better get that idea across as soon as possible, would you agree, Dr. Brewer?"

I nodded glumly. "My daughter Abby will be delighted by that conclusion."

"So will a lot of animals, I imagine," said the chair. "The other thing is that if we fail, in year one or year two, the Bullocks will eliminate human life from the planet Earth in some unspecified way. And finally, it appears they are quite capable of doing this, as evidenced by their ability to make certain well-known structures and their human inhabitants disappear and reappear at will." He paused again to sip a glass of water. "The purpose of this sub-committee is not to determine how all these things can be accomplished, but how to convince the rest of the world that it is necessary that we do so, and that every single country in the world will need to co-operate in this endeavor. That there can be no doubt about the outcome if we fail to comply. Did I leave anything out?"

"I don't think so," I said wanly, wishing I had had a little nap, "though it should be pointed out that there are inducements. An earlier visitor, this one from K-PAX, left us with a veritable encyclopedia describing in a language we can't yet decipher, everything we might want to know about the sciences – space and time travel, the origin and fate of the universe and all that, as well as medical advances such as how to manipulate our DNA, and a lot more. I have personally experienced both types of travel, and I can assure you that they are feasible. It even seems that I can do these things on my own, though I couldn't begin to explain to you how I do them. I'm still trying to figure that out."

The former Secretary of State asked: "Would you be able to give the Security Council a demonstration of these things when the time comes?"

I hadn't thought of that. I stammered, "I – I don't know. Even if I could, the members wouldn't know about it. While I'm gone, time would not move for them."

"How is that possible?"

"The Bullocks told me that time is like the pages in a book, where each quantum of time is one page. You can travel in another dimension without turning the pages, so time doesn't pass for anyone else."

"Could you bring something back from one of these 'journeys'?"

"No. There is no interaction with the three spatial dimensions we know about."

The former President said, "That's not quite true, is it, Dr. Brewer? You could conceivably bring back information."

"I don't understand."

"Let's say you visited the year 1492. If you could tell us something that only a scholar would know about, something about Christopher Columbus's family, or what he might be wearing, that should convince at least the scholar that you were there."

"Yes, I see what you mean."

"Or what if you took a camera?"

I felt like an idiot. "I hadn't thought of that."

Someone else in the group (wasn't he a former patient of mine?) suggested, quite seriously, "Let's make it easier. You could visit any of the permanent members at home the morning before your speech and tell him what he had for breakfast. We could give you his co-ordinates – "

"Hold it, hold it," interrupted the chair. "Perhaps we could set up another committee to figure out the best approach to this. In the meantime, Dr. Brewer, maybe you could practice your technique. Apparently you've got all the time in the world once you're in the – uh – fourth dimension. Let's move on, shall we?"

Someone added, "Could you bring the cone and demonstrate the kinds of things that might be available on that?"

The chair said, "We're already working on that."

"By the way," I asked, rather meekly. "How long should the whole thing be? The speech, I mean, and any videos I can show?"

"The former President replied, "As long as you need. Within reason, of course. But don't drag it out with anecdotes or the like. It's strictly business there. Set a goal of fifteen to twenty minutes for the speech itself."

"I don't know any anecdotes."

More chuckles, but perhaps they were only humoring me.

"Okay," said the chair. "We all have some thinking and some homework to do. How about we re-convene here at eight o'clock in the morning and begin to seriously draft Dr. Brewer's speech?"

There were no objections, least of all from me.

Scraping of chairs. Mike, as always, escorted me to the door. "How are you feeling, Gene? I mean, any unusual symptoms, like those associated with stress or nerves? Remember, there are doctors who are always on call."

"Nothing unusual, no."

"And you have an effective sleep medication you can use tonight if necessary?"

"Yes, of course."

"Good." We reached the door, where we shook hands, something we had forgone in the past few days, as friends are wont to do. He looked into my eyes as if trying to find any indication of weakness, a hint that I might want to back out of my duty, if that's what you would call it. "I'll see you in the morning. Would you like me to come to breakfast with you and Karen, or would you rather it be more private?"

"No, I think you'd better come in case I have questions, or the heebie-jeebies."

"See you then, my friend."

I nodded and turned past the agents guarding the door. The short walk to the house seemed to take a million years. Partly because I expected to hear something from Walter. But the other thing on my mind was whether I would find myself flying through space toward K-PAX or some other distant planet, not knowing where I was going or how to stop myself and turn around. And if I got to K-PAX again, would I encounter anyone I knew? I would love to see my daughter again, but how would I find her, or anyone else?

I was halfway there – I had almost made it – when I saw Karen in back of the house cutting the tops off some plants in the garden. Preparing for winter, I supposed. I was almost upon her when I noticed that she was wearing her hair like she used to in the first years of our marriage. How nice! Then I saw our son Fred behind her, and I realized that I was forty years in the past. Freddy started running around, and our first dog, Daisy, came out from under the porch and chased him, barking. Fred giggled and ran and ran. My lovely wife looked up and smiled. How beautiful they all were, how young! I was overcome with joy. How short life is! And when it's gone, it's gone, never to return. Even when you're alive everything from the past exists only in memory.

I watched them for a while. I tried to speak to them, but of course they couldn't hear me. I even tried to touch my wife, but she didn't notice. Just once I would love to pet Daisy, feel her short stiff hair in my fingers. All for naught. No one knew I was there. I wondered whether even the Bullocks knew I was there. If so, there was no sign of it.

Then I started to panic again. I would love to stay here forever, but I had a job to do (I was still carrying the reading material I had been assigned), and had no idea how to get back to the present. If I just thought about it, would I be able to go there? I thought about it, hard, but went nowhere (no*when*?). *Everything that was happening was beyond my control!* I felt sick; no one was there to help me – not Walter, not fled, not prot. I knew, at least, that time was not moving. Not the usual present time, anyway. If I stayed here for twenty years before returning, I would find myself making my way from the Nerve Center to my own house, only a short walk away. How bizarre. The universe is so unfathomable, a fact first glimpsed by Albert Einstein, who, in a moment of sublime inspiration, realized that time and space were not constants, but symbiotic variables. And here I was on the other side of the coin, I suppose, able to manipulate time and space in some way, but without the slightest understanding of how I could do that. Einstein would probably have loved to be in my running shoes. But not me. "Help!" I shouted. "Get me out of here!"

I needn't have worried. In another moment Flower came barging out of the dog door and wrapped herself around me. I was home.

But the work day wasn't over. The President was waiting for me in the living room (along with a couple of Secret Service agents). We chatted for quite a long time, an hour and a half, perhaps, about everything under the sun: his childhood, my childhood, sports, climate change, American history – you name it. Finally, of course, the Bullocks, and how we were dealing with them. He knew that the particulars of my speech hadn't been set, or even discussed yet, and he didn't offer any suggestions on what to say, just that I would do fine as long as I tried to do my best. "That's all anyone can do in any given situation," he assured me. "And your best is quite good enough." He shared a couple of stories about how he had misspoken during a campaign speech or two, which eventually rebounded in his favor, owing partly to the empathetic nature of the American people. I reminded him that I wouldn't be speaking to Americans, but to the whole world, and I hoped they would be empathetic as well. He told me that he had spoken all over the world, and people were basically the same everywhere. That most people of whatever race, creed or nationality wanted the same things: peace, a loving family, and productive employment. "Talking to the Russians or Chinese is exactly like talking to a bunch of Americans," he contended. I wasn't so sure of that, but it was comforting to hear him say it. I almost felt as if he were telling me that if things didn't go so well at the UN, he would be sharing the blame. Whether that was his intention or not, I suddenly had another motive to provide a clear, logical message to the Security Council: to win one for the Gipper.

As he stood up to leave, the President informed me that I had been firmly inserted into the Security Council's agenda, where I would be reading my speech at 2:00 P.M. a couple of days hence. And with that he left, whether to return to Washington or somewhere else he didn't say. Karen and I escorted him and his entourage to the door, where we both received a warm hug. But perhaps he gave that to everyone he met. Even Flower got a good ear scratch from the President, who observed, with a broad smile, that he knew a couple of dogs much like her. How could anyone be so upbeat at a time like this? So confident, so unafraid? Of course I had no clue as to how he really felt – maybe it was all a front.

After he had gone, my supportive wife informed me that dinner would be on the table soon, and asked whether she could help me with my "homework," something I had already forgotten about. I said yes, of course, and started looking over the booklets I had been given about the history of the world and the workings of the United Nations. The first thing that struck me about the former was that our history was indeed a violent one. Wars, assassinations, murders – most of civilization's major turning points hinged on vicious acts of one kind or another. As Karen handed me a stiff drink, I remarked that the only way we, the people, could get out of this mess was to entirely change society's outlook toward other nations, other people. She countered with the observation that things are better now than they were centuries ago, and were getting even better all the time. I asked her how long, at our present rate of progress, she thought it would take for people to stop killing each other entirely.

"A thousand years?" she ventured.

I reminded her that we only have one.

"Maybe Walter can cut us some slack."

"I think they would probably say they have given us 100,000 years to get it right and we aren't even close yet."

I could see tears forming in her eyes when she asked, "What do you think they're going to do to us if we don't meet their demands?"

"I suspect they'll make us disappear from the Earth, like they did the Eiffel Tower."

"Where did the Eiffel Tower go? Is that where we're going, too?"

That I couldn't even begin to tell her. But I said that all of time and space is open, and maybe they would just let us start over with a warning not to let it happen again. I thought she would be comforted by this, but instead she cried out loud. I got up and gave her a hug like the one the President had given us. What else could I do? Then I told her about my trips to K-PAX and to the past of forty years earlier, describing in detail her and Freddy's activities. She sobbed even louder.

"Honey, we just can't let this happen. Somehow I've got to convince the world that human life is worth saving, even if we have to give up some things in order to survive. Doing without wars and an eye for an eye and all that crap can't be so bad. Once we try it, we might like it."

She nodded and smiled, took the booklets, and started quizzing me on the day-to-day operations of the United Nations.

DAY SIX

Because of heavy rainfall overnight, half the leaves had been knocked off the trees during the night and now there was a brisk wind and the rest were falling fast. The colors never last long enough, like life itself. Then I remembered that a year from now there might not even be anyone to witness this, and the duration of human life would be moot. It was only a couple of days before I had to go to the United Nations, and the demons had started roaring around in my head. I stayed in bed a few more minutes grappling with that reality before deciding, as anyone facing a difficult ordeal must, that it was time to get up and face it. How bad could it be, after all? If the Security Council wouldn't listen to reason, was that my fault?

Partly, at least. If I couldn't convince them that the end was near, like some of the patients at MPI used to scream, I certainly wouldn't be blameless.

Mike came to breakfast, as promised, but none of us said much about the upcoming meetings or anything else. The three of us did enjoy one another's company, however. He reminded us of our son Will so much that he almost seemed to be part of the family.

After breakfast Mike and I returned to the conference room we had left, it seemed, only minutes before (how arbitrary time seems to be). Everyone was all smiles, another feeble attempt to boost my confidence, I suppose. I saw that both the former President and the current one had joined us, sitting in the back, not taking an active role, for the present, at least, chatting between themselves as only those who knew their awesome responsibility could. Nor did my putative shrink, Dr. Schultz, though I caught him studying me from time to time.

A first draft of my speech had already been prepared, and everyone who hadn't been involved in its actual writing, including myself, was given a copy.

My hands were shaking as I took it. The good news is that it wasn't a long one – I guessed about fifteen minutes – and there were no surprises, though I was impressed by the tone, which was much more conciliatory than I would have thought. Not exactly pleading, perhaps, but certainly making it plain that the United States was fully committed to appeasing the Bullocks, and that the very survival of the human race depended on the unanimous support of the other four members of the Security Council, followed immediately by the rest of the world. My first thought, however, was quite self-serving. Rather than analyzing the words and their possible effect, I found myself thinking: I can do this! Perhaps a natural reaction to being put in such a spot, but I nevertheless felt ashamed for internalizing something so vastly important. Be that as it may, the head speechwriter opened the meeting with, "You've all read the draft. Any comments before we begin?"

There were, of course. Indeed, they went on all morning, and it occurred to me that the Gettysburg address might never have been delivered if it had been written by a committee. There were some (out of the two dozen or so participants) who thought I needed to go deeper into proving that the Bullocks were who they said they were (much of the world still didn't trust this fact, it would appear), and others who wanted more solid data showing how a 20% reduction in human killing could best be accomplished (though that was the work of another subcommittee). It was also suggested that the mention of my travels through space and time ought to be minimized because the presence of the cone should be enough of an inducement to comply with the Bullocks' demands without going into bizarre tangents. The President's science advisor asked how much of the cone had been deciphered, and whether its contents would be available for presentation. On and on the discussion went, including arguments about a couple of grammatical points and syntax. The Vice-President, noting perhaps that I was feeling a bit flustered, remarked perceptively that I shouldn't worry; this happened all the time with important speeches. I nodded and smiled weakly. I found that I couldn't swallow without difficulty.

During a brief coffee break (with donuts), I was assured again and again that I would do fine, that I had been reading all my life, and that delivering a prepared speech was "a piece of cake." Even if I never lifted my eyes I would do fine. I nodded unhappily over and over again.

By then another draft had been prepared and distributed. A few lines had been changed, but the thrust was about the same: we were coming to the UN with hat in hand, and everything depended on the cooperation not just of 95% of the world, but 100%. Someone asked the question, already raised days before by a different task force, whether the majority of the world's population might have to agree to wipe out a country that would not agree to stop the killing, for the benefit of everyone else. As before, it was decided that the Bullocks might take a dim view of such a course of action. The former President noted, however, that some third world countries might demand something from us in exchange for their co-operation. And on and on it went. I found myself wondering whether a demonstration by Walter during the Security Council presentation wouldn't be worth a thousand – or a million – words that I could give them.

"Why do you need another demonstration?" the Bullocks roared.

"There are some who don't believe the ones you've performed," I told him as calmly as I could, forgetting, as usual, to say it aloud.

The roar became deafening. "Then why would they believe another one?"

I actually covered my ears, even though I knew it wouldn't do any good. Almost no one noticed, though I saw Schultz staring at me quizzically. "Let me tell you something about our race that you may not understand, Walter. We may not be a logical species, but we are far more convinced by something we see with our own eyes than we are by being told about it. Even with a video, which can be altered with certain tricks. We call these tricks 'photoshopping.'"

"Thousands of your beings saw the last one with their own eyes!"

"But the United Nations representatives did not!"

"Should I make the UN disappear while you are there?" he sneered.

I shouted out loud, "You want me to succeed or not?"

The room immediately became silent. Mike ventured, "Walter is here?"

"They're always here!"

The chair calmly asked whether they had offered us any suggestions.

I took a deep breath. "I suggested they give the Security Council a demonstration of their capabilities."

"What did they say?"

"They said we've already had enough demonstrations."

The room was silent for a long moment before the former Secretary of State asked me, "Can you twist their arms?"

I restrained myself from pointing out that they didn't have any arms. "I can try, but they don't pay much attention to what I want."

The Vice-President concurred with the others. "I think another demo, especially while you're giving your speech, would be a good idea. Keep trying."

"Whatever the Bullocks do shouldn't affect the thrust of Dr. Brewer's speech," said the chair. "For the time being, let's try to finalize that, shall we?"

I had no idea how every phrase in the English language, and probably all the others, was so nuanced. Every paragraph, every sentence, every word in the working draft had to be pondered, analyzed again and again, decided upon, and later changed to mean something even more clear (or less subtle). I didn't envy diplomats, government officials, or politicians their jobs, which must be composed mainly of endless minutiae, at the cost of a fortune in time spent. I thought; how boring their lives must be! We didn't even stop for lunch except for some sandwiches and coffee. As the meeting droned on an on I found myself resting my eyes for a moment, but when they came open I found myself in the past again. "Walter, are you doing this to me?" But there was no response from the assholes of the universe.

I wasn't sure what year it was, but I found myself inside our home of several decades ago. It was daytime, perhaps after school. Two of my sons were there, along with my daughter Jennifer, who was on the phone. Fred was playing with a model airplane he had built, while Chip was apparently doing his homework on the kitchen table, something he rarely seemed to do. My wife wasn't there, nor was Abby. I presumed they had gone shopping or the like, but there was no way to know. I wandered around the house. Funny – I neither walked nor flew, I just *went* from one place to another without thinking about how I got there. There was our old sofa, our shiny dining room table, the old TV set without disc player or Tivo. I had almost forgotten how nice it was then, but it was all coming back. I started to sniffle a little because it was all so *peaceful*. It occurred to me to wonder where I, myself, was at that moment in the distant past. Probably working at the hospital. I tried to will myself to be there, but that didn't work. Would I have to return to the present and start again from there to get to another place?

But couldn't I just go there if I could flit from room to room? I floated out the door and somehow wandered down the street toward the subway station, as I had done a million times before. It took awhile – perhaps I would eventually learn better techniques for "past-traveling" as I became more accustomed to it – but I eventually got there. Based on the ages of my children I had a pretty good idea of what year it was, but now I saw that it was early spring: for example I spotted daffodils here and there.

I found myself on the train heading into the city and downtown. Still weeping because I missed all of this so much, and because I didn't appreciate it enough at the time, I watched people getting on and off; they all seemed so blasé – didn't they realize how wonderful their lives were? Eventually I made it to the familiar stop, where I somehow got off the car and rose up the steps near the Manhattan Psychiatric Institute, where I had spent more than thirty years of my life (and my wife and children's lives, I realized), and approached the building slowly. I tried to go faster, but I still could manage only one speed. Sluggishly I drifted inside, where I found myself in the lounge, a place so familiar that I could have found my way to every table and sofa in the dark. I headed directly to my office, where I found myself talking to a patient, one of hundreds from the past, none of whom I had forgotten about. In this case it was a young woman, barely out of adolescence. She was curled up in a ball in my "analysis chair," her slippers lying on top of each other on the floor in front of her.

I took a good look at myself at work. (How many of us get to do this? I wondered aloud, disturbing no one, of course.) My eyes were fixed on my yellow pad and I was concentrating intently on what Susan was saying. Parents! It's always the parents! At that point something occurred to me, something I had forgotten to ask Walter about: can visitors from the future see *each other*? There was no one else around as far as I could tell, but perhaps no one would want to visit this particular time and place. Still, I hadn't seen any evidence of a past world choked with "ghosts." Maybe we're all invisible even to one another! Or maybe the number of visitors is limited by some Einsteinian physical parameter, or even by regulations established by future societies. Maybe you need a ticket. I could see a waiting room a thousand years hence, filled with people lined up to depart for the year 1955, say. Or maybe the duration of each visit is limited, and there aren't enough minutes in the whole of past time to worry about running into someone else from the future. They might all be a drop in time's ocean, so to speak. (Or maybe not many people would want to revisit the past. Or maybe there *is* no future . . .)

I watched myself ask a question or two – the wrong ones, probably. I could see Susan tense up on the second one. At least she hadn't attacked me, something that had happened two or three times in my career. Nevertheless, I had probably pushed her too far, something I had never overcome in all my years of experience. I had long realized that I wasn't really a very good psychiatrist, had never wanted to be one in the first place. I didn't want to be a doctor of any kind, but when my father died, I had tried to fill his empty shoes. What I *really* wanted to be was a singer and actor on the Broadway stage.

I left the hospital and took the downtown #1 train. The theater district! My parents had brought me to Broadway shows any number of times when I was a kid, and Karen and I went to a few when we were dating and for years after we were married (until the kids began to take up all our time). We had seen the original productions of *My Fair Lady* and *West Side Story*, and a few of the later hits after the kids were grown. *A Chorus Line!* Even *War Horse*, of late, two of the best ever. We had seen the greats: Barbara Cook, Alfred Drake, Mary Martin, and so many more. Gielgud. Burton. Fonda. How wonderful life is! I was so engrossed in memory that I almost forgot to get out at Times Square. No matter. I left when the train was between stations, and floated up to the street.

Karen and I hadn't been to mid-town for a while – I'd forgotten how bright the lights are (prot whipped out his sunglasses there). I wandered around like any first-time tourist, gawking at the signs, the tickertape, the traffic. At 47th I turned toward the theaters there just to see what was playing. At the Helen Hayes I slipped inside without a ticket and went backstage, where the stars were applying their makeup. I watched for a while (I had always been curious about that, and whether the actors were ever bored doing the same job over and over again, sometimes for months). They didn't seem to be. Some were rehearsing their lines, others were listening to a concert or opera on the radio or a cassette tape player, some chatting with their fellow actors or their dressers. I ached to be one of them.

I hung around for almost an hour, until the first curtain calls came. Throats were cleared or rinsed with gargles, and tested for clarity and volume. I tested mine, too. At last the final calls came, the audience was seated (except for a few latecomers – there are always latecomers!) – and the most thrilling moment in all of theater: the raising of the curtain. I was onstage! I paused for a moment and intoned, "Ladies and gentlemen, I'd like to do my rendition of the theme from *Oklahoma*! I cleared my throat loudly and belted out, "Oklahoma, where the wind comes sweeping – " Halfway through the first bar, however, I was interrupted by the maid, who came onstage with her duster. All eyes were on her and no one was paying any attention to me. Shoulders slumping, I slunk offstage. Though somewhat disappointed, I was nevertheless elated. I had made my Broadway debut!

Feeling better about having achieved my lifelong ambition, I left the theater and drifted toward the subway. I use the term "drifted" for want of a better one. To me, at least, it seemed like drifting. I tried again to vary the pace, but my attempts to speed up ended in failure. Flapping my arms or pumping my legs had no effect at all. I suppose that made some sense: since there was no passage of time in the "present" I had left behind, there was certainly no hurry about getting anywhere in the past. Apparently I could stay here forever and come back to the same instant it was when I left. Yet – what determined the seemingly slow pace I was making? Why should it be *that*, and not something else? How could one travel back decades and then be stuck in one place? Could it be a mental, rather than a physical process? I decided to set a speed record to get to the next traffic light – and there I was! Is that how I got here in the first place? What if I decided to travel forward by ten years? I wasn't sure whether I had accomplished that goal, but when I got back to the house (in an instant!), things were a little different than they had been a short time earlier. Some of the furniture had been moved, for example, and the television set was bigger. But no one was home. Where the hell were they?

Can a visitor to the past get tired? I was exhausted. I closed my eyes, and when I opened them I was back in the committee room at exactly the same moment I had left. The endless discussions about grammar and semantics were still going on. Soon thereafter, thankfully, the chair announced that we would move on to an analysis of the political content of the speech – i.e., whether there were words therein that might offend any of the other four major nations with veto power, or weak terms that might not effectively convince the delegates of the Bullocks' intentions and their ability and *willingness* to act on them. As that discussion began, and dragged on and on, it occurred to me that Walter had led me to begin my travels both to the past and into the realm of space as well. Was this happening so that I could tell the world about the wonders we would encounter if we played our cards right? Or was I supposed to find something else on my travels through space and time? Something more personal, perhaps? Or perhaps there was some way to change events in the past after all?"

Not likely. There was the unbeatable grandmother paradox, for one thing. If someone went back and steered his grandmother away from his grandfather, he wouldn't have been born and couldn't go back and meet his grandmother, etc., etc. For another, a visitor to the past is invisible, and can't interact in any way with the people living at that time.

But maybe it was more subtle than that. What's in the past, anyway? Everything! If everything in the past hadn't happened *exactly* the way it did, the present and future would be different. Could a visitor make some infinitesimally small change to events that would affect some other event, which would affect another event, and on and on? What if they did something because of this that they wouldn't have otherwise? What if I were to determine who the first killer was, and somehow change his or her mind about what he was about to do!?

No. Same problem: the grandmother paradox.

I decided to try again, maybe to see something I hadn't noticed before. In a trice I was back at the place I had just left. So why was I here? Some of my family drifted in: my wife and I, soon followed by our son Chip, perhaps ten years older than he was before. Where were the others? Grown up and gone due to the inexorable passing of time?

I gazed at my wife for a few minutes, remembering how lovely she was then, which I calculated to be about 1989 or thereabouts, so she (and I at that time) would have been about fifty, the prime of our lives. I stared at myself, too. It's impossible to describe how weird it is to gaze at oneself at a time in the distant past. One is filled not only with nostalgia, but also with sadness that time rushes forward and all must end, and much too soon.

I hung around until everyone started to get ready for bed. I didn't follow anyone to their bedrooms – even Karen's and mine – that seemed a bit too prurient, despite the unusual circumstances. But I did ponder another question: now that I was in that past, could I travel to K-PAX or anywhere else I might wish to go from there? Probably, but I would save that for another day. Shasta got up and stretched, wandered to the kitchen for a drink of water, settled back down on the carpet. I watched her sadly, remembering the day she died, the day we all comforted ourselves by telling one another that she had lived a long and happy life. This was one of those moments in the life she loved so well, perhaps more than the rest of us.

Another weird thing occurred to me: perhaps we had all been to the same theater at which I had performed my rendition of Oklahoma a decade earlier, to no acclaim whatsoever . . .

I went to Abby's room, hoping she would be there. It was filled with all her things: photos of the Beatles and a few other bands I didn't recognize or remember, an anti-Vietnam war poster (she hated that conflict), as well as dolls and toys from an earlier time in her life. No computer or other electronic gadgets, only a record player and a few dozen LPs. A portable radio. A little makeup on her dresser, clothes and books scattered around. But no Abby.

Could I move quickly ahead to another month or year? I closed my eyes, but didn't seem to be going anywhere. Walter? Are you here? I floated through the wall and into the backyard, wondering where to go from here. Shasta was relieving herself along the back fence, after which she trotted to her door and went back inside.

It occurred to me that I didn't have to go back to that goddamn meeting for ages – time would not have moved and they would still be writing my speech. I could take centuries if I wanted to visit ancient Greece, or sail with the Vikings, or sit with Mozart as he composed the Jupiter Symphony. I could visit the locker rooms of both teams after a World Series game. I could indirectly participate in anything that *ever happened*! But I wasn't in the mood. All I could see in my mind was the upcoming Security Council meeting with me at the microphones. When I opened them I found myself back in Room Two and the Task Force on Brewer's Speech. A week ago I would have been shocked to find that the proceedings were at the exact same moment as when I left, even though it seemed to me that I had been gone for hours. No more. Even this was beginning to seem routine.

The final touches of the damn thing were just being finished. It had been broken down into six main paragraphs. The first, the introductory one, would briefly summarize my background and my earlier experiences with prot and fled. The second, that another alien race called the Bullocks were now on Earth, and were demanding that we stop killing each other. The third would present their specific demands, that we stop 20% of the killing in the first year, and so on until there wasn't any at all (except for accidental deaths). The fourth would encompass a plea to immediately phase out hunting and fishing, laboratory experimentation, and even animal husbandry, with the goal of ending the slaughter of Earth's animals as well as ourselves. Fifth, the evidence that the Bullocks were for real and, for all intents and purposes, all-powerful, at least compared with us, and could do anything they said they could do (as evidenced by the videos of the disappearance and reappearance of various huge structures around the world; a sample of what was on the cone would follow). And sixth, what would happen to us if we failed to comply. There would then be a final summary and desperate plea for the world to comply with Walter's demands.

The Secretary of State apologized for changing the subject, but he nevertheless asked, "Dr. Brewer, do you have any further indication of how the Bullocks are going to eliminate us?"

"They aren't saying precisely. I suppose they could sterilize us, but that wouldn't stop the killing for decades, so I don't think that will happen. Or perhaps they could make all the weapons disappear, but we would just make new ones. The only thing I can suggest is that we will probably be taken to a remote planet and dumped there." I didn't mention the cannibalism part.

"This is all speculation, Mr. Secretary," the chair correctly pointed out. "It isn't really relevant to the issue at hand, is it?"

"It might be if it's going to be a horrible experience. People might change their way of thinking simply out of fear."

"Point taken, but it's still speculation at this point, right, Dr. Brewer?"

I had to admit it was.

"Very well, let's move on with the speech, shall we?"

After that I lost my focus for a while: it occurred to me that since I could leave for days, months, even years, and come back to the same point in time as when I left, did this mean I could live forever (and delay my presentation for that long) if I just left this space and time and wandered the universe until it collapsed back upon itself? It would be a tempting option, of course. But not, I quickly realized, if I had to do it alone and couldn't take Karen with me.

I suddenly realized that I was being spoken to again. "Sorry? I didn't quite catch that."

The chair repeated, "Now that your speech is essentially complete, we could start working on your delivery tonight. Or, if you'd prefer, we could start fresh in the morning. Do you have a preference?"

"What's the right answer?"

This time the titters were sympathetic ones. "The sooner we get started, the better your presentation will be. But we also know that the stress must be taking a toll on you. After we finish here, we're going to ask you to stop by the medical room for blood pressure readings and the like. If everything's okay, we could start rehearsals after dinner."

I thought: rehearsals? It sounded like a movie. "If you could print me a copy, I'd rather practice it at home tonight, and then we could begin to go over it here tomorrow morning."

"Objection?" asked the chair. There were none. "We'll get you a fresh copy right away, Dr. B. Thank you all. Do you have anything you want to add, Mr. President?"

"I think everything is going as smoothly as it possibly could. I would only like to remind Gene that we're all behind you a hundred percent, and that you can ask any of us, including me, anything at all during the next couple of days. If there is anything any of us can do to help you get through this, all you have to do is ask."

"Mr. President, will you be with me in the Security Council chamber?"

"I'll be right beside you, and the ambassador will be on the other side. Others of us will be right behind you throughout your entire presentation."

"Can my wife come with me?"

"She can come to the UN with you, but it probably wouldn't be a good idea for her to accompany you into the Security Council chamber."

"Will *your* wife be there?"

The President smiled. "That can be arranged. She loves New York."

"Anything else?" queried the chair. "If not, the meeting is adjourned until tomorrow morning at eight o'clock."

As everyone was streaming out (some paused to shake my hand and offer words of encouragement), Mike sidled up to me and said, "You didn't ask for me to be present at the UN."

"Oh. I'm sorry, Mike. Of course I hope you'll be there. I guess I just assumed you would be."

"Just kidding, doctor. You won't need me there. My job will be finished. For now, it's still to act as liaison and make sure everything's okay and on schedule." He and Dr. Schultz escorted me to the clinic for temperature and blood pressure readings, which were normal. Schultz asked if I was sleeping well. I told him I was. I don't think he bought it, but what could he say?

Mike walked me to the door. "You go have a nice dinner with your wife, and I'll see you in the morning."

I had almost forgotten about Walter, but he was there (and had been the whole time, no doubt). "Did you enjoy the trip to your past?"

"Not especially, though I did take care of some unfinished business."

"Is that what passes for music on this planet? O-kla-ho-ma?"

I was in no mood to argue to point. "Something occurred to me while I was in the TF meeting. Will you be present when I speak to the Security Council?"

"Wherever or whenever you are, I will be there."

"You've demanded a lot from us. Here's one for you: I demand that you give another demonstration there."

There was a pause before they said, "How many times must we prove to you that we can do what we say we can do?"

"Only once, if it comes at the right time."

No response.

"Walter?"

No Walter.

Flower came out to greet me and sniffed around as if someone else had been there. Did Walter have an odor? I looked into the woods and the hills on the other side of the house. The leaves were almost gone, and the world looked dead or dying. With that unpleasant thought we went into the house.

Karen had the usual beverage waiting for me – she must have seen Flower run out and assumed I would be coming in. As we munched on some nuts, she told me that my grandchildren had called again. I reminded her that there were only two days left and we would spend as much time with them as they wanted after that. I took a long drink and told her also about the trip back to our old house in 1979 and '89 (or thereabouts), the one that Will and Dawn and their children, two of my grandchildren, live in now. She gave me the same look that she had before – half believing, half not believing me. I understood what she was thinking; if she were me, I would be skeptical, too. What could I tell her? I wished

I could have brought back a souvenir to show her, but I explained to her why it didn't work that way. She wondered whether I had told Dr. Schultz. I promised to do so next time I saw him, which would probably be tomorrow.

"I'll tell you what. After dinner we'll go for a jaunt in space or in time together. You choose."

She stared at me as if I were crazy, or at least joking. "Can we do that?"

"I don't know. If we hug each other and don't get separated, it might work. Let's try it."

She thought about that. "If it does, maybe you could link arms with everyone in the Security Council! If you could take them on one of your 'rides,' they would surely be convinced that you were speaking the truth."

"I'm hoping Walter might do something along those lines."

She broke down crying, something that was happening with more and more frequency. "Oh, I wish this whole thing were over!"

I got up and put my arm around her. "It will be soon, honey. In the meantime will you go with me tonight after dinner? It won't take any time at all, I promise."

"I'm scared. What if we don't come back?"

"That's never happened. For all I know it can't for some reason."

"We'll see."

Another nice dinner – Italian, with a nice chianti. I reflected again on how well government officials eat. Afterward, I let her read my copy of the latest draft of the speech. "Not very poetic, is it?" she remarked.

"No, it's pretty straightforward. Want to hear me deliver it later on? I'm practicing."

"Of course."

After coffee I asked her if she were ready to go to the past. She tensed again, but agreed to try it "this one time." We came together as if we were going to dance. I thought hard about the last trip and how I got there. Nothing happened. We stood in the living room for several minutes, but went nowhere, notime. "I don't know what happened," I confessed. "I guess I don't really know how it works. Walter never gave me any instructions. It just seemed to happen."

She looked relieved, but put on a game face. "When you figure out how to do it, we'll try it again." As soon as I backed off from her, though, I suddenly found myself back on K-PAX (there is no mistaking the ambience of that planet) even though I had expressed no conscious desire, to myself or anyone else, to go there again. This had to be Walter's doing. But why? "Walter?"

No response.

"Why, Walter, why?"

Although the position of the sun and a couple of moons were about where they were last time, I was in a somewhat different place – perhaps thousands of miles from where I had been before. I hovered there for a while, trying to figure out which way to go to find Abby, or anyone else. I wandered for a while in what I thought might be a westerly direction when I suddenly realized (I almost slapped my head): why am I creeping along when I could move at any speed I chose? Suddenly I was flying like a low-level jet. I probably zoomed halfway around the huge planet in less than an hour. It was like watching a movie on ultra-fast speed. I passed over countless human-like beings (dremers?) and even more ape-like creatures and all the rest of the fauna of this nearly waterless world, which was sparsely covered with all kinds of low vegetation of many hues – reds, yellows, oranges and blues. Few trees, though, so I could see far, far into the distance in all directions except for where a high purple mountain range dominated the horizon. Even at this incredible speed I realized that it would take me a very long time to find a particular K-PAXian (or human, for that matter), but I realized I had all the time I would need to find Abby, and/or prot and/or fled and all the MPI patients who had come to this world to escape their dismal lives on Earth.

I tried a different direction and was immediately rewarded by spotting my namesake, Robert and Giselle's son Gene, who was conversing with an individual I didn't recognize, somewhere between human and ape in appearance (could that be fled's child?). My godson was a handsome boy, a late teenager by now, who strongly resembled Robert in physical appearance, and Giselle in his bubbling vivaciousness. They were juggling some kind of plum-like fruit from one to other, and when one dropped to the ground, they stopped and ate it. I wished I could have joined them. For that matter, I wished I could ask Gene where my daughter was, though it was unlikely he would know. I watched for a little longer before making my departure.

Much of the surface of this world was the same as every other part, and I realized that it must be hard to meet someone at a particular place. But, of course, K-PAXians were different from us in most ways, and perhaps they never met anyone, but merely ran into someone accidentally. If Abby or any of the others ever came back to Earth, I would ask them about this and a million other things.

I must have stayed there a couple of weeks or more – I lost track of time – and I did finally find fled once, as well as Robert and Giselle and their other child, a girl, and many of the former patients I knew – separately, not together – sometimes more than once as I crisscrossed the globe at a brisk speed. But I couldn't find Abby. It finally occurred to me that perhaps she had already left K-PAX, and was on her way back home!

I wanted to go home, too, but I still didn't know how. If I thought about the date and time . . . That didn't work. But I remembered where I was and what I was doing when I left for K-PAX, and focused on that, *pictured* that scene, and voila! I was back in the dining room with my wife. Even though I had been on K-PAX for what I was sure were several days or weeks, no time had passed in the house at all.

I told Karen about the trip. She listened carefully as I described in detail where I had been and what I had seen there, including my godson, and when she heard his name I could see that she suddenly understood that I wasn't crazy, but that there were things that were beyond human conception and we simply had to accept them. When I told her I believed that Abby had to be on her way home, she grew excited. "It will be so nice to see her!"

"She's been gone a long time," I agreed.

We went to my study, where I read aloud the "final" draft of my speech to the UN. Karen suggested I put more emphasis on certain things, but otherwise thought it sounded pretty convincing, especially if Walter were to give another demonstration. "But will that be enough?" I said. "The Russians and the Chinese veto everything that's put up for a vote."

"They would vote for more killing even if it meant no humans would be left on Earth? Including themselves?"

"It's not that they wouldn't want to survive. It's that they will probably doubt that this would happen."

"Then it's your job to convince them otherwise."

"That's exactly what I'm worried about."

"What about the Eiffel Tower and all the rest?"

"They may think all that was faked by Hollywood or something."

"But there are interviews with people who were – "

"There are countless interviews with people who have been taken aboard alien spacecraft, too."

"Oh. Yes, I see what you mean." She thought a moment. "Then your speech doesn't really mean much, does it?"

"Probably not, unless the Bullocks perform something else during the Security Council meeting. Something that everyone in that chamber can see with their own eyes."

"Why wouldn't they be willing to do that?"

"They think they've done enough of those to convince 'reasonable' people."

"Who says people are reasonable?"

"Yeah. I know."

"So what is the speech for?"

"I don't know. To make their demands official, I suppose. But they said it has to come from me."

She nodded. "I think you should do the best you can with it in case they don't show up with more 'proof.' Want to read it again?"

I read it through another couple of times, and on the last try I was beginning to stumble on every other word. "Let's try again in the morning," my understanding wife suggested.

As we were lying in bed, I did a little experiment. I thought about the scene, just minutes before, where I was stumbling on the phrase, "We must try to make – " and there I was, watching it happen again. I thought about being back in bed with Karen and there I was. That must be how it works. There are no two situations in a lifetime that are exactly alike. If you can picture the furniture, the people who are present, what is being said, and so on, there is only one such scene in all of time, and that's where you end up. Could anyone do it? Probably, with a little experience and a lot of practice.

"Well done, Gene."

"Walter?"

"Were you expecting someone else?"

"No. Where have you been?"

"There are less than two days before your United Nations debut. We visited the Security Council chamber to get a sense of the dimensions."

"Are you planning something, Walter?"

I could almost see their dead eyes twinkling. "It's going to be a surprise."

"Oh, how nice. I love surprises. Especially when the survival of the human race is at stake."

"Good night, Dr. B. Pleasant dreams."

They weren't, but at least I was able to get some sleep knowing that Walter was covering my back, and with thoughts of our daughter Abby's return dancing in my head.

DAY SEVEN

I've had many patients with severe anxiety or depression who woke up one morning and felt none of their usual symptoms. This happens only rarely, but it is a wonderful sight to behold. A patient who shuffles around the hospital is suddenly bright-eyed, smiling, even laughing at almost everything. The other patients gather around them as if trying to catch the "infection." It usually lasts only temporarily, a few hours or sometimes days, but it is a beautiful thing to see, if only for a short time. Those who experience this sudden "remission" usually report that the fear and sadness "just left me." There is no known explanation for this temporary "cure," but it is quite uplifting both for the patient in question and for everyone else who knows him or her.

It was with such a feeling that I awoke on the seventh day of the Bullocks' visit. I felt happy, buoyed, ready, even eager, to go. Karen and I had a very nice breakfast (I wish prot could have been there to share the large bowl of various ripe fruits), I dressed in one of my nicest casual outfits, kissed her good-bye, gave Flower a good head scratch, and bounded out the door.

There were still a few leaves coloring the woods, the sun was shining, and birds and squirrels were everywhere, fattening themselves for travel or winter. Even the government men seemed to be smiling, if ever so slightly, and both of them nodded to me as I approached. One even said, "Good morning, Dr. Brewer!" A breach of the rules of conduct? With the future of the entire population in jeopardy, of course, I suppose no one would have cared except for the toughest-minded military man. I certainly didn't. By now I knew the guy, having seen him several times, and I murmured a good morning. That broke the bubble, and his blank demeanor reappeared immediately. For some it's business as usual even when Armageddon comes.

And then I remembered Walter. They didn't say anything, but of course I felt their presence. The feeling of elation evaporated, and I was back to the usual crush of anxiety and dread of speaking to some of the most important people in the world. Tomorrow!!! I almost turned around and went back home, but of course that would accomplish exactly nothing. It occurred to me that I could delay my appearance by delving into my past life, continue looking for my daughter, find out why she was never home. But it would just be a stalling tactic, and I would eventually have to return to *now*.

Or would I? I could be gone for a year, or a century, or even a millennium, and nothing in the present would change. Nor could it. But how long would I want to be without my family and friends, and especially my wonderful wife? Nevertheless, perhaps I could stay somewhere long enough to gather my wits, obtain some perspective, even discover how some people learned to deal with situations similar to the one I found myself embroiled in.

It occurred to me that the past emcompassed more than my own experiences. Could I actually visit ancient Egypt, for example, or watch Leonardo da Vinci paint the Mona Lisa? Witness the signing of the Magna Carta? Maybe even experience dinosaurs roaming the Earth? Could I go anywhere I wanted throughout the entire history of the planet, or was I limited to my own tiny past?

"Anyone can travel to times past, Gene. Go anywhere, visit any time period you like. If you survive the next year, this will some day become one of the chief forms of recreation for your species. You'll find the instructions for this and so many other things on the cone."

"But Walter, I don't have the cone, and couldn't read it anyway. You never showed me how to go to a specific place and time."

I heard a grunt. "You've done it before, doctor."

"Yes, but I don't know how I did it!"

"How did you get back to your childhood?"

"I don't know! I just sort of pictured it in my mind. But what would I picture in my mind for the time the pyramids were constructed? I don't know exactly what to picture, and wouldn't be able to conceptualize any particular person or scene there."

"Try it. If you make a mistake, try again. You've got all the time in the world."

"But – " I sensed, however, that Walter was gone for now. I saw that the expressionlesss guards were still frozen in time. What would I like to visit most of all if I could? How about Beethoven conducting his Ninth? I closed my eyes and ran a few bars through my mind, and when I opened them, I recognized immediately the figure of Ludwig von Beethoven at the podium, hair flying, with the soloists and chorus coming to the climax of the final movement. Even though I couldn't hear the music, the sight was so powerful that I literally gasped. I was a foot away from him! I watched for a minute before I turned and saw that some members of the audience were angrily yelling. Fortunately, the maestro couldn't hear any of this (nor could I), and the expression on his face was so intensely beatific that I shouted (to no avail) to the audience to shut up. It frankly amazed me that people could be so dense as not to realize genius when they witnessed a new idea that transcended all other musical creation up to that time. I watched as his pudgy, though immensely graceful, hands conducted the musicians, his tails dancing in syncopation with the music.

The barbarism of the audience led me to the realization that violence and cruelty have always been characteristic of humanity. Why is it that people take such pleasure in killing not only anything with legs or wings or fins but even their own *neighbors* if the opportunity arises? Why do we get so much satisfaction from executions, which put us in the same category as the rapist or murderer? Why are we all so eager to go to war with another country – any country – under the illogical pretense of striving for peace? I wept for the hardworking Beethoven, who was able to rise above our base nature to ascend to the heights of human achievement. Perhaps that's why we are so moved by great works of art: for a moment we understand that beauty is counter to our very being, and it suggests what we could be if we could break away from the meanness of our nature. If we could only *evolve*, and eliminate the stupidity, the cruelty and violence. How stupid we are. We really don't deserve to survive the Bullocks!

The symphony was finished and poor Ludwig turned to face the snarling crowd. True, there were many who were applauding, but the ugly reaction of some forced him to quickly make his exit from the stage. I followed him into the backstage area, where he was hustled to a waiting coach by some of the concert's organizers. I watched sadly as the driver urged the horses forward, leaving behind the great man's top hat, which lay in the dust. For once I wanted to be corporeal so that I could at least touch the silky fabric, hold the brim for even a moment. Take it home to the present time! A few members of the audience chased the coach a little way, but gave up after a block or two. Would they have killed him? Perhaps not, but I knew they were capable of it. I found myself glaring at them with disgust because I knew that inside all of us . . .

"So you understand now why you have to be removed."

"You're here, Walter?"

"I'm always with you, doctor."

"Did you send me here to tell me that we are all killers?"

"No, you found your way here yourself. Congratulations."

"Thank you, I'm sure," I said sarcastically, much as the Bullocks themselves might have responded to something I had said or done. I felt myself wishing I were one of them, having broken free at last from the shackles of our limited minds and bodies, our atavistic need to repeat and repeat and repeat the mistakes of the past with no awareness whatsoever of a bigger picture. "I suppose I should go back and tell the committee that I can't do it. That our species – we – have always been killers and always will be."

"That is one option."

"Is there another?"

"Proceed with the original plan."

"Why?"

"Because no matter how miniscule the odds that you will all suddenly become pacifists, humans also have the characteristic feature of hoping that things will get better. And you have made some progress over the centuries."

"If you hadn't come to Earth, how long will it have taken before we would have reached the point where killing would be something we would no longer be proud of?"

"Your wife's estimate was a reasonable one. Perhaps another millennium or two."

"But you can't let us reach that stage naturally, on our own?"

"We've explained that to you days ago. Think of all the lives that will be lost in the next thousand years, with your endless retaliatory wars and all the other forms of brutality. We can't wait forever for you to evolve. Enough is enough."

"Yet you think I should go through the motions of this farce."

"No, we think you will want to go through the motions yourself."

"Thanks again. I'll take that as a compliment." After a moment, I added an afterthought: "Did you take a look at the score? The symphony was beautiful, wasn't it?"

"To a human, perhaps."

"Aren't there things that are intrinsically beautiful to anyone?"

"No. Beauty comes only from past experience. Your music would make no sense to most of the universe."

"A pity."

They completely ignored this pithy remark. "We encourage you to wander through your history. Take your time. The present isn't going anywhere . . . ."

"How do I – ?" But of course he was gone again.

I had lost track of Beethoven, who was probably home by now, or drinking away his sorrows in some biergarten or other. I could probably have found him sooner or later, but the past was so vast! I closed my eyes and pictured as best I could the beatific smile on the Mona Lisa. The next thing I knew I was floating above a canvas, the painting nearly completed, with Leonardo himself studying what he had done so far. After a moment he mixed a little more oil on his palette and changed the tone of the face just a little, enough to give her cheeks a bit more of a rosy hue. I watched, fascinated, as the model for the work sat placidly, completely at home in the presence of the great man. Once in a while he would murmur something to her (I couldn't hear the words, of course), and she would shift a bit, perhaps to catch the light a little better. I hovered up, down, and around her, gazed close-up into the craggy, bearded face of the artist, who seemed to be utterly lost in his occupation. The session lasted perhaps an hour and a half, after which he nodded to her and smiled a little. Without a word she arose and disappeared into the next room where, I supposed, she found a cape or other wrap and left the building. The great man left, too, maybe for lunch. An assistant picked up his paints and brushes, washed the latter with some kind of solvent, and generally cleaned up the area. After that I was left alone in the huge studio.

I floated around the room, absorbed in the tables of models – aircraft of one sort or another, ships, human bones, several notebooks and drawings, any of which would be worth a fortune in the "present." The history of it all was staggering. Although I could see no one else, the artist-scientist's studio might have been filled with time travelers coming from all eras of the future. Who could blame them? I hoped I would be able to come again.

But there was so much to see in the past that I hardly knew where (and when) to go next. Furthermore, it was wonderful to forget about the United Nations and Walter if only for a little while. A little while? I could stay here forever if I so chose. In fact, if I *never* returned, mankind would be safe, frozen in time. But it would be a lonely existence, if you could call it that. As many of my former patients used to remind me, you can't win.

So I knew I would have to return at some point, and relentless time would start up again. Nevertheless, I decided to linger awhile in the past. After all, how many more opportunities would I have?

I couldn't decide when to visit next. What would *you* do? Would you visit the era of the dinosaurs? Watch the signing of the Declaration of Independence? Listen as Mozart plunked out a new opera on the harpsichord? At this point I became confused. As warlike and vicious as we all are, there are so many good things about us that I suddenly saw everything from a different perspective. A moment ago I realized that we cause so much pain and suffering that we as a species didn't deserve to live. Now I badly wanted us to survive. To create more music, more literature, even more touchdowns and home runs. There was no point in further delay. I had to go back and face up to my duty, with Walter's help if necessary, as well as that of all the good people who were in the committee room and elsewhere working night and day to come up with the best way to save our species. I took one last look around Leonardo's workplace, felt a little more amazement and awe (who wouldn't?), and thought about Mike and the President waiting for me back at the Nerve Center.

"Good morning, Gene," Mike said as I shuffled into the pre-fab structure, which would be gone in a few days, as if it had never been here. "Anything new from the Bullocks?"

"Not much," I said. "But I've been . . . Well, never mind."

He stared into my reddened eyes. "Anything you want to tell me? Are you okay?"

I waved him off. "Yes, fine. I'm ready for my close-up now."

"Your close-up?"

"It's a line from a movie."

"Sunset Boulevard, right?"

"Yes."

"One of the great ones."

"Let's hope it lives forever."

"Amen to that, Gene."

We came to the familiar yellow committee room, which was stuffed with even more people than were there the afternoon before. Only the President was missing; apparently he had a few other things to attend to. This time the meeting was chaired by the Vice-President, who brought everything to order. Someone may have realized that his avuncular presence (even though he was younger than I) was somehow soothing to me and, indeed, I liked the man very much. He started off by asking me how I was doing and whether I needed anything.

"Only for this thing to be over," I said.

"I think we can all sympathize with that," he said with one of his wide smiles. He turned to the other members of the task force. "Okay, let's get on with this, shall we? Everyone have a copy of the 'final' draft?"

Everyone did but me; I was quickly supplied with one. It began this way: *Ladies and gentlemen of the Security Council, I bring greetings from the citizens of the United States of America and the world.* No more time was wasted in pleasantries. *Today we are here to discuss an ultimatum brought to us by an alien race called the Bullocks. One week ago we were visited* – Well, you know the rest. It seemed to me to be a perfect speech: concise, to the point. Every word was necessary; those that weren't had been cut. The only thing I didn't like about it was its coldness, its lack of emotion, despite the fact that everyone on the planet was faced with total annihilation. Nevertheless – what did I know? – I assumed protocol and experience dictated such an approach. Even though it was already perfected to the standards of diplomatic speechwriters, it apparently wasn't good enough. For the next several hours the subcommittee went over every line again – every *word* – until most of the participants (though not all) were satisfied with the syntax, continuity, and all the other grammatical necessities to make sure that there would be no misunderstanding, and that no one could accuse the United States of being too arrogant or demanding. Though I was tempted to go watch Babe Ruth hit a home run, I stuck it out through the whole thing.

I spent the time trying hard to imagine what it would be like sitting at the big round Security Council table reading the damn thing. But I could not. It was all so unreal: is this *really* happening? I asked myself, or was it just a bad (if vivid) dream? It was all so out of the blue, so to speak. One week ago I was in the grocery store looking for *pickles*, for God's sake! Now I could pick anytime in history, anyplace in the universe I could visualize, and go there. This just couldn't be happening, despite the fact that it was. The Vice-President wasn't a figment of my imagination. He was *here*, as real as you or I. I had shaken his hand! And that of the President, too! And countless other dignitaries that I had never seen before except on TV. So I listened to the discussion with increasing trepidation and decreasing confidence. Then it was over. Suddenly the Vice-President was saying, "We'll take an hour and a half for lunch, and reconvene at 1:30. If you have no objection, Gene, after that we're going to show you a short film that will demonstrate what it's physically like to be in the Security Council chamber, what you will be seeing and hearing when you are there, what the protocols will be, and all of that. The idea is to get you intimately familiar with the environment, so that it will be almost like a visit to your own living room. After that, we'll ask you to read the speech again in its entirety. There won't be any surprises – you've already gone over it with us several times. When we hear you read it we'll know what, if anything, needs further work or further revision. Sound okay to you?"

"Can't wait," I said, to the usual encouraging grins and nods.

"Incidentally," he added, "the President couldn't be here this morning because of pressing business, mainly that of negotiating the details of your presentation – who will be allowed in the room, things like that. But he will be in attendance this afternoon. The meeting stands adjourned."

I felt my shoulders noticeably slump. Everyone nodded and smiled yet again as they walked out, on their way to further discussion and nice lunches, I presumed. As always, Mike escorted me to the door. 'I could probably find my way out," I told him.

"I'm sure you could," he said with a kindly laugh. "But for one more day it's still my responsibility to see that you get home safely and back here again." He shook my hand. "Don't worry about practicing the speech in front of us today. You're already intimately familiar with it, and it's simple and straightforward. Just come relaxed and ready to go."

"No problem," I lied, and started across the lawn to the house. Halfway there it started to rain. More importantly, something occurred to me. "Walter, are you here?"

"Is the Pope Catholic?"

For some reason that struck me as uproariously funny, and I laughed loudly. The Secret Service, of course, pretended they heard nothing. I don't know whether the Bullocks were practicing their version of our humor, but it just seemed – Well, I guess you had to be there. "I was just wondering what you think of the speech the task force has come up with. Do you think we can make it better?"

"One thing we have noticed about Homo sapiens is that with you *nothing* is ever perfect. *Of course* you can make it better, Gene. But don't worry about that. It's sufficient that you got your foot in the door."

"What do you mean by that?" I asked, shielding my eyes from the raindrops. No response.

"Walter?" What was he saying? That it didn't matter *what* I said to the Security Council? Were they just using me to get to the chamber themselves? "Walter?" I continued to the house where Flower greeted me warmly in the little entryway. I hung up my jacket and went into the living room. Karen, of course, was waiting for me there. But so was someone else: my son-in-law. "Steve! What are you doing here?"

"Ah came to speak to the aliens."

"But how did you get through the security people?"

Karen spoke up. "I told them it was all right. Steve is very persistent, honey. I thought it was better to get it over with."

"They're not here, Steve."

"They're not? Where are they?"

"I have no idea."

"C'mon, Gene. Are you telling me you're doin' all this on your own?"

"No. It's just that they come and go. Too bad. They were in the backyard a few minutes ago."

He ran to the front door, yelling, "Then maybe they're still there!"

"It doesn't work that way, Steve. They come and go without warning. Maybe they're here in the living room right now. Should I ask?"

His eyes darted around the room. "Ah don't see anyone."

"They're not corporeal in the usual sense."

"What does *that* mean?"

"They can occupy someone else's body, even an insect, maybe even a rusty nail. But otherwise they're like a – I don't know – a vapor or a spirit."

"Can you find out if they're here?" He was pleading now. "Ah'm only asking for five minutes."

I knew they weren't, but I asked anyway just to get rid of him. "Walter?"

"Yes, doctor?"

"Walter!" I spoke quickly before he had a chance to leave again. "This is my – "

Surprisingly, I heard them speak out loud for the first time since Day Two. "I've been waiting for you, Steve. What would you like to know?"

Steve audibly gulped, but didn't waste a minute. "Just one thing. Is there a Grand Unified Theory?"

"No. Why should there be?"

"According to current theory – "

"Theories change. It's all on the cone."

Steve turned to me. "What cone?"

"It's a long story. I haven't had a chance to – "

Walter ignored me and went on. "I'll give you a hint. The 'dark matter,' or 'missing mass,' as you like to call it, is real."

I could actually hear my son-in-law panting. "What is it made of?"

"Gravity, of course."

"It's gravity itself?"

"What did you think it was?"

"Well, uh – " I could tell that Steve was overcome with emotion. He knew something now that no one else in the world knew, and apparently that was quite enough for the time being. He couldn't think of a single follow-up question. But he quickly regained his wits and asked, "And dark energy?"

"There is no such thing as 'dark energy.' It is a figment of the human imagination that attempts to explain the absurd hypothesis that the expansion of the universe will go on forever. It's all on the cone."

"What about string theory?"

"Another crude attempt to explain something you don't understand. Strings don't exist, either. Nor does the creation of the universe from nothing. It has always been here and will be forever, even when it collapses into a black hole."

"You're kiddin'!" Steve squealed.

But there was no answer. The interview was over.

Steve grabbed his hat, the beret that he was so fond of, and literally ran again for the door. He didn't say good-bye or ask me to tell him about the cone. I never even got to ask him whether he would like to help decipher it.

"See?" said my perceptive wife. "He won't be back. It'll take him the rest of his life to digest that information. C'mon into the kitchen. Lunch will be coming soon, and you're wet. I hope they bring some hot soup."

I took her hand. "Just one thing."

"What, hon?"

"I saw Leonardo da Vinci painting the Mona Lisa this morning. And Beethoven conducting his ninth symphony. All I could think of was how I wished you could have been there with me."

"Did Walter send you there? Or have you figured out how to do it yourself?"

"I think I've got it figured out. Maybe I can teach you how to do it and we can go back to those places together."

"Oh, that would be wonderful. But – "

"Do you want to try it?"

"What if I go somewhere and you aren't there?" As I said, she is perceptive, far more so than I am. "And if that happened, are you sure I'd be able to get back?"

"Just look around and picture what you see now. The way I figure it, this is the only moment in all of time that we will see this exact scene."

"But what if I get it wrong? What if *you* get it wrong?"

"What if we get it right? Isn't it worth the risk?"

"I don't know. I just don't know. And what about lunch?"

"Won't matter. Time stops while we're gone. We could stay away a century and everything will be just like this when we get back."

"Would Walter help us if we get stuck somewhere?"

"Good question. I don't know. But I think they're here to make sure the Security Council meeting happens tomorrow. I don't think he will let us disappear and not make it to that meeting."

"They won't let *you* disappear, anyway. But what the hell – we only live once," she accurately predicted. "Let's go for it!"

This is why I love her so much: even though she had grave doubts about the outcome, she was game to try it. How many spouses do you know like her?

"So what do I think of?"

"Let's try something I've already done; it should be easier than, say going back to the building of the pyramids. Which, by the way, is on my list of things to see. You know I've always been fascinated by them."

"What have you already done?"

"Well, I've been to K-PAX a few times . . . ."

"Can we try something a little closer?"

"Do you have a suggestion?" I asked her. "Something that would be intimately familiar to both of us?"

"Our wedding day?"

"Perfect! Okay, let's take the very moment when the minister said, "I now pronounce you . . . Uh, I forget the rest of it."

"Very funny. All right. How do we do it?"

"You just close your eyes and picture exactly what that moment looked like, and felt like. But remember, no one will be able to see you or hear you. You will be something like an invisible 'spirit.' Are you ready to try it?"

"I'm scared. I'm afraid I'll get lost."

"Look around you. Remember what *this* moment looks like. If you end up in the wrong time, just come back here. I know: I'll put this candle right on the edge of the table. Focus on that when we're ready to come back."

"You make it sound easy."

"I guess it isn't, but it gets easier with practice. We could also ask for Walter's help if we need it. Walter?"

There was no answer, of course, but nevertheless I said, "If we have a problem, will you find us and get us back to this moment?"

"What did he say?"

"Nothing. But I'll bet they heard me. Okay, are you ready?"

"I now pronounce you . . . I now pronounce you . . . I now pronounce you . . ."

I said the same thing, but silently. In a nanosecond I was standing beside the minister (Reverend Dole, his name was, and he had a big mole on his nose, and everyone called him Reverend Mole) watching Karen and I get married. ". . . man and wife," said Rev. Mole. I looked around: Karen wasn't there. At least I couldn't see her. Then I remembered that maybe I wouldn't see her even if she were there.

I have never seen anyone else from the future when I've gone to the past; like the people who are there, maybe we can't see other "ghosts," either, even a traveling companion. I had thought there just weren't many of them around, but – So maybe Karen was here somewhere, even though I couldn't see her. Damn it, I should have asked the Bullocks about that.

Or maybe she wasn't able to make the trip work. I decided to head right back, but I waited a few minutes to watch the kiss (I remembered it well because it lasted longer than wedding kisses usually do, and there were "ooh"s from our friends and relatives. I watched as we strode back up the aisle, everyone smiling and applauding. I wondered whether I was really there, or just remembering everything. But I didn't have time for such musings. I needed to get back to the present to find my wife of nearly fifty years. I focused on the dining room as it was when we left (or I, at least, left), and in another nanosecond I was back. With a huge amount of relief I found Karen still there, murmuring "I now pronounce you . . . I now pronounce you . . ."

"Never mind, honey. I'm back and I guess you never made the trip."

"You're already back? As far as I could tell, you never left."

"That's how it works. Time stands still when you're gone. Don't ask me to explain it."

She looked at me doubtfully. "Gene, are you sure you aren't imagining these 'trips'?"

"Pretty sure. I don't see how I could have seen things so clearly otherwise. What Beethoven looked like, or Leonardo da Vinci. Their dress and mannerisms. They seemed as real as you are. And there's the candle on the end of the table that I put there before we left, remember?"

"Yes, but that doesn't prove you left."

I realized she was right. There was no way to prove I had been gone, then or any other time, even though it was as real as anything I had ever experienced. "No, it doesn't. But I think we must have done something wrong. Want to try it again? Tell you what: I'll put the candle somewhere else and we'll both try to go back only a few seconds to this very moment, with the candle on the edge of the table, okay?"

"Not now. Maybe after your United Nations speech. We'll have plenty of time for games after that."

"You won't think it's a game when you've done it."

After lunch (vegetable soup) and a little nap, my wife woke me with, "Are you ready to rehearse your speech?"

Reluctantly I got up. "As ready as I'll ever be, I suppose. I hate having to do this."

"I know, sweetheart. But it will be over soon." She hugged and kissed me and I felt better, as always.

"Want a roll in the hay before I go?"

She laughed a little. "Later, alligator."

"Is that a promise?"

Another kiss. "Promise."

"I'll be thinking of you when I give that goddamn speech."

"I'll be thinking of you, too."

"See you later, kiddo." I gave Flower a good ear scratch and left for the Nerve Center. I heard a "Good luck!" as the door was closing. The rain shower, I noticed, had stopped.

No Walter in the backyard. Maybe he had nothing more to say. After all, it was only another twenty-four hours until Message Day.

Mike was waiting for me outside the trailer, as usual. "I wanted to have a little chat before we go in," he said.

"What about?"

"Just wanted to make sure you're okay. Are you sleeping well? Would you like to see Dr. Schultz again before we go down to the UN?"

"No, I'm okay. I'll be even better when this thing is over."

"We'll *all* be glad when this is over."

"I guess that's true. I'm so focused on my own role in this that I forget it involves a lot more people than just me."

"In fact, it involves everyone in the world. It would be a shame to let seven billion people down."

"I hadn't thought about it that way. Thanks, Mike. I think that will help me get through this."

"Ready to go in?"

"Yep."

When we arrived at the meeting room we were greeted by the President and all the others. He gave me a fist bump. "Afternoon, Dr. B. It looks like the moment of truth has finally come."

"I'm afraid so."

"Let's win one for the Earth," he said.

"Not the Gipper?"

"This time it's for *all* the Gippers." I suppose that's what separates the goats from the sheep. I almost said, "Baaaa." "Seriously, Gene. This will be much easier than you think. Your speech is already written. It's only sixteen minutes long. All you have to do is read it and it will all be over except for the voting. Once that's done, your job will be finished, and we can all go home and live our lives."

"For a year?"

He frowned. I think he didn't much care for pessimism. "Possibly," he replied.

"I'll do my damndest to make it forever," I said, almost believing it.

The frown segued into a brilliant smile. "Good. Okay, let's get on with it, shall we? Will you take your seat, please?" He pointed in the general direction. A copy of the speech is already there."

For the first time I noticed that all the chairs in the room had been placed in a circular arrangement resembling those occupied by the Security Council members. I had seen this setting on TV a hundred times, and chills ran up and down my spine, my whole body. Obviously this was the point: to make the setting as near as possible to what we would see in the chamber so that I would be less intimidated when the time actually arrived.

Though my legs were weak, I managed to find my seat at the round table. As I looked into the faces of those gathered, I realized again that I knew some of the most important people in the country, or at least in the federal government. The President nodded to an aide, and the room went dark. On the wall at the end of the room a video presentation showing another former Secretary of State explaining why we had to go to war in Iraq appeared. I watched, fascinated, as the camera went from the speaker to various Council members, some of whom couldn't conceal their obvious doubt. Nevertheless, everyone listened politely, and a few even applauded at the end.

When it was over, the President said, "Any questions, Dr. B?"

"Looks like a piece of cake," I said as confidently as I possibly could.

The President nodded. "Okay," he said. "Showtime!"

I looked at the speech, which I had already read several times in various drafts. Still, I paused for a few moments to catch my breath before I plunged. I practically had the thing memorized, so I read through the first couple of paragraphs as rapidly as I could.

"Gene?" said the President.

"Uh – yes?"

"I think the purpose of this session is to practice reading it as if we were in the Security Council chamber. You need to slow down and put a little emotion into it. As if it's the most important speech that's ever been given at the United Nations. Which it certainly is, wouldn't you agree?"

"Yes, sir, I would."

"At the risk of sounding like a film director, please begin again, with feeling."

I took another deep breath. As I did so I suddenly realized that I could take a break any time I wanted by merely going somewhere back in time, or even to the moon or another planet, and perhaps gather my wits so that I would be less nervous, maybe make fewer mistakes when I got back to the table. In no time at all I found myself outside of Cairo, gazing at the Great Pyramid of Cheops, which was about half-finished and under active construction. When I say "active construction," I mean the commotion was frenetic. It was like being inside a giant beehive or ant colony. I had no idea what year I was visiting, though I knew it had been finished some 4,500 years before the "present" time. I watched in wonder as *hundreds* of men hauled a single massive stone surely weighing several tons up perhaps a 5° incline using wooden rollers. The earthen ramps almost completely surrounded the gigantic structure, which was under construction on all sides simultaneously. There must have been tens of thousands of workers altogether – were they all slaves? There were a number of oxen and donkeys present, also, but with so much cheap human power, why waste the animals, which were better used for transporting equipment and supplies. The donkeys, apparently, were used to carry the engineers and foremen to and from wherever they went for the night. The workers presumably slept on the ground. I watched in awe as a giant cube was laid perfectly in place without the benefit of concrete or mortar of any kind. As I floated overhead I could see the burial chambers under construction inside, wooden forms outlining the walls and ceilings, and dozens of artists already painting the murals and friezes which would adorn the enclosures.

I could have stayed around another few decades to see how the burial chamber was sealed with the pharaoh inside, or perhaps hopped back and forth in time to get a time-lapse picture of the whole process, but I decided to save that for a later day, when, I hoped, Karen could enjoy it with me. (I wondered whether Walter had visited this or any of the other significant periods in human history.) And, though violent, I realized that there was so *much* past time that it would be a travesty to lose it all for stupid, selfish reasons, including the desire to kill someone for any motive whatever.

For a little while I had forgotten all about the speech I was reading, felt happy and relaxed, so I decided to go back, where, of course, I found myself facing the same critical bunch as before. I began to read the damn speech again, this time with all the feeling I could muster. Soon I began to hear chuckles, and I looked up to see everyone grinning, even the President. I became a trifle pissed, and I asked him, "What the hell is so funny?"

"Sorry, my friend." It's just that now there is *too much* feeling. It's not a high school play. We just want you to read it slowly and carefully, with some emphasis on certain things, but not too melodramatically. Want to try it again?"

Somewhat peevishly I started again, but didn't get five words spoken before I began to titter myself, which turned into a guffaw. Everyone joined in. A light bulb had gone on and I thought I knew, at last, what was required of me. When the room was quiet again I started over. This time I read the whole speech without stopping, and without interruption. When I was finished there was a heartfelt round of applause.

Then the real work began. Little by little we combed yet again through every word, every sentence, every paragraph, until every single iota was smooth as custard, and there were no foolish or redundant phrases, it was solid from beginning to end. "Let's take a break," said the President, and with that, assistants came roaring in with coffeemakers and cakes and other treats. Rather than head off for a relaxing visit to another time period, I stayed. I wished I hadn't.

"It's missing the point," said a voice which I recognized immediately as Walter's.

"Goddammit, Walter, what point is missing?" I asked him. Everyone else in the room was frozen in time, with mouths full of cake, and coffee being poured, the stream stuck in a perpetual rivulet of rusty steel.

"You covered all the necessary points, Gene, but you – all of you – have forgotten that you are merely Homo sapiens. When you try to convince the important people of your world not to kill anyone, you make it sound as if it's a matter of numbers. As we have said before, the 20% figure is just a minimum, not a goal. The idea is not to kill *anyone*. I have studied your cultures. Only by trying for 100% will you be able to even get close to 20."

There was a minute of silence, apparently to allow me time to digest this along with the chocolate cake. "I'll tell them," I said.

"Another thing. It won't be like the people on the Eiffel Tower, who came back after the demonstration was over. If you fail to meet our demands, none of you will *ever* come back. You will not be allowed to live in some comfortable world where you will go on with the killing, either. Your species will simply cease to exist."

"Will anyone be spared?"

"No. If we spared even one man and one woman they would still be human, and they would just begin again to multiply and subdue the Earth. This is your only chance."

'So we'll all just disappear?"

"Something like that."

"I'll note that, too, Walter."

"Your speech makes it sound as if you have a choice in this matter. Listen carefully to this: you do not. There are two possibilities: one, you survive, two, you don't. Do you understand?"

"Yes. But you'll be there, too, right? Why don't you – Walter?"

The din returned, and someone was speaking to me. It was Mike. "Were you conferring with Walter?"

"Yes."

"What does he think of the speech?"

"He thinks it sucks."

"Let's speak to the President."

I didn't want to speak to the President just then, so I made a trip to the past – a few hours past. It was a scene I had told my wife about, with the candle on the corner of the dining room table. I just wanted to see if I could do it. And there it was: she and I were talking about that scene, and how we would return to it if either of us got into any trouble finding our way back. Karen was her usual radiant self, but I couldn't help notice that I, on the other hand, looked old, tired, beat-up. I reminded myself that this whole mess would be over in ONE MORE DAY, then I would be able to relax or even sleep 24/7 if I wanted to. I knew I wouldn't, though. I would be visiting all the great moments of the past, re-living, in a sense, all the events that led to the present time. Unless, of course, Karen and I couldn't figure out how to go together. Then, to hell with it.

I hated to come back to the present, but there were things to do.

The President was deep in conversation with a number of advisors, but he saw us out of the corner of his eye and wrapped it up. "Good job on the speech, Gene," he said, shaking my hand again. "Maybe one or two more rehearsals and you'll be ready for the big leagues."

"There's a little problem," I told him. I'm sure my shoulders were sagging. "The Bullocks don't like the tone."

The President was never one to waste words. "Why not?"

I told him about Walter's objections. He whacked a copy of the speech against his other hand. "All right. We'll take care of it." He nodded to the head speechwriter, who didn't even finish his coffee, but strode to a little table in the corner and got to work on it, along with a couple of his colleagues.

I took the opportunity to get some more cake while the President conferred with the writers. When he was finished, he came over to me. "Let's sit over here," he indicated to me and to Mike, who was never far from my side. We did so, and had a nice conversation about the events of our own individual pasts. I learned, for example, that Mike had once been a state champion high school quarterback. The President himself confided that he wasn't sure he had wanted to run for President – some of his advisors thought he would do better at a later time. It was his wife who had talked him into it. "Wives do that," I agreed, and so did Mike.

"Or husbands, in some cases," the President pointed out.

After that pleasant interlude, which I shall remember as long as I live, the speechwriters came back with a revised draft, which the President read silently and carefully, pen in hand. His only comment was, "Yes," and passed the copy to Mike, who perused it quickly and handed it to me.

"Read that through, Gene," he said, "and then we'll try it again."

"Can I have a clean copy before we start?"

One of the writers said, "It'll be ready in a moment, but we thought you might like to see the changes we penciled in first."

I quickly read through the revisions. "Walter?" I said to myself. "What do you think?" But, of course, if they were there they ignored me. Apparently they had said all they had to say about the matter and it was up to us whether to follow his advice. "They look okay to me," I told the committee.

As soon as they came out of the printer, the newly-revised copies were passed around. "Okay, everyone," the President called out. "We're ready to start again."

I took several deep breaths and read through the latest version with as much feeling as I could muster without going overboard. When I was finished the President said, "Well done, Gene." He looked around. "Comments?"

There were only a couple, one a grammatical mistake pointed out by an English professor I hadn't met, but who reminded me of Jackie, another former patient. Otherwise the damn thing was apparently ready.

At this point *everyone* breathed a sigh of relief. There was nothing more to be done with the text except show up and read it at the Security Council meeting tomorrow. There was some chatter about whom I should see next, what other preparations needed to be made. While this was going on I found myself thinking about the passage of time. What does "tomorrow" mean? Tomorrow it will be "today," and then it will be "yesterday," and on and on. How odd that the perception of time depends on whether you think about the past (which went by in an instant), and the future (which takes forever to reach). And yet time simply amounts to pages in a book. It can be stopped at will if you travel silently into the past or to some distant place. But what about the traveler? If I stayed in ancient Greece or Rome for an extended period would I be far older when I got back to the present? Isn't this what Einstein said about travel near the speed of light? No, time travel is different from light travel. It takes no time whatever to get to the past. There is so much to learn! I could only hope the Security Council would understand that it could be far more rewarding to study the contents of the cone instead of how to make better weapons.

"Did you hear that, Dr. B?"

"Oh. Sorry. My mind must have been somewhere else."

"That's okay," said the President. "Here's the plan: we suggest you go from here to the doctors to make sure you're ready for a strenuous day tomorrow. After that you can go to a room down the hall to make a video recording of your speech, just in case of any problem. If you're unable to get to the UN we can show it to the Security Council."

"You mean – ?"

"I only mean that no one can predict the future. A hurricane might come up the coast. The United Nations Building might be locked down by a bomb threat. You might fall and break an arm getting out of the shower. None of that is going to happen, of course, but with the future of mankind at stake, we can't afford to take any chances."

"Sure. No problem."

The President shook my hand for the umpteenth time and looked me right in the eye. "Your part in this is almost over, Gene. I have absolute confidence in you. Get a good night's sleep and don't worry about a thing. You'll do fine."

"Thank you, Mr. President. I appreciate that."

Mike took me down to the room with the men in white coats for a final physical and blood tests. After that it was Dr. Schultz again. I had grown to find him repulsive, but I went through the motions. Once more he tried to give me some sleeping pills, which I declined. "Dr. Brewer, this is a once-in-a-lifetime affair. You may find it difficult to sleep without something to help you. I would strongly encourage you to take these with you."

I looked at the vial of tablets and snorted. I had prescribed the same thing hundreds of times to my own patients. Nevertheless, to pacify him, I took the pills even though I had no intention of using them. He seemed quite pleased (with himself).

After we finished making the video, Mike prescribed a good dinner and a restful evening of TV or anything else I found enjoyable. Maybe a visit from the Siegels, our oldest friends from our college years. "There's nothing more to do, my friend. I'll see you tomorrow morning at nine."

"Nine?"

"We have plenty of time. Sleep late and have breakfast at home with your wife."

Sleep late? I thought. When's the last time I've been able to sleep late? "Are we flying on Air Force One, or what?"

"No. You and I will be with the President in a motorcade. As you know, the UN is less than a two hours' drive from here."

"We'll be riding with the President?"

"No, and there are reasons for that. Besides the security considerations he thought you might prefer riding into the city alone with your wife."

"Well, he's right about that."

Mike walked me to the house, where Flower came running out through the dog door. He gave her head a good scratch before heading back to the Nerve Center. "Have a nice evening," he called out. I wondered how he would be spending his. How long had it been since he had seen his own wife and family?

Karen was waiting for me, as she always has. We were both looking forward to a nice, relaxing dinner. That's when she told me that Will and his family would be eating with us. "That's wonderful! We haven't seen them for quite a while."

"Are you sure this won't interfere with your schedule? Don't you have to rehearse your speech tonight?"

"No. In fact, they advised me not to."

"Good. Then we can *all* relax tonight."

I told her I had been thinking that maybe before anyone else comes we could try a trip to the past again.

"Oh, honey, I don't know. I don't think I have the knack for it. I can't seem to visualize all the details about a room like you can."

"I don't think many people can. But here's what I thought: maybe we could set up the dining room like we did before and take a picture of it. If you focus on the picture, maybe we could both get there."

"What then? You can't take a picture of something from the past, can you?"

"Maybe there are old pictures that we could look at. Like the Wright brothers on their first flight – something like that. What do you think?"

"Okay, I guess we could try it. But don't be disappointed if it doesn't work."

"Sweetheart, I could never be disappointed with you."

"Thank you. That was a nice thing to say."

"Okay, where's the digital camera? I'll get it while you set up the table in some way it's never been set up before."

She went about that while I looked for the camera. As soon as I found it I took a picture of my study before hurrying back to the dining room to snap a picture there. Then we went back to the study and uploaded the photos onto my computer (we don't have a smart phone) and printed them both.

"We won't be able to hear each other, so we'll need something to write with." We grabbed a couple of note pads and pens. Okay," I said, "we'll just stare at this picture of the dining room for a minute and see what happens. The next thing we knew we were both hovering over it, staring at the table setting, which of course was identical to the printout. "Well," I said. "That was easy."

"I don't believe this is happening!" she wrote.

"You should see the Earth from space!" I wrote back. "The nice thing about this is that we can stay as long as we want."

"I can see us both, but *we* can't see *us*," she replied. "It's kind of scary. Can we go back now?"

"Sure. This was just a practice run." I held the other picture in front of us, the one of the study, and instantly we were back. I noted that the clock read exactly the same time as when we left. "After the speech tomorrow we'll have at least a year to learn to do this better. We can practice it until it becomes second nature."

"I hope it's more than a year."

I hugged her. "Me, too."

I won't bore the reader with the details of the family talk we had at dinner. Our son Will was deeply immersed in his life and career, writing papers and treating patients, some of whom we discussed briefly over dessert. Neither of us wanted to talk shop that evening, nor did he or his wife Dawn want to know what I was going to say the next afternoon. It was their older daughter Jessica who asked me point blank whether the aliens were going to destroy the Earth.

"Not if the people I will be talking to are reasonable, and if I convince them that it's time for human beings to stop killing each other and focus on the future."

"What if they're not reasonable or you can't convince them?"

I told her truthfully: "I don't know, sweetheart. Let's hope it doesn't come to that. Anyway, we have a whole year to figure it out."

My granddaughter is no dummy. She observed that we should get started right away. "Otherwise there'd be too many dead people by Christmas."

"Yes," I said, not wanting to be untruthful, but also not wanting to terrify anyone. "I'll do the best I can, honey. But it's really not up to me."

Allyson started crying. "I don't want all my friends to disappear from the Earth!"

I could only offer, sympathetically, "I'll tell them that."

There was no more talk of the United Nations the rest of the evening, and soon after dinner the children went to bed. The adults stayed up a while longer, but I excused myself early in order to try to get a good night's sleep. Before turning in I looked at my new supply of meds, kindly provided by my next-door colleague. Reluctantly I took one of the little pink pills and quickly passed into the land of oblivion.

MESSAGE DAY

Day Eight was a blur from the moment I woke up until I found myself sitting at the round table in the United Nations Security Council chamber. I remember little incidents, of course, like getting into the motorcade on the road outside the Nerve Center (Will and his family returned home after an early breakfast, and we left Flower with a neighbor). There were about a dozen big black limousines, along with Dr. Greaney and his staff in the ever-present ambulance; our car was near the rear. I don't know which one held the President (the Vice-President had returned to Washington), or anyone else. Karen and I must have been the last to embark because we were moving almost as soon as we were ensconced in the limo, which, we were informed, was nicknamed "the Beast" because of its five-inch-thick windows and other amenities. We settled back and looked out the smoky windows like any tourist. Perhaps the President did, too, though I suspect he was on a phone or working at a desk the whole way. In any case, I doubt his heart was pounding like mine. Not long after we left, I noticed that we were driving down the same highway that Walter, the corpse, and I had traveled seven days earlier. I couldn't be sure, but I could swear that the tree he had vaporized had reappeared.

I held a copy of my speech the whole way, had been planning to look through it again, but I just couldn't do it. The truth is I wanted to forget about it. I thought about going back in time to watch the signing of the Declaration of Independence or something, but I would have had to go alone at this point, so I stayed and held hands with my wife the whole way. We weren't alone, of course. The ever-present Secret Service agents sat in front of and behind us in their usual attire. The highways were empty all the way except for the motorcade. Occasionally I saw several red flashing lights a couple of blocks away, presumably where the regular traffic was being held back. The whole trip took barely an hour and a half, but it seemed more like a minute. By noon we were settled into a small, comfortable dining room, where we presumably enjoyed a light lunch, though I can't remember anything we had. The President had joined us by that time, and he related a few stories about certain speeches he had delivered and how nervous he was at times. "Learning to give speeches requires a lot of practice in seeming to be relaxed while being scared shitless," he informed us.

"Tell me about it," I replied dismally.

"Jack Kennedy was a master at that. Everyone in his shoes, or your shoes, is scared, even terrified, under extreme conditions like these. Why? Because you can never be sure that you're right. On the other hand, there is a living ex-President who got the willies with every speech he made." He shook his head. "You have to admire his courage. Press conferences, too. Of course it has a lot to do with self-assurance. If you have doubts about yourself they show, and you have to try to overcome them beforehand, mainly by being well-prepared."

"I haven't done that yet, Mr. President. Can we postpone this for a few years?"

"I've always appreciated your sense of humor, Dr. B. What would the Bullocks say about that?"

"I think they would take a dim view of any delays."

"That's what I thought they'd say."

Otherwise it was probably a nice lunch, with pheasant or the like. I remember ruefully thinking that a year from now we had better not be killing birds, or anything else, to eat. That, of course, assumed we would survive Year One, which was a dubious proposition at best. Just before two o'clock I went to the bathroom, and when I came out Dr. Utt handed me the cone, reluctantly, I thought, encased in a plastic cube with locked door. Immediately thereafter we were on our way to the Security Council chamber, leaving my wife behind with Mike and the First Lady. Only the President, our U.N. representative, the Secretary of State, and I represented the U.S., or more properly, the Earth. I suppose, in fact, we were representing the Bullocks, or perhaps the entire universe. Karen waited with the others in an ante-room, which, she told me later, was equipped with a closed-circuit television monitor so that they could watch and hear the proceedings.

There were some formalities, of course. The chair, in this special case the Secretary General of the United Nations himself, introduced us and briefly explained the situation. There wasn't a murmur in the chamber – I presume the delegates had already been thoroughly briefed about what was about to transpire, and any gasps of disbelief had been wheezed long before. While this was going on I felt myself beginning to tremble, and my chest rising and falling. I told myself to relax, it would soon be over, but it didn't help much. I looked around and found myself in the UNITED NATIONS SECURITY COUNCIL

CHAMBER. The huge round table had an opening at one end, like a donut that someone had taken a bit out of. When I saw the enormous mural on the back wall, the full gravity of the situation fell on me like the Great Pyramid of Cheops. I couldn't believe I was there. The delegates, however, seemed to ignore me, as if I were somewhere in the past and invisible. All of a sudden the President literally punched me in the arm and grinned at me. That did it. I relaxed immediately. I could almost see myself tightly gripping the speech, as if I were coming back from the future, a disembodied observer watching myself preparing to make the most important speech ever made. It was such an impossible sight, almost like a dream, that I found myself grinning and, in fact, I almost laughed out loud.

At last, at *long* last, it was time to go on. I need not recite the whole event here – God knows it has been reported in thousands of newspapers and websites – but I will recount the reactions of the various representatives of the fifteen governments representing the peoples of the world. (At that moment, incidentally, I wasn't the slightest bit nervous – all the preparation had paid off, and I had worried myself almost sick for nothing.) The first thing I concluded was that all of them were taking me seriously – no one was looking around at his or her colleagues, yawning (though I held back a few after the lunch we had), checking watches, etc. In other words, everyone else was quite aware of the seriousness of the situation, the stakes involved. In fact, they all had a copy of my speech in front of them and had probably read it before I even started. For a moment I thought this strange: if I were giving a speech, why did they need a copy? Or if they had a copy, why was I giving it? But I soon realized that there were certain formalities that had to be observed, that there should be no misunderstanding of the words that I, as a kind of representative of everyone in the universe! was bringing to them.

Indeed, when I gave them the background of my encounters with Walter (his occupying a corpse and all the rest, with video accompaniment), I think I detected a muted hint of wonder, or even envy. Maybe everyone secretly wishes he could have an encounter with an alien – which may say something about our own world (are we all hopefully wishing for something better?). When I mentioned (briefly) that I had gone to distant places, and to times past, there were eyebrows raised, but I again sensed that the reaction was one of surprise, not doubt, especially when the videos were shown of the Taj Mahal and the other structures disappearing and coming back without harm to anyone (though I had been told there was still some uncertainty in the minds of many that they weren't photo-shopped, or faked in some other way, just as some still believe that no human ever went to the moon). Indeed, I knew for a fact that there are people who still think the Earth is flat, or has existed for only a few thousand years.

I reached forward, unlocked the hard plastic cover, retrieved the cone, and turned it slowly a fraction of a degree at a time. Instantly the walls were filled with equations, videos of solar systems forming, time-lapse pictures of animals evolving and atoms colliding, and a dozen other remarkable visuals. Everyone stared in silence, though there was the occasional "Ooh," just as any ordinary citizen might have uttered.

I returned the cone to its case, and proceeded immediately to the matter of what the Bullocks wanted of us: not to kill at least 20% of the people who had been murdered at the hands of their fellow men over the past year. Though they had almost certainly been apprised of this demand earlier, there were still grumblings and mumblings among the VIPs assembled for this meeting. "Impossible!" someone shouted in a foreign language.

"Then we'll all die!" I responded without thinking. The President frowned a bit, but said nothing. I realized, as I often do, that I should have kept my mouth shut.

I don't know exactly what the protocol was – I was under the impression that no discussion would take place immediately, though these were certainly extraordinary circumstances. In any case a delegate, speaking English with a French accent, informed us, in beautiful, dulcet tones, that even if the world wanted to comply with the demands of the "aliens," (said with a hint of a smirk) the problem was that there was still considerable doubt among the delegates about the authenticity of the Bullocks (and, by implication, the authenticity of *me*). I felt a certain amount of chagrin, of course, and I whispered to the President the suggestion that I give them further details about my travels. He shook his head, leaving me to fend for myself. Before I could respond, however, every delegate's seat started rising slowly toward the heavens. There were screeches of terror, demands to be put down, but every chair around the table (except mine and those of the others in our party) rose well above the floor and continued rising, everyone hanging on for dear life, until they reached the ceiling. Some of the grizzled veterans, who could have fearlessly faced down a rival in a duel, were wailing, though a few actually seemed to be enjoying the ride, laughing all the way. After hanging near the ceiling for several minutes, all the chairs suddenly plummeted toward the floor, with renewed screeching, before stopping and softly landing where they had started. There was a brief hiatus as medical personnel rushed out to revive a man from somewhere in the Middle East, I think, who had fainted. After that, the Secretary General quickly restored order.

When everyone had finally quieted down, I informed the participants that Walter had obviously done this, and that surely there could be no doubt that the Bullocks could do whatever they wished with us. I reiterated that we were not the most important species in the universe, merely one of many, just as our sun is only a drop in the ocean of the heavens. Finally, I recited my granddaughter's heartfelt appeal: "I don't want all my friends to disappear from the Earth!" There didn't seem to be anything more to say.

"Dr. Brewer," said the chair, "will you and your party please excuse us?" I glanced at the President, who nodded to me and rose. We all stood, I grabbed the cone, and we left the chamber.

In the large waiting room, actually a banquet hall, my wife told me that I was wonderful, and there were handshakes all around. Dr. Uttley relieved me of the cone (and was visibly relieved, himself), and quickly vacated the premises.

There was nothing left to do but wait. I asked the President how long it would be before a vote would be taken. He said it could be anywhere from a couple of minutes to never. "A long time to wait," I said.

"We'll stay awhile, have a cup of tea. If nothing happens by five o'clock, it probably won't take place today."

For the next two hours the President and others tried to make small talk, tell jokes and the like, but it was no go. Everyone was exhausted, most of all me. The time passed excruciatingly slowly. Finally, just before five o'clock, the Secretary General came into the room. His face showed no emotion. I wondered how he could maintain that inscrutable countenance regardless of the news he was carrying. He made a gesture to the President, but came directly to me. The President came over to join us. The Secretary wasted no time in preliminaries. "The vote was 13-2 in favor of reducing the death rate."

"Yes!" shouted the President. Then he asked, more quietly, "Who were the two?"

"Nigeria and Rwanda."

"We have some work to do there,' he said. "But at least they don't have veto power."

"Does this mean – ?"

"Exactly." He held out his hand, which I took, though he did all the shaking. "You've done it, Dr. B!"

"I didn't do it alone, Mr. President, as you well know."

"Nevertheless," he said, "your name will go down in history as the man who saved the human race. Assuming we can meet our quota, of course."

"The Secretary General reminded him that it would first have to be approved by the General Assembly, though that should be a mere formality, given the Security Council vote. Another round of handshakes and congratulations, sighs of relief, laughter.

"So let's get started," said the President. "I won't be joining you and your lovely wife on the trip back to upstate New York – I'll be flying back to Washington. There will be more meetings, decisions on how to implement our goals, convince other nations to help us reach them. You would be welcome to – "

"No, thank you, Mr. President. Karen and I have done our duty, and we're retiring from politics. But good luck to you. To all of us."

He gave each of us another hug, as did the First Lady. "Thank you both," she said. "And enjoy your retirement. You've both earned it."

The President's familiar grin reappeared. "After all this is over we'll play a round of golf or something."

I laughed nervously. Mike said, "Don't worry, Gene. The President is an even worse golfer than you are."

The next thing I knew the motorcade, or part of it, was on its way back home. We actually made it in time for a late dinner. But we would have had to prepare it ourselves. The Nerve Center was gone.

We ordered in pizza.

*   *   *

The General Assembly voted 'yes," though it was a surprisingly close vote. It appeared that some countries had a different agenda. "What if we're attacked by our neighbors?" was the refrain. "Or by terrorists?" It became a kind of mantra. Certain well-known terrorist groups, in fact, vowed to make sure there would never be a day when no one was killed. They were perfectly willing to martyr everyone on Earth for their cause. Some of the third world countries took a different approach, asking for money in exchange for their co-operation, just as the former President had predicted. However, most nations went along with us, and diplomatic efforts were begun to change minds around the world.

Over the next several months there was the occasional call from Mike or the President (we never did play a round of golf, however, or have the party promised by the Vice-President), with encouraging messages about the reduction of killings in the Netherlands, or Japan, or some other country that didn't kill many people anyway. Many leaders around the world were still unwilling to co-operate, calling the Bullocks' demands a "trick" of some kind. With COMPLIANCE DAY (some were calling it CAPITULATION DAY) rapidly approaching, the murder rate in the United States was slowly falling, but only by a few per cent after four months. The military was actually faring much better than the general population after having withdrawn early from Afghanistan, and refraining from engaging anyone elsewhere. Certain nations in the Middle East, Asia, Africa, and South America were not doing so well. The trend was in the right direction, however, and diplomatic solutions continued to be firmly pressed. Envoys were even sent to a few of the more radical and violent political organizations, to no avail, and some never returned.

In the meantime, efforts to decipher the cone were going ahead full steam, and hundreds of scientists had been conscripted for the project. It reminded me of the constructions of the pyramids. After several months, however, Mike informed us that they had come up with virtually nothing.

So it appeared that all the efforts on my part and that of all the others were going to result in abject failure. I didn't say this to the President, but I knew that the responsibility had been mine and I had failed. Perhaps if I had been more forceful? Or if I had better conveyed my ability to travel in time and space . . . I began to rely more heavily on Schultz's happy pills for the anxiety and insomnia

I felt. A safe drug, but I actually thought briefly about checking into MPI, under the watchful eye of my son Will, to see if someone could help me deal with my problems.

During those months I never heard from Walter. I presumed they had returned to Bullock, though they could have been traveling the Earth, watching and waiting – who knew? Wherever they were, I was sure they would be back on the anniversary of MESSAGE DAY. I can only tell you this: during that time I refused to go to the mall for pickles.

In the meantime, Karen and I practiced time and space travel. After many, many failed attempts, she finally got the hang of it, mostly by studying pictures, including works of art, etc. We visited ancient Greece, hung out in the Roman Forum for a while (it reminded me of the Security Council meeting), watched the signing of the Magna Carta and the Declaration of Independence, and attended literally hundreds of other events: the Gettysburg address, the crowning of kings and pontiffs, great sporting events (my wife loves to watch Olympic figure skating, and she completed beautiful triple axels of her own on Olympic ice), including many World Series' and Super Bowls, historic battles (where we witnessed cruelty and bravery on an unimaginable scale). And, of course, dozens of original Broadway shows. For my part, I loved hovering over the hood of an Indy 500 car as it roared down the straightaway at more than 200 miles per hour. I wish we could have taken pictures, but our camera didn't work in the fourth dimension. Another mystery for someone to solve.

But the highlight of these visits was a trip to 0 A.D. to attend a sermon by Jesus Christ. It was quite remarkable. We had never seen a crowd so transfixed by a message (I wished he could have given my speech), which, after all, was one of love and kindness, perhaps entirely new ideas for the time, and one (we could argue) that was brought to us again by the Bullocks. Whether Jesus was the son of God, or just a charismatic carpenter, there was no way to determine from the sermons he gave, especially since we couldn't hear or understand them. Nevertheless, it was a fascinating experience, and we vowed to come back to this era later on.

After all that, we tried a simple experiment: travel to the moon. After a number of failures to do that, we finally succeeded. This was followed by a brief visit to the deserts of Mars, a pretty dull place to tell you the truth. At last we were ready to visit prot and fled and all the others on K-PAX.

On a sunny April morning, exactly six months after the declaration by the United Nations that the world would stop all killing of other humans insofar as was possible, and begin to reduce the slaughter of animals for food and all the rest, we left the house for that now-familiar planet, promising to return to the dining room if we got lost somewhere in the ether. Miraculously, we made it on the first try, and after a short time in this remarkable place we decided to stay for a while. Whatever happened, we knew we could always go back to our own beautiful planet at the same moment we had left it.

We stayed on K-PAX for five years, mostly just floating around watching the K-PAXians, including the various animals, living their peaceful, yet rewarding lives, and watching the heavens at "night," which is often not much darker than in the daytime, thanks to the planet's two suns. Here, no one killed anyone or anything. If there were some way to become corporeal, we would have stayed forever. We spent considerable time in the company of prot and Robert (though they didn't know it) and many of my former patients, but we never ran across Abby. Or for that matter, Giselle and her son Gene. We finally concluded that our daughter must, indeed, have been on her way back to Earth. So we finally returned to our dining room, which, of course, looked exactly as it had when we left.

It was a few months after that, on a hot summer day in August (one of the hottest on record, in fact), that we were surprised and delighted when Abby appeared at the door with Giselle and her son Gene, by now an athletic and handsome young man. Of course we all started talking at once. But after the greetings and all the questions had been asked (they had never seen our retirement home), I said to Abby, "Why did you come back? Are you planning to stay?"

"Are you kidding, Dad? Human beings will soon be gone from the Earth. I came to take you both back to K-PAX!"

I was stunned. "No one can predict the future," I told her. "How do you know we won't stop the killing?"

"You know human nature as much as anyone, Dad. You'll be lucky to get 20% for the whole five years. Maybe in another thousand."

"But Walter came *now*. We have to at least *try*."

"This is the only chance you'll have. Do you want to go to K-PAX or not?"

"You mean in real time?"

"Yes."

Her mother and I looked at each other. Would we want to give up our new-found ability to travel around the galaxy?"

"You can still do that," Abby said, with a little smile.

"Can you read minds now?"

"Not very well, but I'm working on it. But your facial expressions were pretty transparent."

"So you'd take us there on a – ?"

"On a beam of light. Yes."

Karen's and my eyes met again. "I'm willing if you are, honey," she said.

"I can't think of anywhere else I'd rather be," I replied.

"Give us a day to say our good-byes."

"No problem. I've got a few people to see, too."

"Is Steve going with us?"

"I doubt that he'd ever leave his telescope. Anyway, he's got a new girlfriend now." She giggled. "His assistant in the observatory."

"Oh. We didn't know that."

"Nobody else does, either."

"What about your kids?"

"I'll ask them, but they have their own lives here, too."

"Maybe not for long," I pointed out.

"Like a lot of people, they probably don't believe in the Bullocks. Or that you can speak to them. If they truly believed that, all the killing would stop immediately. Just as it would if they truly believed the Bible."

"Maybe you could help us convince the world's leaders that the Bullocks are who they say they are, and that they can do what they promised."

"No matter what you do, a lot of people, maybe most people, still won't really believe it, or can't break old habits even if they did."

"So there's no hope?"

"Oh, there's always hope. Even if you have a terminal illness. But you know how that usually plays out."

"So when do we leave?"

"Noon tomorrow?"

"Why noon?"

"It's already programmed. It's the only time we can go."

"Oh. Do we need to take anything?"

"Nope. Everything you need is already there."

"Can Flower go, too?"

"Of course."

I glanced at my lovely wife, who smiled and nodded. "Okay," I said, with very mixed feelings. "We'll be ready."

She grinned. "Don't take it so hard, Dad. I guarantee you'll love it there."

"I'm sure we will. I only wish the human race could find some way – "

"Don't worry, the Bullocks aren't going to kill anyone. They're just going to make all us humans disappear, like they did the Taj Mahal, until the end of time. No one on Earth will kill anyone ever again."

"Where will everyone go?" her mother wanted to know.

"Just into another dimension, where they'll stay in the present until the end of time. Until then, of course, they'll be able to visit the past, like you and Dad did. Who knows – maybe learn something from that and convince the Bullocks to give them another chance."

"But why don't they just change our DNA, like fled did with Jerry? Evolve us so we would lose the desire to kill?"

"Then we wouldn't be human anymore. We would be a creation of the Bullocks. They don't want that. They do have their principles, after all. We have to figure it out for ourselves. Anyway, the answers are all on the cone if anyone wants to find them. The human race still has a few months to do that." She headed for the door. "Okay, Mom and Dad. We'll see you tomorrow at noon."

Karen and I talked late into the night discussing what we'd be leaving behind and what might lie ahead. Both of us agreed that the richness of the Earth, our family, our friends, and all the rest didn't make up for the fact that the killing would probably never stop. And if it did, we could always come back. K-PAX was just the opposite – filled with peace and beauty and compassion. We went to bed with mixed feelings, yet eager for the morrow.

*   *   *

That morning we spoke to everyone in our immediate family, as well as our good friends, the Siegels. There was some wavering, but no one really wanted to come with us. We understood it would be a difficult decision, and we couldn't fault them for wanting to stay where they had been all their lives. They hadn't experienced everything we had. We wept for them but we had to go.

We were in our usual travel base, the dining room, when Abby and the others returned just before noon. "Ready?" she asked us (our daughter never minced words). "And you're sure you both want to go? And Flower, too?"

We both looked around the familiar room and the adjacent kitchen. Would we ever see this sight again? "We're ready," we said simultaneously.

"Gene? Giselle?"

"Beam us up, Scotty," they both said in unison.

Abby pulled out a little mirror and flashlight. The last words we heard, and the last thing I wrote on my yellow pad, were "Here we go!" She held the mirror in front of her so that everyone's reflection showed in it, and switched on the light.

AFTERWORD

My father, Gene (actually "Eugene," though he hated the name his father gave him) Brewer, disappeared into a state of catatonia on October 15th, 2013. Before that he had been a long-term patient at the Manhattan Psychiatric Institute in New York City. Although I am actually a psychiatrist, and my name is William (also described in his books as "Will" or "Chip"), I was not his doctor, who was, in fact, Dr. Bernard Schultz. Dad had long ago been diagnosed with intractable psychotic depression resulting from the death of my mother and my sister Abby. Both were raped and murdered by a deranged man who had escaped from a New Jersey prison more than two decades ago. I would prefer not to go into the details here, but the events of this tragedy paralleled, more or less, those that befell Robert Porter, a prominent character in the fictional K-PAX series.

The reader may be wondering how such a person as my father, a severely ill mental patient, could have written five books (*K-PAX I* through *K-PAX-V*), one of which was made into a successful motion picture by a top Hollywood studio, with A-line actors and producers. I still wonder about it myself, though it goes to prove what all psychiatrists know: there is no limit to what the human mind can do. The brain is actually divided into compartments. The "multiple personality" syndrome, more commonly called "dissociative identity" disorder, for example, allows a person to live in one of these compartments while those souls "residing" in other such areas of the brain are often unaware of his or her existence.

To put it more plainly, my father was a very sick patient who became someone else when he was writing, someone who had become intimately familiar with the workings of a mental hospital. When he was scribbling on his yellow pads (he never used a computer), he was so absorbed in what he was doing (and thinking) that he could escape for a time the agony of remembering his life with his beloved wife (my mother) and daughter. When he was too tired to work any more, he lay down his pad and slept for a while, or tried to. I doubt that he ever got more than four hours' sleep a night. (Dr. Schultz has tried for years to get him to take one or another sleeping medication, but he managed to hide and discard almost everything he was given.)

How did he get his novels published? In the usual way, I suppose. As Gene Brewer the writer he was able to do everything other writers do, submitting his manuscripts to agents and publishers in an attempt to get them into print. We at the hospital had no problem with his "moonlighting" in this way – it was far more pleasurable to see him at work than weeping or rigidly staring out the windows for hours at a time, and it was quite gratifying for all of us to find out that his first novel (K-PAX) had been accepted (by St. Martin's Press, a well-known New York publisher) after forty-eight rejections by others, including various small presses throughout the country.

His success is not entirely unprecedented. The man who contributed so heavily to the Oxford English Dictionary, for example, was a mental patient, and some artists and musicians have also been quite insane (Vincent van Gogh comes to mind). The mental patient retains many capabilities; when they are incarcerated it is for reasons unrelated to their creativity.

But where did he get the idea for the K-PAX series? To back up a step, Dad was a practicing astronomer at Columbia University before Mom and Abby were so brutally murdered. That was his background, and his basis for coming up with a story about an alien visitor he called prot (short for protagonist). In fact, he may have created 'prot' thinking that only an alien would understand his dilemma.

The other half of the story has to do with his utter devastation at the hands of a killer (still serving a life sentence in upstate New York) who represented, in his mind, a sort of encapsulation of the human race, which, he felt, was capable of anything. Dr. Schultz has informed me on numerous occasions that Dad spent most of their sessions together railing about our civilization, especially our eagerness to go to war, to kill one another over the slightest provocation, and by extension, to kill anything else that inhabits our planet.

His writing was a kind of outlet for his deep frustration about being able to do nothing to change what happened and to get Mom and Abby back. Although there are many parallels to his own life, he was able to rectify his terrible situation in the sense that he could re-create my mother and sister (and even their beloved and long-deceased dog, Flower) in his books, and live a relatively normal life with them. At the same time, he needed to tell his story (purge it from his memory) in such a way as to indict the human race for its callousness and cruelty.

The genius of his creations, I think, was that somehow he came up with the idea of prot and the planet K-PAX, where none of the terrible things that befell him (and me) could ever happen. No one ever killed anyone else on K-PAX, not even a fly (if there were any there). By comparison with the Earth, K-PAX was a kind of paradise, and as such he could indirectly indict the human race for its inherent viciousness, as evidenced of late by the almost daily shootings in schools and shopping malls, not to mention our never-ending wars (they go together, Dad would frequently declare, and are triggered in part by the desensitization of children to killing by the films they watch and the games they play).

When he was writing, he spent considerable time in our library reading the literature on psychiatry and related subjects, becoming intimately familiar with the ins and outs of the subject as well as the routines inherent in any psychiatric hospital. Some of the patients described in his novel are purely fictional, others (under assumed names, of course) actually reside at MPI, and his descriptions of them are an accurate reflection of their often horrific existence. He followed everyone's progress (or lack thereof) closely, and often helped them to overcome the little obstacles that their doctors wouldn't have nearly enough time for. Howie, for instance, and Ernie are real people whom Dad helped treat, if not entirely cure, and who are still productive members of human society. (I was amused when I read that he made a character in one of the novels (*K-PAX IV*) a patient named Claire, who pretended to be one of the clinical staff.) Many of the others he mentioned are still here, and will probably never leave MPI. The point is that if you read one of Dad's novels, you can be sure the settings are real. It's almost like being here. Similarly, some of the characters mentioned in *K-PAX V* were based, I am sure on these patients. Some of the reporters and committee members mentioned in *K-PAX V*, for example, are pretty recognizable to those of us who work here.

Where he got the idea for space travel "on a beam of light" is anyone's guess. As I said above, he was an astronomer, and concerned with all aspects of nuclear physics and cosmology, but whether such a thing is possible is extremely unlikely, according to certain other professionals I have talked to. The same for his theory that the speed of light varies with time, and that the universe recycles over and over again, ideas which have little support within the scientific community. As does his latest one, that the "missing mass" is a form of gravitational energy. As prot would say (if he weren't fictional), that doesn't mean much. Many of the greatest scientific discoveries were scoffed at by the discoverer's peers. The human mind seems to resist anything that smacks of the new and unfamiliar. Once we settle into the familiar picture of how we fit into the world, it becomes uncomfortable, and even unpleasant, to change our way of life, our way of *thinking*. According to Dad, this is why we haven't evolved much in the last hundred thousand years. We started out as killers, he said, and we will end up by killing ourselves.

I don't happen to subscribe to this philosophy, but his books weren't about me, they were about *him*. If you've read any of them, you have a pretty good idea of what my Dad's life was like. His father, my grandfather, was, in fact, a small-town physician who died of a heart attack and a relatively early age. He was quite a domineering man, however, who left his son with an inferiority complex and a serious need to be loved and respected by others. He finally won that respect in his final book, becoming literally the most important person on the face of the globe (note how many times he was congratulated or applauded, for example), rubbing shoulders with the leaders of our country and the world. How happy this must have made him!

Mom was quite an interesting person in her own right. As Dad reported in his books, she was a psychiatric nurse as well as a terrific athlete, an all-American lacrosse player in college, among other things. (I think he resented, at least a little, her ability to beat him in certain sports, such as golf and bowling). But it was a deep, lifelong love few have attained, until a hot day in the August of 1989, when he came home and found her and Abby tied up, gagged, and lying dead on their beds. My father, of course, was never the same after that, and he ended up at the Manhattan Psychiatric Institute.

It was another decade before I joined the staff, in part to keep an eye on Dad, who was like Howie in some ways, always working at his desk, trying desperately to forget what he had seen and felt on that fateful day. But at present he lies in a catatonic state in his room in Ward Three, much as he wrote that Robert Porter, prot's alter ego, also remained, for a time, unresponsive to the world around him. What he is thinking about, if anything, remains a mystery.

As for the current book, he must have finally come to the conclusion that the visits by prot and fled would do nothing to alter our violent natures, and that the only way we humans would be able to change our decidedly unpleasant habit of killing each other was with the intervention of an all-powerful alien who would put the fear of God (so to speak) in our heads. Thus, he created "Walter," a sort of ant colony of beings from the planet Bullock (or, in a larger sense, the universe). The desire for retaliation for a perceived injustice is so strongly imbedded in our DNA, Dad believed, that it could only be removed by someone else. We can never do it on our own, we will never *evolve*.

Dad could never understand how our society, *all* societies, actually *encourages* violence in a dozen different ways. We call anyone who puts on a military uniform a "hero," but what do we call those who refuse to do so? We produce films and games (all virtually identical) filled with blood and gore which can only desensitize those who participate. We murder anything that walks the Earth (except, ironically, our pets, which are often considered part of our families), especially for food, but even for "sport" and a dozen other reasons. People love their guns, and society respects those who produce them. And while capital punishment is perhaps on the wane, some states still eagerly kill criminals for retaliation, and to what purpose? Why do we have so little respect for life, even human life, which only happens once?

Of course, Dad was led to all this by the violent murder of his wife and daughter, without which he might not have thought much about it, nor do most other people. But in fact that is almost *all* he thought about, and who can blame him? In the end, after saying everything there was to say about the horror of his experiences, he could no longer take it and, for all intents and purposes, disappeared from the Earth by riding a beam of light with Mom and Abby and Flower to the idyllic planet K-PAX. Like his fictional character Robert Porter, he may hear everything anyone tells him, including reports of former and current patients, but there is no way to know this. Though he lies like a stone, he may, in fact, be creating a new novel even now. Or a book of poetry, or painting beautiful canvases or composing songs or even symphonies or operas. It would be nice to know.

Will he ever return to us? Possibly. In the meantime I hope he's living a truly wonderful life with Mom and all the other beings on K-PAX. If he does return some day, perhaps we'll hear all about his experiences on that faraway planet. I hope so, for I deeply miss him.

PROT'S NINE SUGGESTIONS FOR PLANET EARTH

- If you must hate something or someone, it should be your own idea, not one formulated for you by someone else.

- Set aside half of each country, state, province, etc. for the other species you share the earth with.

- If you feel the need for a flag, make it the flag of the united nations. Discard all the rest.

- Read the bible of your choice and decide for yourself who wrote it.

- Create a common language learned and spoken by everyone in your world.

- If your planet's human population is increasing, don't add to it.

- Boycott violent films, tv shows, games, and other forms of "entertainment."

- Before you eat your next sandwich, spend a day in a slaughterhouse.

- Eliminate the word "fight" from your vocabularies.

NOTE ADDED IN PROOF

On May 1, 2014, my father awoke and, without a word, began writing on his yellow pad. This is what he wrote on that day:

EPILOGUE

After five happy years on K-PAX, including reunions with prot and all the others, Karen and I decided to return to Earth (we had mastered the art of light travel and had practiced it extensively) to see whether the human race had been able to comply with the Bullocks' demands, or if anyone had survived the "purge" of its human inhabitants.

We landed in Russia, and were shocked but not surprised to find no human beings anywhere. We traveled around Europe for a while, and then to America. No matter where we went, however, there was no one to greet us. Stained coffee cups, decayed meals, unfinished puzzles and the like indicated that everything simply came to an end on a certain day. Lawns were unmowed, subway cars unattended on routes no longer used. Churches and theaters and shops – all devoid of people. In a couple of cases bank vaults were left open, and we could have confiscated millions of dollars in worthless money. The overall effect, which was not at all unpleasant, was the absence of traffic and other noises, especially in the big cities.

There were, however, animals of all kinds everywhere, wandering among the buildings, squares, and plazas. Evidently there was plenty to eat, for they looked well-fed and healthy. We had to hide from a bear once; otherwise the entire world was like an open zoo. We visited a few of those, by the way, fearing that the animals there had starved. But someone (Walter?) had opened the gates and let everyone out. The same for laboratories, farms, slaughterhouses – anywhere that anyone had been incarcerated or made use of without their consent. (There were undoubtedly many animals who could not have survived on their own, and we like to think Walter took them back to Bullock, or to other suitable planets.) In any case, the elephants and tigers and whales and so many others were on their way back from the brink of extinction. It was like another Garden of Eden.

From the evidence shown by calendars, whose pages were left unturned on the day everyone vanished, we deduced that the Bullocks had transported everyone off the Earth on the second anniversary of Compliance Day, which meant that Homo sapiens had survived the first and second years before failing the command to stop the killing. This was confirmed by our finding old newspapers, which reported that the human race had managed to end just over 20% of the killing of other people, worldwide, during that first year. Later articles indicated that the next 20% was proving more difficult to attain, and curtailing the killing of even 1/5 of the other fauna living on Earth even more difficult. It appeared that Homo sapiens had failed in both endeavors.

We didn't stay long – a few days at most (there was plenty to eat: canned goods were available in every market). But the prospect of a longer visit was too heartbreaking. All of our family and friends (not to mention everyone else) were gone. Somehow I never got a chance to tell the Bullocks about many of the things that made the human race worthy of surviving and becoming even better – things like our arts, music, and literature, not to mention brilliant accomplishments in the sciences and humanities. I should have told them also about the countless acts of selflessness and even heroism that are reported daily on the news. People who rush into a lake to save someone who is drowning, or leap down to pull someone under a moving subway train after he or she has fallen onto the tracks. Now, none of these things will ever happen again. There will never be another Mozart, or Gandhi, or Einstein (on Earth, anyway). Or, for that matter, another Taj Mahal, Eiffel Tower, or World Trade Center. Our dark sides may have outweighed our better selves, sometimes, but I truly believe that the balance was shifting. If only there had been more time . . . .

At first I held myself responsible for failing to convince the world of Walter's readiness to remove us from our beautiful planet. That was, after all, the charge bestowed upon me by the Bullocks, and I blamed myself for not being up to the task. But prot assured me that *no one* could have stopped Homo sapiens from killing both our fellow humans and all the other creatures that walk, crawl, or swim the Earth, even with the inducement of complete knowledge of medicine and the sciences and a thousand other things. It's part of our nature, embedded in our DNA. Nothing short of a mutation can change that. Even so, I still felt the weight of the entire world on my shoulders.

Nevertheless, it was pretty devastating to discover that the Bullocks had carried out their program so successfully. Where everyone has been taken, of course, we hadn't a clue. Our only consolation was that we were sure that no one had been killed, but were only "sleeping." If the human race is ever permitted to move forward in time once more, no one will have aged even a second. Maybe the Bullocks will one day allow those who were taken to return, perhaps a few at a time, for another chance, hoping that once they see what the Earth can be without the endless killing, they will begin to evolve into beings the universe can respect. We hope so, and we plan to return every decade or two to find out.

In the meantime, we love our lives on our peaceful planet, where wars and other forms of violence are not seen, and there isn't even a term for killing. The saddest part of all this is that the Earth could have been another K-PAX if its human inhabitants had only wanted badly enough to make it the garden of Eden it could have been.

After writing these final words, Dad reverted to a catatonic state, where he has remained to this day.

ACKNOWLEDGMENTS

I thank Bob Brewer, Ron Chase, Charles Palmer, Mary Mikalson, and Karen Brewer for valuable suggestions and encouragement. Each of them made this book a little better.

Visit the author at www.genebrewer.com

Printed in Great Britain
by Amazon